THE
PATIENT

THE
PATIENT

TERI TERRY

bookouture

Published by Bookouture in 2024

An imprint of Storyfire Ltd.
Carmelite House
50 Victoria Embankment
London EC4Y 0DZ

www.bookouture.com

ISBN: 978-1-83525-175-1
eBook ISBN: 978-1-83525-174-4

PROLOGUE

It's dark. I can't see – can't move – can't feel anything, not my own body or if my eyes are even open. Where am I? What's happening? Splintered memories, of fear, pain – the pressure of hands around my neck. The world fading away...

But there is no pain now. I'm still alive? Am I alone? I listen. There are footsteps, distant voices.

I shout – scream: *help me, please help me...*

No one comes.

This has happened before. Hasn't it? Many times. They can't hear me.

I begin to drift from what seems to be real and present, to dreams, remembering. I can't always tell them apart. Some things I know happened, others I'm not so sure about. They merge together.

A door opens, closes.

'Hi, Flora.' It's Mum. There's a pause. I imagine her brushing my hair back from my eyes, holding my hand. 'Are you sure this is the right thing to do?'

'I'm sure.' It's Fern, my sister. They don't usually come together.

Now Mum is crying. She often cries when she visits, but this sounds different, somehow. 'My baby girl,' she says. 'Beautiful child.'

Can I be beautiful still after what happened to shut me inside of myself? But I shy away – don't remember that. *Don't.*

Mum and Fern say they love me.

Why are they saying goodbye?

I drift away. When I come back, there are new voices, ones I don't recognise. They must be doctors or nurses – they're talking respiration, heart rate, other measurements.

'She was such a beautiful girl, and so young.' A woman's voice. 'It's so sad.'

Was? Past tense?

They think... I'm dead.

I'm not, I'm here! I'm howling as loud as I can, but not even a whisper escapes.

'Now we'll have minute of silence,' one of them says, and movement and voices cease. I imagine a clock – the second hand – winding around.

A minute of silence?

To mourn the dead. To mourn *me.*

There must have been a mistake. Can't they tell I'm still here?

Maybe it wasn't a mistake, and I've been attacked all over again.

'It's time.' It's one of the doctors, but another voice also said those words – the last voice I heard before I became like this. Panic swirls inside of me.

Please. Let me go...

No. I will remember what *I* choose.

Benji's eyes held something no one else's ever did when he looked at me – like he saw me as more than I was. I could never live up to that. There was no chance it would ever end anything but badly, was there?

Don't go there. Go further back.

The day we met – the day that set so many things in motion. If I could travel in time, stop it, never meet Benji, would I do that?

No. Never.

ONE

SAPHY

The first thing you should know about me is that I'm dying. The second is that I'm almost sure that I want to. It's the *almost* that keeps me hanging around – it's not the sort of thing you can take back.

Everyone has to die. Life and death are two sides of one coin; it's part of the deal and there is no opt-out clause or higher court of appeal. But most of us are good at avoiding talking or even thinking about death, until forced to confront it personally – saying goodbye to a close friend, a lover, a parent. Or a doctor looking in your eyes and telling you that your expiry date is coming rather sooner than you thought, as mine told me some months ago.

Dying and uncertainty about its pros and cons are what brought me to today.

'Are you sure, Saphy?' Zoe says. My best friend forever, her eyes are anxious, and not just for me. I'm warm inside that she's come with me when I know she's scared.

'I'm sure,' I say, and take her hand. 'And thank you.' Zoe understands me better than I do myself, sometimes. She gets why I need to do stuff like this – take risks, face fear – to feel like I'm still alive.

But that is only part of the reason, isn't it? It's facing mortality, too, and surviving. Showing it can be done. It's feeling the reach of death – a cold hand around my heart – and saying, *fooled you! Not today.*

Zoe takes a selfie of us to commemorate the moment. Zoe, the golden girl, and me, her opposite: long dark hair tied back so it doesn't get in my face when we jump. Dark eyes too big on a face too thin, pale.

'Saphy and Zoe? You're up first,' the jump master says. 'Ready to go?'

'Yes!' I answer, for both of us.

We're harnessed together and half walk, half hobble to the crane, Zoe almost carrying me. They help us on, attach the bungee to our harness.

Adrenalin is flooding through me, heart stumbling along. I tell it to hang in there a bit longer.

And we dive headfirst into nothing, in each other's arms.

Zoe's eyes are shut tight, mine are open: the world lurches as we hurtle down, down, down. She's screaming when we hit the limit of the bungee. It recoils, sends us flying up, up, up, and I'm laughing. Zoe finally opens her eyes but then closes them again.

Down, down, down again, and on the way to the bottom, my phone – tucked in my bra – is vibrating. Then we're back up, up, then down, repeat a few more times. All too soon, it's over.

We're lowered to the ground and the jump master and his mate catch us, undo the straps. Zoe is shaking and I'm laughing, laughing, losing my breath, and then she's rubbing my back. She helps me to a bench and I sit down, my vision going grey, but it starts to come back.

'OK?' she says.

'OK.'

'Thank God, because you need to buy me wine – *all* the wine.'

My phone is vibrating again and I fish it out of my bra. A voicemail from an unknown number? Zoe's is also beeping with a message now.

'It's Mum. She says, tell Saphy to check her phone. And about a dozen exclamation marks?'

My hands are shaking. Zoe's mum is my backup contact for only one thing I can think of. I go to voicemail, listen to the message but can't take it in. I play it again, then just sit there, staring at my phone.

'Saphy? What is it?'

I look up, meet Zoe's eyes. She's the one who has stuck with me when most friends disappeared, stopped calling, got on with living and having weddings and babies, and didn't want to be reminded that one day, it could all be taken away. That they are mortal, too.

'Saphy?'

'It's a message from the transplant team, asking me to call as soon as possible. They must have a match. A heart – a match – for me.' Despite being on the transplant list, the chances of finding a compatible heart were low. I'd tried to put it out of my mind. After all, when have I ever been lucky?

There are tears in Zoe's eyes, mine too, as she hugs me. 'Don't just stare at your phone. Call them.'

The number is in my contacts. It's hard to find, hands shaking, and Zoe takes it from me, finds it and hits call. Hands it back.

'Hi, this is Saphira Logan. I got a message to call.'

A woman's voice asks me to confirm my identity, then tells me there is a possible match for a heart transplant. That if I want to be considered for surgery, I have to come to Harefield in London today to be assessed. She asks me what I want to do.

Do I want to be taken apart, put back together? Maybe live longer. Maybe not. And I know what the answer is *supposed* to be: to hope. To put my faith in doctors – like the ones who couldn't save my mum from cancer all those years ago, or my dad from Covid more recently. To keep my coin spinning mid-air for as long as possible. But I'm tired. Beyond tired, to a point of exhaustion so severe it's hard to imagine ever being free of it. Tired of being ill. Of hospitals. Of having no say in what is happening to my failing heart, my body. My life. Is agreeing to this wresting back some control, or is it the total opposite?

'Saphy?' she prompts.

There is no guarantee it'll go ahead no matter what I say. I should, at least, go and see if it is even possible. And I hear my voice saying *yes*.

TWO

By the time we get to London, fear and uncertainty and more fear are buzzing through me, making my heart flutter so much that instead of a taxi from the station, I'm in an ambulance.

Getting a transplant was never any more than a maybe. For ages, my consultant has wanted me to check in to hospital, to a ward of patients, like me – all on a death watch: who will die waiting, who will get lucky? Moving in, knowing chances were I'd never be able to leave.

I couldn't face it. I'd rather die sooner, at home, not eke out my last moments half alive and hooked up to a bunch of machines. But now that a transplant might actually happen – what does it mean?

Someone else's heart beating in my chest – a heart that might keep me alive longer than the original model.

Or not.

They said maybe tonight for surgery, and I've looked into all of this enough to know that hearts have to be transplanted within a few hours after someone dies. Does this mean someone is in the process of dying? And they're thinking it'll happen tonight, so they're getting me ready?

Some unknown person, dying – someone else's heart beating on inside of me after they're gone. What could be a new life for me is the end of another, the sorrow of some other family, friends.

We arrive at the hospital. Once inside I get transferred from the stretcher to a wheelchair, and taken for assessment – questions to answer, blood pressure, temperature, chest X-ray, leads here and there on my chest to transmit my heart rhythm, an oxygen monitor clipped to my finger. They take so many tubes of blood I'm surprised I have any left. Afterwards, I'm wheeled to an office, where Zoe and Claire, her mum, are waiting.

Claire gets up, leans over my wheelchair – a hug with a wave of spice and chocolate. She's been baking again, hasn't she? Making me treats, convinced enough of them will keep me going for longer. 'Is it happening?' she says.

'I don't know yet.' *I don't know what to do.*

There's a light tap on the door. It's the nurse who has been taking me around the houses for all the tests, and Dr Thornton is with her – one of the transplant surgeons.

'Here you are, Saphira, and it's not even Monday,' he says. The day they'd been trying to convince me to check in.

'I know, right? So, tell me about this heart.'

'A woman, a few years younger than you and a good antigenic match. No contraindications beyond all the usual risks. Which we must now go through. There is a consent form, and you have to be sure you understand everything that is involved.'

'Can't I just sign it now?' *Do I want to?*

He shakes his head and begins to go through the litany of terror. I could die during surgery. I could die afterwards without regaining consciousness. I could die in a long list of ways in the first hours, days, weeks. If I get through that critical time, I could still die in the months that follow. I'll have to take immunosuppressants to stop my immune system from rejecting this new heart for the rest of my life, and they will make me more susceptible to cancer and all types of infections. Infections are more likely to kill me. There's a long list of checks, appointments, heart biopsies, to check for signs of rejection, that must be done all along. If I make it to a year, we'd be hoping for years and years more at that point. I can see the shock on Zoe's face. Claire's is more stoic – she's a nurse, probably already knew most of this.

Then he goes through what will happen in the surgery. I try very hard not to listen to the details but can't shut them out. One of the worst is a heart-lung bypass machine pumping my blood, breathing for me – not the same as the ventilator I've had before, when I had Covid, and I'm pushed back to remembering another day, another time, that I almost died.

Finally, he seems to think he's freaked us out as much as he possibly can: his job is done.

'Do you have any questions, Saphira?'

'No. I just – can we have a minute?'

Zoe and Claire exchange a glance. He's not surprised, though. I'm sure he's read my psych evaluation and all the rest.

'Of course.' He and the nurse leave us, close the door.

'Saphy?' Zoe says.

'I'm dying. No matter what. Maybe in weeks or months as I am now, maybe months to years if I have a transplant. But if I have the surgery I could also die tonight.'

'Survival rates after transplant surgery are good and getting better all the time,' Claire says.

'I know that. I know I should be happy and excited and hoping I'm one of the ones who sails through it all and lives for decades. I'm just not sure I can believe it. If things I hoped for came true, I wouldn't need a transplant. Dad wouldn't have died.' I swallow, trying to stop the tears but they won't be blinked back. 'My mum wouldn't have, either.'

Claire takes my hand and Zoe's, Zoe my other hand. A circle of three. Tears in both of their eyes now, too.

'I believe in the power of hope,' Claire says.

Zoe nods. 'I hoped you wouldn't die and you didn't. I hoped you'd get a transplant, and here it is. Now I'm hoping that one day you'll be a fearless old lady, dragging me skydiving on your seventieth birthday.'

'We can hope for you,' Claire says.

Dr Thornton comes back in and I sign the consent form a short time later.

I'm still almost sure I want to die – or, at least, that I want to do it on my own terms. The thought of the surgery – and recovery – terrifies me. But I can't say no to the only people in the world who love me. I can't hurt them like that. And as reasons go, it's a pretty good one.

THREE

Showered, scrubbed, gowned. One IV line in, another follows. Leads replaced, oxygen monitor clipped. A nurse is telling me about all of it, but her words aren't getting through. I'm the strangest mix of fear and elation. Elation, because this is the heart patient equivalent of winning the lottery. Fear, because – well, all of it. The thought of someone sawing through my breastbone, opening my ribs, and – I make myself stop there. And underneath it all are two small words I try so hard not to resort to, because they don't help. They just make things worse. But right now, I can't push them away.

Why me?

I was born with a heart defect that was almost bad enough for surgery – at the sort of level where they weren't sure if surgery would help enough to make the risks worthwhile. I didn't have surgery and I was doing OK. Better than OK, really, so long as I didn't push things too much physically. I survived A levels, got a first at UCL in English Lit. I had a job I loved in a bookshop and I was writing, always writing. I was sure my next novel – or the one after that – would be published, that I would be the author I always wanted to be. Despite the constant ache of missing my mum, Dad and me were close, and it was enough. But then I got Covid, and Dad did, too. He died. I didn't, but it damaged my not great heart even further. I couldn't manage my job. I gave up writing, because what was the point? I knew that it was going to get me. I could feel it, that it was coming soon – that no matter what drugs or procedures they could come up with, my heart had had enough.

Can this surgery give me back my life? I want to dare to hope, to dream, but I'm afraid. It could go wrong and all be for nothing.

'OK, Saphy, we're off to the waiting room now.'

I'm lying on a trolley, being wheeled down a hall, through doors. Another hall. A lift. I watch the ceiling change as we go and want to go faster – for this to be over – and slower, too. To never get where we're going.

I wonder what would happen if I said I've changed my mind. Is it too late?

'Shouldn't I be asleep?'

'Not yet. Only sedated for now.'

Sedated? I don't feel sedated. I feel wired. I feel like I could jump down from this trolley and run, and no one would be able to catch me. It's been so long since I've been able to walk fast, let alone run, that I giggle at the thought.

'Here we are.'

Another room – softer lighting. We come to a stop. Claire and Zoe are here, gloves and masks on. Claire takes one hand, Zoe the other.

'Hey, babe. This is pretty wild,' Zoe says.

'It's going to be OK. Isn't it? I can't be due any more bad luck.'

'All the good luck is yours now and forever, I promise,' Claire says. And that is what she wants – Zoe, too – but they don't have that kind of power.

I try to believe her, just the same.

They're coming for me now.

Claire and Zoe say they love me. I know. I love them, too.

More moving ceilings. A last room, brighter lights. So many people.

Someone asks me my name and birthdate. It'd be bad news if they got this far and had the wrong patient, wouldn't it? Too late, I think I should have said I was somebody else and it would all have stopped.

I'm lifted, moved, by many hands – slid across to the operating table. It's cold.

Faces are masked. All I can see are eyes. They're not human. They're robots, and they don't know I'm still awake and they're going to start the surgery—

'Hi, Saphira.' A masked face swims into view above me. 'I'm Priya, your anaesthetist. Can I get you to count backwards from a hundred?'

'A hundred? Isn't it usually ten? Does this stuff work?'

'I promise you: it works. So go on, give it a try.' Her eyes hold mine – calm, steady. She knows what she's doing.

'OK. One hundred...

'Ninety-nine...

FOUR

Warm arms hold me close. I look up, grasp a curl of hair tight in my hand. She tickles me until I let go, giggling...

Daddy's hand holds mine as we go through the gates. I'm squirming in unfamiliar school uniform, new shoes. Other children are here, more follow, some with two parents, some with just one – always a mum. I haven't got a mum. I'm different. I don't want to be left here...

Zoe takes my hand and announces that we're best friends. Why? We are light and darkness: blonde ponytail and a face that always smiles. Dark braids, afraid of teacher, of standing in corners, of the lights going out...

A kaleidoscope of now and then unspools faster and faster, a blur of everything that made me who I am and then was gone. Isn't that what happens before you die?

Now there is another gate.

Why are Mum and Dad saying goodbye?

No! Don't make me go. I want to stay with you...

. . .

There are footsteps, voices. Repetitive, mechanical clicks and beeps. Whooshing sounds.

I open my eyes. Ceiling above, but it's not clear. Either mist is in the way, or my eyes won't focus. I'm confused, disconnected – drifting. Now I'm not even sure if that is the ceiling, as which way is up?

Something connects inside: transplant. Heart transplant.

Is it over? Did I survive?

A masked face swims into view above me.

'Saphira? Hello, there. I'm Johnny, one of the ICU nurses. It's all gone splendidly.'

It has? It really has? He must read it in my eyes.

'Really. I promise. I heard them say after that the surgery went like a dream. Now, rest.'

My eyes close even as his words are looking for meaning inside of me: splendidly. A dream.

I'm alive – I'm still here. But for how long?

FIVE

FERN

When we said goodbye to Flora, it didn't feel real. After months of grief that was suspended, waiting, I was almost numb, confused by a mix of feelings that I couldn't sort out. Part relief that it was over and guilt for feeling that way, but also doubt, disbelief. Flora was such a whirlwind of colour and life. Could she really be gone?

Mum and Dad went home afterwards and asked if I wanted to go with them, but I needed to be alone for a while. The thought of being around anyone else, even my parents – just no. So, I'd gone home on my own.

It wasn't until late that night that I could cry.

The family liaison officer for Flora's case calls in the morning. Tells me that now that Flora has died, Benji has been arrested again – charged with murder. He had been on bail with the previous charge of GBH. She assures me bail is unusual for murder charges, that he'll likely stay in on remand.

I suppose I knew this would happen, but I was so carefully avoiding thinking about it that it is still a shock. Suddenly the four walls around me are too much. I go for a long walk in the afternoon, not thinking where I am, where I am going. Just walking. Anonymous on London pavements full of shoppers, tourists, people going to or from work. And I wonder that I can still walk around like this, with a normal-enough expression that no one recoils or gives me space. That no one knows that I am screaming inside.

I'm surprised when I notice how low the sun is in the sky. I've been walking for hours. I'm tired, hungry; I should go home. Instead, I'm drawn to the Devonshire, Flora's favourite pub – her friends regularly meet up here.

My steps slow when I reach the street. Even more so as I get closer to the door. Music and light spill out into the night. Vapers and smokers huddle close to each other – it's chilly for May.

I go past them, through the open door. It's noisy and crowded, claustrophobic in the press of bodies. I'm thinking of backing out, but it's too late.

'Fern? Oh, darling.' I'm swept into a hug – it's Owen. Flora's friend. He came to that dinner party we had – the one where Flora met Benji. He draws me towards the bar. 'How is Flora?' And others are all around, waiting for the answer.

Now there are tears in my eyes. I shake my head. 'She... she's died.'

They find me a seat. One of Flora's friends offers me tissues, but I'm done with the gut-wrenching sobs of last night. Now it is just silent tears, slipping down my face, one by one. Around me, there are more tears, hands held, shoulders leaned on, and the word is spreading. The music is turned off.

I haven't come here since it happened, more than four months ago. Since Flora was drugged, tied down, strangled – but in a very specific way. Carotid artery compression for long enough to deprive her brain of oxygen and cause brain damage. The press were all over her story – the beautiful It girl who'd been on all the society pages, now in a coma? They couldn't resist. There was speculation that she might have been a willing participant in some bondage game, half-strangled to get a rush, but I didn't believe it. She wouldn't do that. Maybe she was different – wild, impulsive – to those who didn't know her as well as I did, but no matter what she got up to, she was always in control. She somehow needed to be. She'd never let someone tie her up like that, make her helpless. And anyhow, if that were so, why would she have been drugged?

She must have been so scared. I've had nightmares that I've stood there, watching, didn't help her.

At least now, after so long, she's free. And that's what I tell myself, over and over again: she's free.

'How – I mean, why – did she die?' It's Owen again. 'Marley said they thought she was starting to regain consciousness. But then she got worse, and they'd had to put her on a ventilator.' Marley is – was – Flora's best friend. As if saying her name conjures her up, I see her coming through the door now, making her way towards us.

'She was deteriorating,' I say. 'There was nothing that could be done anymore.'

The manager is out of his office now. Someone must have told him. 'Prosecco – on the house,' he says. 'A toast to Flora.' Prosecco: her favourite. Bottles are opened, glasses passed around. Room made for Marley next to me. Her eyes are red, like mine.

'To Flora!'

I don't leave early like I always have before. Everyone has stories to share – Flora, as they knew her. Rebel girl, wild thing; she burned bright, and now she's gone. Tonight, Flora's friends are my friends. They hurt, too.

But I knew her before they did. Six years older, I carried her around when my arms were barely long enough. I loved her for so long – hated her sometimes, too. She had a way of taking over, taking everything for herself. Once she was born it was like I receded into the background, forgotten. I was only known as Flora's sister, as if I didn't have a name or identity of my own. But I still loved her. Didn't I? Didn't everyone?

Owen stays close, his arm around my shoulders. It feels good to have someone warm, alive, to lean on. I know that he'd come home with me tonight if I wanted him to, but Benji was the only one for me.

Now Flora is dead and Benji is in jail. What do I have?

Nothing.

I was her big sister. I was supposed to look out for her.

Instead I introduced her to her murderer.

SIX

SAPHY

I'm a radio, tuning in slowly, cutting through static: the background sounds of the hospital. Beeping, shuffling, footsteps. Voices.

I'm still alive.

Is there pain? I feel more numb, disconnected. I don't try to move, scared to even think about it, but then, all at once, I want to know that I can. Toes – toes sound safe. Can I wiggle them? But my legs feel dull and distant, toes lost somewhere beyond.

Footsteps are coming towards me, a masked face above. Her eyes are smiling.

'Hi, Saphira, welcome back. I'm Pat, one of the ICU nurses.'

'Hi,' I croak. Two letters, one word: I can speak. I'm still here.

'We need you to move, OK? We'll help you.'

There's someone else here now. It's important, Pat tells me, to move, to stop fluid pooling in my limbs – to sit up and cough to expel any fluid out of my lungs. All they want me to do is swing my legs around and sit up – without using my arms, which could pull at my incision, breastbone.

My legs are thick, swollen. They don't feel like mine. Trying to move is like reversing a car with a wayward trailer, and every tiny movement is pain. I can't do this, I *can't*. They're helping me and I want to scream, but all that comes out is a pathetic whimper. Somehow, they get me sitting upright and now I'm coughing. Pat is here with a pillow to hug against me, but it still hurts, I don't want to, but she says I must clear my lungs. Even though I want to stop, I can't, and fluid and whatever else is coming up.

Finally, it is over and there are tears on my cheeks, Pat's hand gentle on my shoulder. 'Well done,' she says. 'Rest now.' They help me ease back, lie down, and although every tiny movement still hurts, it's more muted now – whether from drugs damping down the pain or exhaustion or both.

I rest my head back against the pillow. Close my eyes. I hate this. I want to scream and rage at the pain, at this body that is so useless, powerless. But all I can manage is another whimper.

I'm still alive, I remind myself. A faint *beep-beep, beep-beep* nearby on their machines is a reassuring rhythm, one that says I'm alive, I'm alive, over and over again.

But I could have stayed with Mum and Dad, not had all this pain. If I told anyone I saw them, they'd say it was a dream, that it doesn't mean anything. Doctors always want an explanation for things that can't be explained.

When I was younger, Mum watched over me. I could see her in shadows out of the corner of my eye; I could feel her feather-light touch on my shoulder. When my eyes were closed before sleep, mind drifting, sometimes there would be a flash of her face, a smile, there and gone a split second later. When Dad died, I tried to see him the same way but it wouldn't work, as if I'd lost the knack when I lost hope. It wouldn't work with Mum anymore, either.

Now. Try it now.

Eyes still shut, breathing in and out so slowly I'm barely

moving at all. Mind still, body still, so much so I almost lose connection with my physical self. Hold my breath for a moment. Then a shallow breath in, out, slowly.

Thin wisps of colours and patterns begin to dance in my mind, resolve into images I can almost see, then spin out again. This is different to anything I can remember experiencing before. It's the drugs, I tell myself, but I still try to see what is there – who is there. It's not Mum, definitely not Dad. Instead, a shadowy woman in a bright vortex – spinning, dancing. She's almost in view but disappears if I try to look directly at her.

Who are you?
Wrong question.
Who were you?

SEVEN

FERN

Is compassionate leave meant to cover hangovers? I wince when I open my blinds and light streams in. Prosecco is evil. I could never understand why Flora liked it so much.

Flora. A fresh wave of pain hits me even as I'm trying to piece together the rest of the evening. I frown: how did I get home? It's hazy. I'm thirsty, need tea.

The kettle is already warm when I fill it; there is the smell of toast, crumbs on the counter. What have I done? Then the bathroom door down the hall opens, and out steps Marley. I breathe a sigh of relief.

'Good morning,' she says, and winks. 'Or is it good afternoon?'

I glance at the clock. 'Ah, let's say afternoon.' I put the kettle on.

'You looked surprised to see me.'

'Let's just say I was glad it was you.'

She laughs. 'Flora would be impressed. She tried to get you to come out with us so many times, and the odd time that you did, you always left early. Shame she missed it.'

Her smile falls away and tears are filling my eyes. I turn, get the milk out of the fridge. 'Want some tea?'

She shakes her head. 'Got to get to court. A jury is expected back; here's hoping we can get scenes of triumph or despair for the six o'clock news.'

'OK. I'm guessing you saw me home last night. Thanks.'

'It's fine. I'm sorry I have to go – are you going to be all right?'

'Yes. No. I don't know.'

'I know, honey.' A hug. She's picking up her stuff, heading for the door. 'Don't forget about next Saturday.'

'Don't forget what?' I say, drawing a blank.

She shakes her head. 'The candlelit vigil we planned last night for Flora. Owen said he'd take you?'

'He did?'

'Yes. He did. Look, I'll call you later, and see how you are. Bye.'

After she's gone, it's too quiet. I try the radio, but the news comes on. Flora's death and Benji's arrest for murder is one of the top stories. I switch it off. It's going to be all over the papers and TV too, isn't it?

I can't settle, keep wandering around, picking things up, putting them down again. Somehow everything reminds me of Flora.

Her favourite chair: how she'd sit with her feet tucked underneath her like some sort of yoga guru. The vase that I didn't notice was superglued for months after she'd knocked it over. I can see the cracks if I look closely enough.

Marley must have slept in Flora's room. No one has since Flora last did, and now I'm hesitating at the door. It's ajar. I remember coming in here after I first heard what happened to Flora. Lying on her bed, hugging her pillow. Then, it still smelled like her – her favourite perfume.

When the police came, they went over every inch of her room and the rest of our home. They took things of hers, too, like her laptop, letters, cards written to her. Her phone they already had; it was found close to her. It felt like she was the one who had done something wrong – that she was being investigated.

I go into her room. The bed has been neatly made, more so than if Flora had done it, but I can tell it's been slept in – the pillow is at a different angle, the top of the duvet under instead of over the pillow the way it was. I start to put it back the way it should be, then shake my head. Strip the bed, put the sheets and duvet cover in to wash.

I go back and sit on the chair in the corner of her room. I guess this could be my study again, like it was before Flora moved in a few years ago. Dad had wanted me to keep an eye on her. I could never afford to live in a place like this mews house in Kensington; it belongs to Mum, so I couldn't argue.

I knew nothing would be the same once Flora was here. I had life on an organised, even keel – as much as that is possible, being a junior doctor in a hospital. When Flora moved in, everything was upended. Yet she started to change me as much as Dad hoped I could change her. I began to live a bit more. I started to think there might be more to life than work, sleep, work, sleep.

And now she's gone.

I know – better than most – how Flora could torment those who loved her without even trying. She was like a drug that once you had you wanted more and more. When she ended things with Benji, was it more than he could handle? That's what the police and the Crown Prosecution think. They wouldn't have arrested him, charged him, if they weren't sure.

I can think these things but deep down, inside, I still can't believe Benji could have hurt Flora.

But then, I never thought I could, either.

EIGHT

SAPHY

Good minutes. Bad minutes. All there is, is now. Time slows down, speeds up and slows down again, with me trapped in the centre of it. Zoe and Claire – the shock on their faces that first time they saw me. The horror in their eyes, especially Zoe's – I must look a train wreck. It's their fault. They pushed me into a decision I didn't want to make. The doctors, too, cutting me open, knowing what I'd go through after. Anger, reasonable or not, is distraction from pain. From wishing I'd died in theatre and avoided this misery that goes on and on.

It's a good minute now. Zoe is here.

'Tell me, honestly. How bad do I look?' I say.

'You are much brighter today.'

'Don't avoid the question.'

'You look amazing.'

'Yeah, right.'

'Your colour is much better. Honestly. You're not anywhere near as pale as you were before.'

Claire is here, too, and she agrees with Zoe. 'We've getting the downstairs room ready for you,' she says.

The downstairs room? I'm confused. Am I leaving the hospital? My eyes close and their voices fade away.

I'm drifting, in that place between awake and asleep, when I see her again.

She's not spinning now. She stays almost still, but if I try to look directly at her face, it disappears. Her arms are crossed, right hand over the left side of her chest, covering what isn't there.

A tear runs down her cheek, but it isn't clear. It's vivid red and leaves a bloody streak behind.

NINE

FERN

Owen's knock on the door comes just before nine, like his message said it would. I've been ready for a while, psyching myself up. The vigil for Flora has been mentioned all over the place and there'll be crowds, Marley said, and at the best of times I hate that. I can't help but think of all the germ swapping when people gather. The fear and panic of the last wave of the pandemic are too fresh, too recent, for me to feel comfortable around big groups of people. What we went through together as junior doctors is part of why Benji and I bonded in the first place. But I know that isn't the only reason tonight is worrying me: it's all the eyes, looking at me. All the things people will say, want me to respond to. As Flora's sister, I can't be anonymous tonight. It's not like at the hospital where I have a role and know what I'm supposed to do, how to be. This is unknown.

One step at a time: open the door.

'Hi, Fern.' Owen is in a dark suit, but with a bright-yellow shirt – Flora's favourite colour. It suits him, the contrast with his dark skin. It was Marley's idea but I don't have anything yellow, couldn't face venturing out. Flora's stuff would be too small, but I found a yellow patterned silk scarf tucked in her wardrobe.

Pretty, but it feels too bright, too garish, draped around my shoulders. 'Ready to go?' he says.

'Yes. Thanks for stopping by for me.'

'No worries.'

We set off and I'm trying to think of something to say, anything, and, like being uncomfortable is contagious, Owen seems ill at ease also.

'Sorry,' I say.

'What for?'

'Not being Flora.' I flush. 'What I mean is, she always knew what to say.'

'You weren't so quiet the other night.'

'No. It must have been the Prosecco.'

'Maybe that was Flora's secret. We're all going back there tonight. Are you coming?'

'I don't know. Maybe.' I meant to say no, but somehow, another word came out. We walk the rest of the way to Kensington Gardens, not talking, but now that feels OK.

Marley was right: there's quite a turnout, more coming all the time. Flashes of yellow everywhere. Marley sees me, waves, comes over.

She touches the scarf I'm wearing. 'I bought this for Flora – when we went to Paris for her eighteenth.'

'I'm sorry, I didn't know. Do you want it?'

She shakes her head. 'Keep it – it suits you.'

Liar.

Owen is frowning, looking back the way we came. 'I can't believe he had the nerve to come.' I look across. It's Leo, a determined look on his face, making his way towards us. I'm sure most of Flora's friends suspected he was responsible after she was hurt. But the police said his alibi checked out, that he was nowhere near where it happened.

Owen steps forward as if to intercept Leo. I put a hand on

his arm. 'It's all right. No matter what, he's just someone else who loved Flora.'

'Hi, Fern,' Leo says.

'Hi, Leo.'

His dark eyes are full of pain. He leans forwards, gives me a hug.

'You all right?' he says.

'Not really. You?'

He shakes his head. He's rigid, as if he has to knot his muscles to stop from collapsing, falling to pieces.

Gradually everyone stops talking, moving about. Candles are lit, fireflies that dance in the darkness. A minute of silence stretches on and on, and I'm remembering:

That night, when Flora was still with Leo. Everyone – me included – was worried about her being with him. Marley hatched a plan: a dinner party at ours. Leo was invited, and Marley brought Owen – obviously not Marley's date, she's gay. Owen's role was to flirt with Flora like they often did – just banter, they were friends. Flora had brought her boss, Imogen; she wanted to fix her up with Marley. That didn't happen. Marley thought that Leo would react to Owen, show his true colours, and Flora would see him for what he was – jealous and violent. And things did erupt – but not quite how Marley intended. Because I invited Benji, and once Flora met Benji, that was it.

Leo's heart was broken, and so was mine.

TEN

SAPHY

The more hours and days that pass, the more likely everything will be fine – my bones and tissues will knit together and heal, cradle this heart in place inside of me. They've got me doing more light movements and exercises, and learning about all the things I need to do and not do to stay healthy. While part of me is so over being in hospital – I've spent way too much time in them in recent years – more of me is terrified to even think of leaving it.

Yet even as I worry, my body seems to have its own agenda. With each day that goes by, I feel stronger. This heart that beats with so much determination in my chest – in a way mine never did – has me both energised and on edge, at once. It's weird and kind of creepy, feeling it beat, knowing it was someone else's, someone who died. And I can't stop thinking about whose heart it may have been.

Later I'm flicking through channels on hospital TV without enough channels for proper flicking when something on the news catches my eye. Crowds of people holding candles last night at Kensington Gardens.

The vigil was in memory of Flora Hastings-Clifford. Her

name is familiar. There are images on the screen now and I recognise her face, remember hearing what happened to her. She'd caught the media's interest after she was strangled and left in a coma – Sleeping Beauty, they called her. And now, months later, she has died. She was only twenty-five. So sad. I'm reaching for the remote again when it hits me.

All I know about my donor is that she was a few years younger than me. I'm twenty-eight, so Flora's twenty-five fits. Could she have been my donor?

I search her name on my phone. She died the day before my transplant, so it can't be her. Not only was my surgery the next day, it didn't start until late evening. Hearts have to be transplanted within hours; it's not possible.

Why do I feel disappointed? I don't even know.

I search for images of Flora. There are so many: she was always in the society pages, captured on red carpets and at events for years. I can't stop looking in her eyes on the screen, can't stop the conviction that she was my donor, even if it doesn't make sense.

She was truly beautiful. It wasn't just having the right make-up and clothes – she definitely had those things – but beyond that, she had something. I can't work out what it was, and I can't stop looking at her and trying. And she wasn't just beautiful: she had it all. Bet she never had to worry about how to pay the bills like I have lately. It was lucky Dad had mortgage insurance for our terrace house in Islington or I'd really have been in trouble after he died. Even without mortgage payments, it's been a struggle.

What happened to put Flora in the coma that led to her death?

An ex-boyfriend – Benjamin Lawrence – was charged with GBH, now murder.

I stare at his images. He just looks so normal – dark eyes and hair, a little long – attractive but not ridiculously handsome. He was a doctor and had a kind face and eyes, the sort of doctor patients would feel comfortable relying on.

He was Benji to friends, family and colleagues who all swear he would never have hurt anyone, let alone Flora. That he loved her. But she dumped him and then he strangled her. It may have taken months for her to die, but it was murder just the same.

That night, I try to see the woman I've been dreaming about again. As if that is exactly the wrong way to go about things, there is no trace – no colours, patterns, movement. All gone.

After a while I give up, start drifting to sleep. Like that was what she was waiting for, she's back, shimmering on the edges of my consciousness. I stay completely still, barely breathing. Unfocused, not searching, just being.

She comes closer.

I still can't see her face. But there is a flash of red hair.

Red, like Flora's.

ELEVEN

FERN

'Fern, darling.'

'Hi, Mum.' She goes for air kisses, but I stop her and hug her instead. She is pale under make-up that isn't up to hiding puffy circles under her eyes. When I hold her, she seems both rigid and thinner than before – as if she's diminished in just days, since we said goodbye to Flora.

'Come in. I'll put the kettle on.' She follows me to the kitchen, watches as I sort cups, teabags, milk.

'No teapot?' A faintly disapproving tone.

'Sorry. It got broken and I haven't got around to replacing it.' Unsaid – Flora knocked it off the counter with an extravagant gesture late at night, not long before she was hurt. She'd promised to replace it but never did, and once she was in hospital, I somehow couldn't bring myself to do it.

'Biscuits?' I say.

'No, thank you.'

'Have you been eating enough?'

'Who is the mother and who is the child?' A raised eyebrow. Once the tea is ready, she takes her cup, turns and squares her shoulders. I follow her up the stairs to Flora's room. She stands in the doorway a moment and I come behind her, put a hand on her shoulder.

'Flora always liked her privacy, didn't she?' Mum says. 'Even when she was only ten or eleven – her room was off limits.'

'I don't think she'd mind now,' I say, though I'm far from sure.

'No. I suppose not.' She steps in; I follow her. There are bookshelves on one side, fitted wardrobes opposite. The wardrobes have no organisation at all. Either they were always this messy or the police going through made it so – or a mixture of the two – but I'd hazarded a quick check once I knew Mum was coming, for anything obvious she'd rather not see. A box of condoms and a bong are now hidden away under the bathroom sink.

'What do you think Flora would like to wear to her funeral?' I say, as Mum opens the first door, starts looking through some dresses.

'Something wildly inappropriate, most likely.'

'Can we do that?'

'It would be kind of fun, but no.' She picks up her tea from where she'd put it on Flora's dressing table and has a sip, pulls a face. 'I know it's early, darling, but I need a glass of wine for this.'

'Ah, I think I've got some French white?'

'Please.'

I go back to the kitchen, and glance at the clock as I get it out of the fridge. Early? Early is 5 p.m. instead of six. Right now, it's not quite 11 a.m. Mum has always had a bit to drink – sometimes more than a bit. But since Flora was hurt, she seems to drink more and more.

We go through dress after dress, a few skirts and suits as well. Everything offends Mum's sense of fashion or suitability in some manner. We've nearly reached the end when she holds out her empty wine glass for the third time.

'Sorry, Mum, the bottle is empty. And I haven't got any more.'

'No teapot, no wine: what kind of daughter have I raised? Kidding, darling. Now, for the dress. I think we'll have to go for plan B.'

'What's that?'

'One last shopping trip for Flora.'

'Do you want me to come with you?'

She shakes her head.

'Are you sure?'

'Quite. Thank you, darling.' She looks around the room, the open wardrobe doors, shuts them one by one. 'What are we going to do with all her things?'

'I don't want to think about it yet.'

'Me neither.'

TWELVE

SAPHY

Today is finally the day: I'm leaving the hospital. I should be happy, excited. I've spent way too much time in hospitals in recent years. But I'm scared, too. What if something goes wrong? Should I stay here for longer, just in case?

My consultant and a nurse come by for final checks. Claire and Zoe arrive as scheduled to listen to all the reminders about the stuff I must do, all that I can't. How important it is to take immunosuppressants every twelve hours, on an empty stomach – at 10 a.m. and 10 p.m. When to take all the other medications. Avoid crowded places for three months. Don't lift anything heavier than two kilos. Always wear sunscreen when outside and reapply it frequently. No sex for eight weeks.

'Is that from now or from the date of surgery?' Zoe asks.

'The latter,' the nurse says.

'So, five weeks to go. It's good to have a deadline to work towards,' Zoe says.

Claire rolls her eyes. 'Are you ready to go, Saphy? Have you got everything?'

'I think so.'

A wheelchair arrives for me, but I shake my head, insist I'll walk.

Zoe takes my bag. We walk, slowly, down the corridor. Nurses and doctors in our ward all come to smile, wave. Wish me well. I'm a walking success, and other patients – the ones who can – are there, too, at their doors with wistful smiles.

Then along another corridor, down a lift. This is further than I remembered; maybe I should have used the chair. But even though I'm tired, sore, it feels OK, even better than OK, to be moving, walking, myself. We go past other departments and then, finally, there they are: the main doors. I hesitate. One step, another. They open automatically as we get close. I pause, then step over the threshold.

'One small step for Saphy, one giant leap for the pubs of the UK!' Zoe says.

'You heard the nurse,' Claire says. 'No crowded places for three months.'

'Spoilsport,' Zoe says.

A light breeze moves my hair. The traffic sounds are louder than before. Birds, twittering in trees. Distant sirens. A lungful of London city air without background notes of disinfectant and whatever else makes that distinctive hospital smell. Early June sunshine dapples through trees, warm on my arms, and I'm like a flower, turning my face towards it.

'Stay here and I'll get the car,' Claire says. She marches off to the car park and we meander along while we wait.

There's a surge of adrenalin, excitement, a note of fear underneath. My death sentence has wrapped tightly around every moment of my life for so long that even a bungee jump only made it loosen its grip enough to pull me closer. Everything is different now.

Claire pulls in for us now. Zoe is putting my bag in the boot when a man walks towards us. I shrink back against the car, but he comes closer, thrusts a flier in my hand, another at Zoe.

She tosses them both in a recycle bin, but not before I see the words across the front: *Stop the murder of living organ donors now.*

THIRTEEN

FERN

I rest my hand lightly on the polished wood. Flora's last party, and she didn't even get to pick her dress. I can think what she would say if she could have seen the one Mum ended up choosing for her – beautifully cut, but a plain dark blue.

I've seen more than my share of the dead and dying, in Covid wards especially. Mostly I got used to it, managed to stay detached, professional. But then, one day, there was this little girl. Five years old when she died. She got to me, and I think it was because of Flora. She had long wavy blonde hair, very like Flora did when she was small, and I thought... she could have been my sister. I ended up a weepy mess, hiding behind a desk in a corner at the end of my shift.

Benji found me. Somehow, he got me up, out of the hospital without anyone else noticing the state I was in. Took me home.

We were both exhausted, but – in total breach of Covid lockdown rules – he stayed. He held my hand, and we talked and talked, in a way I've never been able to with anyone else. About what we did and what it meant. And from then on, we kept each other going. Well, he kept me going. I don't know if I did much for him.

That little girl – I haven't thought of her in a long time. I can't even remember her name now. It must be standing here, next to Flora's coffin, that brought her to mind. Maybe because I don't want to remember Flora as she is now, as she has been these last hard months, or even the years before. She changed, in a way I could never understand. When I was away at university, my little sister became someone else. She wouldn't talk to me the way she used to. I want to go back to the wide-eyed little girl who followed me around and believed everything I said.

There's a small throat-clearing noise behind me. The funeral director has come back in. 'Your parents have arrived,' he says.

'Thank you.'

They come in a moment later. I'm caught in a hug from Mum, and I catch a faint suggestion on her breath, under the mint. I glance at Dad, catch his eye and he shakes his head slightly. Great. Just great. Her coat is open at the front and I can see just enough of dark blue to get why she chose the dress she did for Flora. She's wearing the same one.

Soon the coffin is closed, carried to the hearse. The three of us are ushered to a black limousine. Other cars follow behind us, with relatives, a few close friends.

Dad distracts Mum while I check her bag, take out the flask. Hide it under the seat and wonder how many nips of courage have been taken in this car, on the way to the funeral of someone you love. I'm tempted to see if it helps. I'm tempted, also, to look under the seat, to see if there is a neat row of flasks hidden and forgotten. Or maybe occasional free whisky is a perk of being in the funeral business? I'm studying the car, the route we're taking, everyone we see on the way. Concentrating on things that don't matter to distract me from where we are going, and why.

We arrive. The pallbearers take her coffin from the hearse. Now we are walking behind Flora's coffin. Relatives, friends, follow. I note who they are, what they are wearing – some splashes of yellow in all the black. I see Leo's parents but not Leo. I hope he's OK. Marley is here, Owen, dozens from the Devonshire Arms. Staff, too – they must have closed for the day. Imogen – Flora worked for her in her gallery, but she was more than a boss; they were close. Everyone I would expect to see is here and there are so many more besides, people I don't recognise that must have been in some other part of Flora's life that I didn't know.

Harry Jennings from the Met – the one in charge of Flora's case – is here. I spot him at the back and wonder why he came. Is it like in crime on TV, in movies? That the detective comes to the funeral, watches everyone, then works out from who comes, who doesn't, what is said or not said, who is guilty? Does that mean they're not convinced it was Benji?

I slap myself internally. Stop it; just stop. They wouldn't have arrested Benji if he didn't do it.

But I can't help hoping, just the same. Is it because of the overwhelming guilt – that if it wasn't for me, Flora would never have met Benji?

Or maybe it is because I still want him for myself.

'To know Flora was to love her. From when she was born – to her first beautiful smile, her first steps – she brought life and colour to the world around her. She had a gift few share to draw others to her. So many of her friends, family, know how caring she was, how she could change your sadness to a smile just by being there.' Dad pauses, as if gathering himself to go on.

His tribute to Flora continues but I'm thinking about what he just said. He's right. Everyone who knew Flora loved her, wanted to be near her. She was beautiful, yes, but beyond that, she had something I couldn't begin to put into words. She could be kind, generous – not always, but she could be – but it wasn't just that. Everyone always wanted to please her: to make her smile fall on them.

She had so many friends, but how many of them did she trust? Marley, yes – at least, she did at one time. I'm not so sure about recently. Imogen maybe, in a different way, almost like she was a big sister. I'd been jealous of Imogen: it was supposed to be me. But Flora didn't confide in me anymore, not really. She hadn't properly for years but it was even more obvious this last year, though that might have been as much my fault as hers. Once she took up with Benji I distanced myself.

But Flora always flitted from one group to another, one boy to another. Her friends – boyfriends, too – loved her, but she was less engaged. Almost like what she needed the most was to be wanted, and once they did, she lost interest. I think only Benji – and maybe Leo – had any kind of hold on her feelings.

The grief in me and around me is real. But did any of us really know her?

FOURTEEN

SAPHY

By the time we get to Claire's I've run out of swears. No matter how carefully she drove, every single bump and pothole in the road – every moment of acceleration, deceleration – hurt, and I'm teary, exhausted. Now I can't work out how to get out of the car. I'm not allowed to use my arms in case I put too much stress on my incision and half-healed bones, and my legs are too weak.

Finally, Zoe gets in on the other side. With her pushing on one side and Claire supporting me on the other, I manage to get out, and stand next to the car. We start to walk slowly towards the front door, but then I see the steps. There are three of them. I've been here so many times it's not like they are a surprise but seeing them now makes me want to cry.

'I'm not sure I'll be able to do the steps today. Back way?'

Zoe helps me while Claire goes through. Along the side of the house, through a gate, Claire has already unlocked the sliding doors to the kitchen when we get there. I step through. I'm in and I'm all in, both at once.

'We've got a surprise for you,' Claire says. 'Come and see.'

We go through to Claire's front room. The sofas have been moved around to accommodate a beige monstrosity.

'A new chair?'

'Check it out,' Zoe says, and sits down, pushes a button on a control that hangs down the side. The footrest goes up and the back reclines.

'Off, Zoe,' Claire says. 'Show her.'

She pushes another button, and the whole of the chair rises up. I back into it. It goes down as I sit back, and the footrest comes up.

'Do you like it?' Claire says.

I relax back into the chair. 'It's like sitting in a hug. Thank you.'

'Tea?'

'Yes, please.'

Claire heads for the kitchen, and Zoe sits on the sofa. The door swings shut behind Claire, and I shake my head. 'This is it, I'm officially decrepit. I'm sitting in an old lady chair.'

'You don't want it? I'll swap. But I think you should stay put. You look wrecked.'

'Thanks a lot. Though I have to admit, it's really comfy.'

'I came around last week to try it out. I can report that it's actually impossible to watch TV in it without falling asleep.'

'I can believe it,' I say, but despite feeling, as well as looking, totally wrecked, sleep feels a long way off.

'Is something wrong? You know, apart from moving in with my mum and getting over major surgery and all that.'

I shrug, then flinch at the movement. I'm not sure I want to say what I haven't been able to stop thinking about, since that leaflet was shoved into my hand.

'Out with it.'

'Please stop reading my mind. It's weird. What was with those protestors? It felt like they were looking for me – knew I'd had a transplant. And anyhow, they couldn't use a living heart donor. That doesn't make any kind of sense.'

Claire, coming back through now, must catch part of what I

said. 'It's complete nonsense. Living donors are used for things like kidneys. A living donor can donate a kidney because we have two and can live with just one. So, one can help someone else, the other will be enough to keep the donor alive.'

'But if that's all it is, then what are they going on about?'

'Don't give it another thought. Organ donations like hearts come from people who have sadly died. And you know your identity and what surgery you had are protected under privacy laws. They weren't looking for you; they were just bothering everyone who couldn't get away from them fast enough.'

'That definitely is you just now,' Zoe says.

FIFTEEN

FERN

Flora loved a party. If she were here – if it was someone else's wake – the atmosphere would ease with her presence. The colour has been leached out of the house.

It would be better if I had died. Who would miss me?

I give myself a mental shake, then steer the waiter and his tray of wine away from Mum. Instead, I take a glass myself and try a sip, but it sits like acid in my stomach.

OK, Fern, I tell myself, Mum isn't up to hostess duties and Flora isn't here. It's up to you. Circle the room. Thank people for coming. You can do this.

'Fern. We're so sorry for your loss. Still can't take it in.' Mum's friends, Roslyn and Brian: Leo's parents. They adopted Leo when he was ten and he is the misfit of their impeccable family.

'How is Leo?'

They exchange a glance. 'Not great. We did try to get him to come.'

I want to ask, but don't. Then Roslyn volunteers it. 'Still clean and sober though,' she says, voice lowered.

'I'm glad.'

I wander the room, speaking to aunts, uncles, cousins whose names I'm struggling to remember. Friends of Flora – many I recognise, more I don't. I scan the room for Imogen – she was at the service, but doesn't seem to have come. I'd meant to speak to her earlier but she didn't come past the receiving line at the funeral, either. Some of the unrecognised guests turn out to be friends of Flora's from primary school, others from university. All the while I'm keeping one eye on Mum. Dad seems oblivious, keeping well away from her now – talking in a corner with colleagues. And I wonder, not for the first time, just what is the situation between the two of them. Neither confide in me any more than Flora did. A headache is beginning to pound behind my eyes.

Marley comes over, draws me to the side and gives me a hug. 'I'm going to have to go.'

'Can I come with you?'

'Sure. Do what you want for a change. But you won't.'

'No.' I sigh.

She hesitates. 'There is some news I'm not sure you want to hear, but you will soon and maybe better from me.'

'Go on. Tell me.'

'It hasn't hit the press yet, but I have it on good authority that Benji's defence team have applied to have the murder charge dropped, arguing he can't be tried for murder, because Flora was actually killed when her organs were removed.'

'*What?*' Are they going to try to prove Flora was still alive? How? My throat tightens, feeling sick to even think about it, what it could mean.

'Fern?' I focus on Marley – the concern in her voice, on her face – like Owen and Flora's other friends. Care for Flora seems to have transferred to me. But Marley is the only one who knew how I felt about Benji – I never told her, but she worked it out. Past tense, because how can I still feel that way after what he's done?

'I'm OK. Really.'

She nods, but her raised eyebrow says she doesn't believe me. 'Call me if you ever want to talk? About Flora, or anything else? I mean it.'

'OK. Thanks.' Another hug. She heads over to say goodbye to a few other friends, starts to make her way to the door.

Dad emerges from his corner, comes over to me now. 'Thank you for stepping in. I know how hard this is for you.' A hug and against him I'm feeling and remembering so many things at once that I can't speak. He pulls away. 'How is Marley?'

I'm blinking away tears, surprised he's asking about Marley; he never liked her. 'She's all right, I think.' He's waiting for me to say more, but I'm not telling him what she said about Benji's defence. Not here, not now. 'She was checking how I'm doing, that's all.' His eyes are following her to the door, but then there is a loud crash the other way. Mum has managed to knock over a tray of wine glasses. I hurry over to her.

'It's OK, Mum, sit down. We'll get this cleared up.' Already a waiter is here, sweeping up the shards of glass, but red wine on cream carpets will be harder to fix. Mum sinks back onto the sofa, looking at the spreading red near her feet.

'It's wrong to outlive your child. It's the wrong way around,' she says.

'I know, Mum. But I'm not going anywhere, I promise.'

Her eyes turn to me, unfocused. Puzzled, as if whether I stay or go is of no importance to her.

It's wrong to outlive your little sister, too. But the shadow she casts will never go.

SIXTEEN

SAPHY

I sleep in the chair most of the afternoon, then try to eat some dinner. Food still doesn't taste right; it's the drugs, I think.

I don't argue when Claire helps me to bed not long after that.

'Thanks for everything.'

'You're welcome.' She bends, kisses me on the cheek. 'Goodnight.'

I'm somewhere past tired, fatigue a tangible thing, like I'm caught in treacle, held down by a thick, heavy blanket. But I can't stop myself looking at Flora's images again on my phone.

It was her funeral today. The same day I left hospital. One last appearance; one new beginning.

SEVENTEEN

FERN

Another sunny day, one without Flora in it.

I get up late and start hunting for paracetamol when my phone vibrates with a message. When I pick it up, I see missed calls, more messages. Before I can check them, there is a knock at the door.

There is a twist of unease in my gut as I go to answer.

It's Marley. 'Have you seen the morning papers?'

'Not yet. Is something wrong?'

'The news about Flora has hit the papers. Wasn't me, I promise.'

'About her funeral?' I'm imagining someone reporting on the grieving mother spilling wine and wearing the same dress. We'd managed to mostly keep her away from drink after the tray got knocked over, kept her propped up well enough that any unsteadiness might be put down to grief. If you're an idiot.

'No. It's about Flora, and this nonsense about living donors.' She comes in, passes me a tabloid – broadsheets are under her arm.

I unfold it on the table and there is the headline: *Sleeping Beauty Harvested for Organs*. A photo of Flora, a year or so ago

– glowing and alive at some red-carpet event. Then in a coma, in her hospital bed – before she was put back on the ventilator. Too thin and pale, but she could have just been asleep. How did they get that photo? And the lead line: 'Flora Hastings-Clifford died when her vital organs – heart, lungs, kidneys – were removed for donation and transplant.'

'That's the line Benji's defence have taken. They're reporting it like it's fact?'

'That's not all. He's been granted bail again.'

'They said bail isn't usual in murder cases.'

'It's not. I'm guessing his fancy KC, impeccable record and public school credentials convinced the Crown Court,' she says, rolling her eyes.

There's also a photo of protestors at the hospital. They are protesting the opt-out – that unless you specifically opt out of organ donation, your organs can be used. Though in practice it isn't done if family objects. And they are also protesting the use of what they are calling living donors, saying doctors should prolong life as long as possible, wait until the heart has stopped naturally before any organs are taken. But there is nothing natural about using a ventilator to keep a heart beating, not in someone who is brain-dead.

'How did they even find out that Flora was an organ donor? There is so much privacy around the process of donation and transplant.' Now I'm wondering if – despite saying it wasn't her – Marley might be involved. She is a reporter, after all, and I know how ambitious she is. And how did they get that photo of Flora in a coma? But Marley's name isn't on any of the by-lines, so what would she get out of it? 'Where's my phone?'

Marley points to where I left it on the counter. Missed calls and messages – Mum, Dad, others.

'I'd better call home.'

It's answered by Dad at the first ring.

'Hi, it's me,' I say. 'Yes. I just found out. I can... what about... OK. Yes. I'll come. Yes. Bye.'

'Your presence is requested, I take it?' Marley says. I nod. 'Want a lift? I might be able to help.'

'Are you sure?'

'No problem.'

We don't talk much on the way to Oxford, my mind going around and around in circles. Benji is out on bail again. If the police and everyone are right and Benji is the one who hurt Flora, I should want him behind bars, for as long as possible. But I can't imagine him in prison, how'd he cope. What other prisoners would make of his posh accent.

That's when it hits me. Maybe Benji getting bail hasn't got anything to do with his background and connections, as Marley implied. Was bail granted because the court thought his defence has merit?

The knot of worry in my gut is growing.

There is something I've wanted to do for a long time. Even though it's against the rules and could lead to all kinds of trouble – and not just for me. Until now I've managed to keep away, but I don't think I can any longer.

EIGHTEEN

SAPHY

'Why are we going this way?'

'The hospital called,' Claire says. 'Suggested this would be easier today.'

'Why?'

She pulls up next to a back door. 'Nothing to worry about – just some protestors out front that are best avoided. Wait inside, I'll park and come back and help you. OK?'

She gets out, opens the passenger door, and helps me up. Pain makes me flinch and I try to hide it.

'All right?' she says. I breathe in and out until it fades again, and nod.

She holds open the hospital door for me to go in. 'Wait just here, I won't be long.'

I lean against the wall, eye a chair, not sure if the pain of getting up and down is worth it and decide to stay standing. Wave as she goes, then search 'hospital protests London' on my phone. And there it is:

Sleeping Beauty Harvested for Organs.

I stare at the words. Despite the date discrepancy of when she died and when I had my surgery, I've felt this certainty that my heart came from Flora, but I didn't know whether or not her organs were actually donated. If this headline is correct – she was a donor.

There are links to news about Flora's murder trial. The defence are putting in an application to say she was killed when her organs were removed, so her attacker can't be charged with murder. Seriously? She was dead already – the doctors said so.

Could they have been wrong? I feel sick to even think it.

NINETEEN

FERN

Marley pulls in, parks. I take a deep breath and we get out of the car.

Dorothy – my parents' long-time housekeeper – opens the door. 'Hi, Fern,' she says, sympathy in her eyes. 'Your parents are in the conservatory.'

We go through.

'Hi.' Dad gets up, a quick kiss on the cheek for me, a wary hello to Marley. I'd messaged that she was bringing me, when we were just minutes away: too late to say no.

'Hi, Mum.'

'Fern. Marley.' She's not in tears. She's rigid, angry. 'How could they print these things? They are as good as saying that we – her family – killed Flora.' She glares at Marley as if it is her fault, but before she can respond Dorothy comes in with a tray of tea things, coffee, and takes a moment to set them out. The door closes behind her.

'That application to have the charges dropped is insane. It'll never succeed,' Dad says.

'I expect not,' Marley says. 'But experts will no doubt be called upon to debate it in court. There are some fringe groups that will shout out about it, and it's shining a light on the opt-out for organ donation.'

'We have to do something!' Mum says.

'The way I see this, you have two options,' Marley says. 'Ignore the fuss and wait for it to go away, or meet the questions head on. Explain the personal and medical situation. Stop Flora being used to derail organ donation. Also, you could write to Flora's recipients, see if any of them are willing to waive privacy and tell their side of the story – what a difference she has made to them and their families.'

'That'd be a media circus,' Mum says.

'Maybe. But wouldn't you rather choose how to play it out, and who tells the story?'

Mum is shaking her head. 'No. No way. I'm not speaking to those vultures.' She glances at Marley. 'Present company excepted.'

Marley tilts her head, one eyebrow raised.

'There is no point in debating at least part of this,' Dad says. 'I've done it already.'

'Done what?' Mum says.

'Written to Flora's recipients.'

Mum and me look at Dad, surprised. 'You didn't talk to me about that,' Mum says.

'No. It's something I felt I needed to do. You don't have to be involved if you don't want to be. Anyhow, it is completely up to the recipients. They may not answer, or they may do so but want to stay anonymous.' He takes Mum's hand. 'Margot, being able to help other people live is a gift. If we can show it for what it is, it might save more lives. Other sons and daughters. Parents who won't need to go through what we are going through, now.'

What else could she say but yes?

I'm back to wondering if Marley had a hand in any of this. If Dad decides to go ahead with what she suggests, that'll be a big story. And it would be hers.

TWENTY

SAPHY

Despite all the poking, prodding, blood tests and the complete joy that is a heart biopsy, plus bouncing around in Claire's car to and fro with occasional swearing, I'm feeling ready to face the steps.

'Let's try the front door today,' I say.

'Are you sure?'

'I think so.' We walk up to the steps. The lack of a railing is worrying me.

'Can I help?'

'Just stay next to me so I can use you for balance.'

Claire holds out an arm and I take it. They seem impossibly steep – bigger than steps I practised on in physio in the hospital. But I have to be able to use the front door, don't I?

'OK, here I go.' One step. Pause. Breathe. Two steps. Same. And then three.

'Well done!' Claire says.

I'm breathing hard, feel the sweat on my forehead. Legs not shaking so much as a faint tremor. Actually, it wasn't that bad.

Claire is unlocking the door when Zoe pulls in out front. I'm more focused on getting myself to the chair than on saying hello. I'm backing into it, letting it scoop me up, as Zoe comes in.

Zoe and Claire go to the kitchen, sorting tea, and I'm back on my phone – checking the Flora-related news I'd scanned through earlier.

Then they're back and I try to nibble a homemade biscuit to make Claire happy, not sure of my appetite. Still thinking about what I read online.

'Earth to Saphy,' Zoe says.

'Sorry, did I miss something?'

'What's on your mind, hon?'

'I was just thinking about those protestors at the hospital. They've been in the news, saying people are being killed for their organs.'

'You know that is total rubbish,' Claire says. 'These people would protest anything.'

'I guess. It's freaking me out a bit, though.'

'Try to put it out of your mind,' Zoe says. 'And this should help. I'm planning a Saturday night out in a few weeks, to cele-brate your amazing recovery. Friends from school and my work – don't argue, it's all set up. We can invite anyone else you want.'

A night out? With a load of people, only some of whom I know, all carrying potential deadly germs. All staring at me with sympathetic, curious eyes.

'Uh, I don't know.'

'You're on a schedule, remember?'

'A schedule?'

'Less than five weeks left of eight: we have to find you a man.'

'But I'm not allowed to go to crowded places for the first three months.'

'I've taken care of that – it's outdoors. A beer garden. Spoke to them about reserving us an area with more space around so you can breathe fresh air and all that.'

I look to Claire, expecting a repeat of the three-month rule.

'That sounds like fun, doesn't it?' she says.

'I'll think about it.'

TWENTY-ONE

FERN

We're finally getting back into Marley's car for the return trip to London.

'That didn't go quite the way I thought it would,' she says, as we head up the drive.

'Dad surprised me. He was always so protective, at pains to keep family private and us away from the world. Especially Flora. Until she was old enough that he couldn't stop her. And now he wants to talk to the press? About Flora? I'm not just surprised. I'm shocked.'

'It makes sense, but I was expecting it to take time for him to see that. And he even talked your mum around.'

'Though it is still a long shot. Even if one or more of the recipients want to meet their donor's family, it's a big jump from that to being interviewed by the press about it. Especially when they find out who their donor was, and all the attention she's been getting.'

'True. Time will tell. Your dad has a knack of getting his way though, don't you think?'

'Not with Flora – not in recent years, anyhow,' I say, but Marley has a point. Even when I think Dad hasn't prevailed and I've won an argument, I usually find in the end that it was how he wanted things anyhow. He's got a way with words, for making anything sound reasonable.

'What do you think?' Marley says. 'You never really said.'

'About talking to the press about Flora and interviewing one of her recipients? Honestly, I'm not sure. My personal inclination is no, but there are other considerations.'

'Such as?'

'If people opt out of organ donations because of this – or families block donation – or the campaign to change donation from opt-out back to opt-in gets traction – people will die. People who didn't have to die if they got a transplant. Try looking someone in the eye and tell them they're dying, that nothing can be done. It's not a part of the job I'll ever get used to. It's a miracle to be able to save lives now, that decades ago we couldn't.'

'Could you write that down? It's good.'

'So long as you don't quote me.'

There is one person we're not talking about with all of this, even though her name is in every conversation.

What would Flora want us to do? I honestly don't know. Even though she was really out there – an extrovert, completely – in many ways she could still be very private. She kept things to herself, probably too much. All I want is what she'd want. But there is an uneasy feeling running through me about all of this, one I can't explain to Marley. I should talk to Dad. Make sure he's thought all this through. Anyway, there's time. If this even happens it won't be quick.

'I think that was a new record for Oxford to London,' Marley says, as she pulls up in front of my home.

'Thanks again.' I hesitate. 'Are you sure that going to the press is the right thing to do?'

'Yes. Trust me – it's my bucking bronco we're dealing with here. I know what I'm doing.'

Trust me, she says. But I'm not sure I would if her interests were different to mine. Marley has always been very career focused: would she give up a story for my sake, or my family? I doubt it.

Marley pulls away and I walk towards the front door, shuffling for keys in my bag. I sense rather than see movement behind me and start to turn when a hand grabs my shoulder, pulls me around roughly and pushes me back against the door so hard that my head smacks against it. There is a lurch of fear in my gut. Then I see who it is: Leo.

'Were you going to tell me?' His grip tightens on my shoulders.

'Tell you what?'

'What you did to Flora – you and your father.' He almost spits out the last word. 'Nothing he could do would surprise me. But I thought you were better than that.'

'Leo, calm down. Let me go, and we'll talk.' His face, so close to mine – rage and pain – bloodshot eyes. Dilated pupils. 'Have you been using?'

'What does it matter anymore? Someone is going to have to pay. Pay for what they did to Flora.' His grip on my shoulders tightens, and there is real fear in my gut.

'Leo! Back off.' It's Marley; she must have seen, pulled in again.

Her phone is in her hand. 'Yes. Police. There is a man assaulting and threatening a woman.' She gives the address, and I see the indecision in Leo's eyes. Then he lets me go and runs.

'Really, I'm fine. Can we just leave this? Leo has been through a traumatic loss. He wasn't thinking clearly. I don't think he'd do anything to hurt me.'

Marley is scowling. 'I'm not so sure. I heard what he said – he threatened you.'

I shake my head. 'It wasn't a threat against me – all he said was that someone is going to have to pay for what happened to Flora. And that person has been charged.'

'Are you sure?' the policewoman says.

'I'm sure,' I say, even though I'm not. Leo was angry about the organ donation, wasn't he? Which has nothing to do with Benji. But I don't want them arresting Leo, hearing the things he has been saying. And Leo might have landed on his feet when he was adopted by Mum's friends, but his life before then left marks that may never go. Despite that, he's been doing so well lately. The thought of Leo landing back in jail, for this? I don't want that on my conscience.

'OK then. Any other problems, call us.'

'I will. Thank you.'

Marley waits for the door to shut behind them. 'I'm worried about you. Leo is a nutter.'

'Look, he really isn't that bad. I've known him since he was a skinny little kid; I've seen his temper before. He'll be over it by now.'

'You're too soft for your own good. I've really got to go. Keep the door locked and call the police if he turns up again.'

'I will. Thanks.'

She's gone and then seconds later, the door opens and Marley peers in. 'It isn't locked. Lock it!'

I follow her to the door, close it behind her and turn the deadbolt, the key lock, too. It rattles seconds later, and I hear her call bye through it.

I watch through the window as her car disappears up the road. I'm alone at last.

A quick change of clothes – dark trousers, a pullover with a hood. I tuck my hair away, put some sunglasses on for good measure and head out the door.

TWENTY-TWO

SAPHY

My thoughts drift back to the protestors at the hospital. I give up on napping and take out my phone.

The protestors are easy to find – they've been vocal all over the place. Trying to understand why they are protesting is more difficult. It's like they're saying someone is alive who doctors say is dead. They might be breathing – with a ventilator, but still breathing – and their heart beating. Their skin, warm. All things that would make me think they are alive. But if neurological tests show that their brain stem is dead, that's it. They have no chance of recovery and are considered dead according to law, even though their heart is still beating.

When I got the call that a heart was available, I was surprised that they seemed to know just when the surgery would be. But it makes sense if my donor was in a coma, like Flora: heart beating inside her, until the last moment.

Something hits me.

I'd thought Flora couldn't be my donor because she died the day before my surgery. But if she failed brain stem tests the day before – then that would be the official day and time of death.

And then she could have been kept ventilated while they got ready to take her organs?

Then Flora really could be my donor.

I search for images of Flora again, and her face fills the screen. She's so vital, so alive – even just in a photograph.

What happened to you, Flora?

Benjamin Lawrence has been charged with her murder. I find his image again, look for what else there is about him but, unlike Flora, until he was arrested there is very little online. Social media links come up but when I try them, the accounts are closed. I'm guessing he bowed out because once you've been branded a murderer – even before the trial – socials could get toxic in a hurry.

I check my email. My inbox is mostly full of junk – sales of stuff I can't afford. Spam. Bills. But hiding in the midst of it all is one from the Donor Family Care Service.

The words blur and swim so that it takes a moment to take in their meaning. They have a letter for me from the father of my donor. Do I want them to send it to me?

There's a twist of nerves in my gut. I might be able to find out if Flora really was my donor.

All along I was so certain that she was. Even when the date of death seemed to preclude it, I'd felt this strong connection to her. Do I want it confirmed one way or another?

Well, they can send the letter. I don't have to read it straight away – I can leave it until I'm sure.

I reply with a *yes*.

TWENTY-THREE

FERN

I get off the bus a stop early. Walk down a familiar street, then a back lane. I count the houses to make sure I'm at the right garden. No one is around. His gate is locked. I push a bin on its side to stand on and manage to pull myself over the fence.

The kitchen window is wide open, faint Radio Four coming from further inside. He must be home. Is he alone? I stay still, listen for any voices. None.

Would his house be bugged while he waits for trial or is that just on TV? I don't know, but instead of knocking I stand back. Throw a few bits of shingle from the garden against the door. Wait a moment. Do it again. There are footsteps inside. The door opens.

Benji stares, not recognising me and I take off the sunglasses. His eyes open wide. He comes out, shuts the door and we're looking at each other, neither of us moving.

He's changed. Aged in just months. There are dark circles under his eyes, he's lost weight, but it isn't just the physical things I can see – it's the anguish etched in features as familiar to me as my own. He makes a sound between a word and a cry and then he's here, close, his arms around me, shaking as he holds me.

He finally pulls away, takes my hand and pulls me to a bench in the back corner of the garden.

'You shouldn't be here,' he says.

'I know. I just had to see you.'

'Being near anyone in Flora's family is a breach of my bail.'

'You didn't come to me, I came to you.'

'Not sure they'd care.' He ruffles his hair back, a familiar gesture, but he's not the same person he was. Neither am I. 'Aren't you going to ask me?' he says.

'What?'

'If I did it.'

'I don't have to. I know you didn't.' I say the words even though I'm not as sure as they sound. He's more likely to do what I want if he believes me.

He asks me about Flora. Her treatment, care. Her last hours. And he doesn't ask but I tell him about the brain stem tests, and how she failed them all: fixed, unreactive pupils; no corneal, vestibulo-ocular, gag or cough reflexes. No response to supra-orbital pressure. The apnoea test that I hated most of all. Her ventilator was switched off; she was watched continuously for five minutes for any spontaneous respiration. Five minutes is so long. I was caught in this place of wanting a miracle, pleading with her to breathe on her own, to make this stop. What I don't tell Benji is that at the same time, I wanted her to fail. For it to end. To let Flora go.

Benji's tears are falling, along with mine.

'You can't let your defence say that removing Flora's organs was what killed her. Please, don't put us through that – it's destroying Mum. And so many other people could suffer, die, if more people opt out.'

He says he'll think about it. And then we say goodbye.

. . .

It's only after I leave that I realise: he never said that he didn't do it.

The changes I saw in him could be because the woman he loved was attacked by someone else and died, and if he is found guilty and imprisoned, they will stay free, unpunished. Or it could be because he did it, and he can't live with the guilt. Which is it?

I thought if I saw him in person, I would know for sure, one way or the other. But I don't.

I stare out the window on the bus home. It's starting to rain, dirty streaks on the windows. I'm going back in my mind, trying to remember every detail leading up to Flora's attack. To see if there was something, anything, that I'd missed. That the police might have missed, too.

Flora wasn't herself, hadn't been for days, weeks. Maybe longer. Did it go back to when she broke up with Benji? Maybe. I'm not sure.

I remember things had been particularly strained that Christmas. Mum had too much wine, Dad was physically there but absent. Flora had been in one of her moods. There was an edge to her that most people didn't see – black moods, getting angry over nothing. Afterwards, it was obvious that something was wrong. It hurts so much that I didn't ask her what it was.

When we got back to London, she was suddenly throwing things in a case, said she was going to go away for a few days. She wanted some time out. I knew she was going to our family cottage in Dorset because she took the keys.

The next day, Benji asked me to swap some shifts so he could have a few days off. I wondered if he was going to Flora – maybe they were going to get back together. But he didn't say where he was going and I didn't ask.

After Flora was strangled but before Benji was arrested, he told me that Flora had called him, asked him to go to Dorset to meet her. Said she had to tell him something. But when he got there, she was unconscious. Tied to the bed, barely breathing. That he'd tried to help her, called for an ambulance, but she never regained consciousness.

What if Benji went to Flora – expecting reconciliation – and then either they argued or that wasn't why Flora wanted to see him? Then he lost it. But then why would he have had sedatives with him? That suggests he planned it all along, and I can't believe that. Besides, the way she was strangled suggested cold control, not a burst of anger.

Then another possibility hits me, one I hadn't thought of before. It's only Benji who says Flora asked him to go to Dorset. Maybe she didn't. Maybe he'd called her and she let slip where she was, but she didn't want him to come, at all. And then he planned it out. Went there. Drugged her, strangled her. Denied it all. Is that how the police see it?

My head is aching as I watch the rain fall on grey London, tortured by questions I can't answer.

TWENTY-FOUR

SAPHY

The evening is like every other I've had since moving in after my surgery. Claire announces bedtime at ten. She watches me take my immunosuppressants and comes in the bedroom with me, shuts the curtains. She doesn't leave and shut the door until I'm tucked in.

She's taking looking after me a little too seriously, hovering nearby as if to check I'm still breathing. That makes me feel like I should be worried about that, too: is there something that could go wrong they've told her and not me? Part of me is feeling annoyed; part of me is relishing having someone who cares enough to do things like this. I mean, I miss Hermione, my cat – a neighbour is looking after her for me – but apart from seeing Zoe and Claire now and then, long months in a house alone with meows the only conversation have been hard.

I can't stop thinking about Flora, her family. Is the letter the DFCS are going to send me from Flora's dad?

A new search on my phone: Flora Hastings-Clifford's parents. Right at the top is Flora's obituary. Her family are named: parents, Dr Charles Clifford and Ms Margot Hastings, and sister Dr Fern Hastings-Clifford.

I read link after link.

Her dad is sixty, an orthopaedic surgeon at the Radcliffe in Oxford. He's got an OBE for services to medicine and charity work. Her mum is a garden designer. She's even won gold medals at Chelsea, though not recently. Flora's older sister, Fern, is in emergency medicine at St Mary's in London.

A garden designer, with Flora and Fern as daughters? It'd be like Charles calling them Knee and Hip.

There is a family photo from four years ago, when Charles got his OBE. Cameras loved Flora. It's hard to notice anyone else in it, though if you did it would be her dad. He's tall, well-built, striking. If he's sixty now he must have been fifty-six then, but despite a sprinkle of silver in dark hair at his temples, he doesn't look it. Margot's blonde hair is carefully styled; she is slim, well dressed, with family around her, but there is something about the set of her face despite the smile for the camera. Not a happy woman. Fern is shorter than Flora, not overweight so much as stockier in build. There's more of her dad in her – dark hair, square jaw, a direct look – yet what looks good on him does less for her.

Maybe that is unfair. Standing next to Flora – in her red dress, red hair – head tilted to one side, Fern pales in comparison. Anyone would. Even in a photo, Flora was magnetic. I screenshot and crop the photo, so it is only Flora. I save it and make it the lock screen on my phone. This way I can look at her whenever I want, without doing searches that lead me from page to page.

I need to get some sleep, but I keep looking into Flora's eyes on my lock screen. Each time it starts to go dark I touch it again, make Flora reappear. I can't stop looking at her. She must be the most beautiful woman I've ever seen. With the light going through her on my screen, she's vital, alive. If I let the screen go dark, she'll disappear. I have to touch the screen over and over again to keep her with me.

This is fantasy: she's dead, gone. I close my phone, throw it across to the chair so I can't reach for it without getting up.

The Flora the cameras saw, the one in the papers and online, was beautiful, glamorous. She had nerve, you could see it in her eyes. She was so alive. If I have her heart inside of me, it might be three years younger than I am but there's no doubt that with its previous owner it has been places and done things I never have. That I never thought I could.

Maybe it's time to live. To stop being so afraid.

* * *

I'm looking in a full-length mirror, but it isn't me that I see. She's taller, though that might just be the heels; willowy without being too thin; vivid red hair, absolutely perfect make-up – blue eyes made up with dark cat's eye flicks to the side – like Cleopatra. She's looking back at me as I look at her, a reflection studying a reflection – staring at each other. But then her eyes narrow, she shakes her head and walks away.

Once she's gone, the mirror is blank. On my own, I have no reflection. I am nothing.

Please, come back!

Flora, help me...

TWENTY-FIVE

FERN

My leave is over and it is night shift tonight. I walk to St Mary's across Kensington Gardens and Hyde Park, hoping the fresh air will revive me.

It's early evening, a taste of rain to come in the air. Dog walkers, couples holding hands, joggers go by. Flora loved walking in the park. She was desperate to get a dog but listened to me for once when I said that it wouldn't be fair to have a pet when we both worked. Sometimes I wonder if we'd got, say, an Alsatian, if it would have protected her – stopped her from being tied up and strangled.

My head aches from hitting the door when Leo pushed me. I'm tempted to cry concussion and get off work, but that would just make it harder for everyone else.

It's not just the headache and lack of sleep that have my steps getting slower and more reluctant the closer I get to the hospital. Going back to the usual feels somehow wrong, almost like saying, *Flora has died but that's all over now, just get on with things.*

Leo was so upset, angry, from what was in the papers. Everyone will either have read about it by now or been told by someone who has. The endless focus and speculation on all things Flora had almost died down, but it'll be back all over again, won't it?

I want to hide, but I have work to do. I pause a moment by the hospital entrance, breathe deeply, in, out, in, out, then step through.

Soon I'm absorbed in work. A child with a broken arm who fell from a slide. A serious RTA – internal and head injuries, broken bones. Some DIY gone wrong, sent for surgery to have a finger reattached. A stroke. Later, stab wounds: children stabbing children. Something I will never understand. Emergency is the usual hectic madness, made worse by colleagues seeking me out, trying to say something kind about Flora, her funeral.

The messages from Leo start at 2 a.m.

I'm so sorry.

Please forgive me.

Why don't you answer? I said I'm sorry.

Are you ignoring me?

I need to talk to you. Please.

Answer me or I'll find you and make you listen!

TWENTY-SIX

SAPHY

The next day I can't stop thinking about my dream of Flora and the mirror. How I vanished without her. I felt so worthless, begging for her to come back, to help me. I tell myself it was just a dream, it doesn't mean anything.

I do have a reflection; I am something. I will prove it to myself. I want – *need* – to grasp this extra bit of life I've been given. At least, I'm ready to try.

Worrying about all the things that could go wrong is no way to live. I can't stay here with Claire hovering over me much longer, but there is only one other place I can go: home. I both want to be there, desperately, and I'm afraid. There was the loss of my mum as a background note, always, but home was mostly a happy place before Dad died – before I knew I would follow him. More recently, it was the place where I wanted to die. And I'm not sure if that will all come back when I step through the door, as if all the pain and sadness seeped into the walls of the house.

But I have to try.

'Claire, there's something I need to talk to you about.'

'That sounds serious.'

'I'm feeling so well. I haven't felt as good as I do now in as long as I can remember. Every day I have more energy.'

'That's brilliant.'

'And I want to thank you for all that you've done for me. It means more than you'll ever know.'

'Why do I get the feeling there is a "but" following?'

'I'm ready to go home. I need to look after myself – prove that I can do it. Before you say, I know all the precautions, all the things I should and shouldn't do. All the tablets and when to take them, the symptoms not to ignore. The exercises and all the rest. I can do this.'

'I think it's too soon. What if something goes wrong and you're alone?'

'Something can always go wrong – from now until the end. I can't live in your spare room forever. I need to live this new life I've been given.'

'Oh, Saphy. I want that for you, too. I'm just worried.' And Claire is out of her seat, giving me a hug and there are tears in her eyes, and now mine, too.

TWENTY-SEVEN

FERN

I get there early. I need some serious caffeine and queue for a triple shot espresso, then sit at a table in a back corner. I'm not sure this was a good idea. Maybe I should go – message that something came up. I'm half out of my seat when Leo comes in the front door. I settle back down, hoping he didn't notice, and wave. He comes over, sits opposite me.

'Hi, Leo. Do you want a drink?'

'Not that sort,' he says, then holds up a hand. 'Before the lecture begins – I'm not drinking. The other day was a one-off.'

'I'm really glad to hear that.'

'Look, I said it in my texts. I'm sorry about what I said, what I did. I just lost it. And I'm guessing from the absence of police at my front door that you didn't send them my way. So, thanks.'

'It's OK. We've been through a lot together, haven't we?'

'Yeah. We have. But we need to talk about Flora. That last time you got me in to see her, her eyes were open. She was blinking when I asked her stuff. She couldn't move, but she was totally there and with it; I know she was. I could see the Flora I knew in her eyes.'

'We all got very excited for a while, thought that she might be turning a corner – might recover, at least partially. Me included. But brain injuries are so unpredictable. She started deteriorating again, had to be put on a ventilator. There were no signs of consciousness after that – none. She was assessed, not by Dad or me. Two doctors in her care team – doctors who have nothing to do with organ transplantation – came to the same conclusion. She was gone.'

He's shaking his head. 'I know she was there; she was fighting – she was going to come back to me—'

I put a hand over his on the table, not wanting to think about the day Flora was tested, but I need to make him understand. 'Leo, if wanting could have made it happen, she would have. Someone who is brain stem dead can never recover.'

'But in the papers – what they said – that she was still alive. That they killed her, by taking her heart and other organs – took them and gave them to somebody else.'

'She was already dead. All they did was keep her body ventilated a little longer than they otherwise would have done, so her organs could save other lives.'

'But if her heart was beating, she was still my Flora. How could they do that to her – just cut into her?'

'I promise you, Leo: someone who is brain stem dead has no idea what is happening at all. They aren't conscious in any way.' I try for the certainty in my voice – the doctor voice – searching for words that will reassure. 'They can't breathe for themselves; they are not conscious and will never recover. Whether or not the ventilator is switched off, they will die, usually within days. Flora's organs saved other lives. Hers was already gone.'

He's shaking his head; he doesn't believe me or doesn't want to. He gets up, pushes the chair so it crashes on the floor, then he tips the table. Espresso and shards of glass fly everywhere. Everyone is looking, someone coming from behind the counter. Leo pushes him out of the way and runs.

I pay for the damages, convince them not to call the police. And hope, so hard, that, with time, what I said to Leo will settle. Make sense. Ease him enough to let it go.

TWENTY-EIGHT
SAPHY

Claire pulls up in front and my eyes drink it in, all three floors –
much too big for me on my own. Sash windows that need paint-
ing. Front garden a mess and back even worse, but it's home.
Maybe these weeks away from it were what I needed to feel that
way again.

'Are you sure you're ready for this, Saphy?' Claire says.

'I'm sure.'

'Any time you want to come back and stay, you'll always be
welcome.'

'I know. Thank you.'

I get out of the car. Open the gate and walk through the
poor neglected front garden. Find the key in my bag.

I open the door. Claire puts my bag through into the hall.

'Call if you need anything.'

'I will. Claire, thank you for everything. You've been amazing. I just need to get back on my own two feet now.'

'I know. But take it easy.'

'I will, I promise.'

She gives me a careful hug. Goes to her car, starts it. I wave
as she pulls away.

I go in, close the door, and lean on it. Shut my eyes a moment, and pretend: I'm just back from school, or work, and Dad is in the kitchen. But he isn't, he never will be again, and somehow, despite all these months of being without him, I still can't believe it's forever.

Light footsteps patter down the stairs. I open my eyes just as an indignant sound halfway between a meow and a howl – a miaowl, Dad called it – fills the silence, followed by a whole chorus of miaowls. How one little tabby cat can sound like an army of them is a mystery of sound and physics.

'OK, Hermi, I'm home now. I'm sorry I abandoned you. I was busy having surgery and stuff. And I know Neeha has been fussing you and giving you extras by the looks of you.' I go into the kitchen, the chorus by my feet continuing. There's a note on the kitchen table, next to a pile of post: *Welcome home! Milk and a few bits are in the fridge. Call if you need us. N.*

I open the fridge and smile. 'A few bits' looks enough to feed a family of four for a week. I find some cheese, break off a piece. Sit on a chair, hold it out and the miaowls pause. Hermi looks at the cheese, considering. She deigns to accept it, her rough warm tongue extracting it neatly. 'Up?' I say; she turns her head to one side, weighing up the pros and cons. Then leaps into my arms, purring.

I hold her close, stroke her. Tell her how beautiful she is and scratch behind her ears. I don't think I'd still be around if it wasn't for Hermi. When I was the lowest, she always seemed to know to stay close. Didn't mind if I cried into her fur and held her tight, didn't care how red my eyes were or if I stayed in pyjamas all day. I didn't have to pretend I was coping when I wasn't.

Tears are close now. I need to think of something else. I take my phone out of my pocket, touch the screen and Flora lights up. I look into her eyes. *Are you my donor, Flora?* Her eyes stare back at mine, seem to say *yes*. Then she disappears as the screen goes dark.

The letter from my donor's dad – could it be in this pile of post? I reach around Hermi, leaf through the junk mail, the bills, with one hand. Somewhere in the mix is an official-looking envelope.

Hands shaking a little, I open it. There's a cover letter from the DFCS and a separate envelope, inside, from my donor's dad.

I open the envelope carefully, take out and unfold a sheet of cream paper – textured and thick, the expensive kind. And it's handwritten. Even, neat rows of black ink swim in front of my eyes.

Here we go. It starts with *Dear mystery girl*. I smile. I like that. Before I read the rest, I scan down: it's signed... Charles. Goosebumps run like spiders on the back of my neck, my arms: Flora's father's name is Charles. I read the rest:

First, to introduce myself. I'm Charles. The brief bio I'm allowed to share at this point is that I'm sixty years old, a doctor, married, with two daughters. My youngest daughter was your donor.

I thought you might like to know about her, but now that a pen is in my hand, it is hard to find the words. She was beautiful. Intelligent. Funny. Generous. Loved by her family, friends and all who knew her. I suppose all parents say these things, but she truly was exceptional in so many ways.

We'll never recover from losing her, but there is some comfort in knowing that she may have saved the lives of others. Wherever she may be now, I know she'd be happy to know this, too. I hope you will write back, or get in touch directly? I've asked the DFCS to give you my details if you ask for them. I'd love to meet you.

Best wishes,

Charles

Flora's dad is a doctor named Charles who is sixty years old; this letter is from a doctor named Charles who is sixty years old. And Flora had one older sister – he has two daughters; the younger one was my donor. It all adds up. There is a flip of excitement in my gut, and my heart rate speeds up – *th-thump, th-thump* – as if with each beat Flora's heart is telling me: I was right.

Before I can think about it anymore, I get my phone and find the number for the DFCS on the cover letter. Enter it and hit call.

A woman answers and I explain who I am, about my recent heart transplant. The letter they've sent from the father of my donor. After confirming my identity – and finding the authorisation of my donor's father to provide his details – they say they'll email the information.

It lands in my inbox soon after we say goodbye. It starts with his full name. I stare at the letters that make it up and look again to make sure I'm not just seeing what I want to see: there are more goosebumps on my neck, arms. He *is* Dr Charles Clifford. I was right.

And now I have his email address and mobile phone number.

I could call him. I could do it now.

What do I want to say?

Thank you: that's pretty high on the list. But after that, I want to give a sense of who I am, and why what they've done is amazing and important. But that's like saying, *I'm amazing and important.* And who am I? What have I ever done to make me useful or worthwhile? Being unwell has become such a part of me that I don't know what else is there.

Hermi jumps down, walks to the stairs. She turns and looks back.

'Good plan, Hermi. A change of scene might help.'

Up one flight – past Dad's room, his study, my room. Now up another. I'm almost walking normally – maybe not skipping up them like I used to, but one step, and another, no stop to rest. I reach the top.

This loft space was my childhood playroom, then teenage hangout. Zoe stayed, often. Later it became my reading and writing space.

Low bookshelves that Dad made fill the wall space under the sloping ceiling all around. My books are lined up by colour, because how else would you organise your books? And notebooks. So many notebooks. Some half started, abandoned. Many more blank. Pages of promise, now dusty. Soon, I promise them and myself.

I haven't used my laptop in so long that the battery is flat. I plug it in, then carefully lower myself to my favourite beanbag, in front of the round window that looks out on the street. Hermi climbs up the back of it and perches half on the beanbag, half on my shoulder.

I open my laptop, log in and begin.

Dear Charles,

Thank you for writing. And a million times, thank you, thank you, thank you for this life-saving gift. It's bittersweet, knowing what I have now is only possible because you and your family have lost someone you dearly loved.

A little about me. My name is Saphira Logan, but everyone calls me Saphy. I'm twenty-eight years old and live in London. My mother died when I was three. I got Covid, and then my dad did, too. I had a congenital heart problem that was worsened by this infection, and it was touch or go if

I'd ever make it out of the hospital. When I finally did, it was alone. My dad fought so hard to not leave me, but he didn't make it.

It wasn't long after that that the doctors told me my only hope was a heart transplant. And that's where you and your family came into the picture. Your generosity in the face of tragedy saved my life.

You said you'd like to meet? I would like that very much. You have my email now; I'll put phone etc below.

Best wishes,

Saphy

I read it through a few times, then hit send.

TWENTY-NINE

FERN

Reading the news is always painful, but even more so lately. All this fuss about the court application for Benji's murder charge to be dropped has exploded, and I can't stop myself from reading every headline, every article. Hoping for an update that doesn't come.

I'm getting ready for work, TV on in the background. Then run to grab the remote and rewind to make sure I heard it correctly.

'It's just in that Dr Benjamin Lawrence's legal team have dropped the application to have his murder charge dismissed. The application had claimed that Flora Hastings-Clifford was actually murdered by retrieval of her organs. They've put out a statement that their client, as a doctor, cannot accept this argument being used in his defence, that he supports the position of the Academy of Medical Royal Colleges and the medical diagnosis of death.'

The news continues. Legal and medical experts and so on are called on for their opinions, and I'm listening, transfixed, flooded with relief, then glance at the time. Go now or be late.

I'm locking up, then walking, tears in my eyes. I can't reconcile the Benji I know – the caring, dedicated doctor – who has done this, because I asked him to, with the one accused of Flora's murder.

THIRTY

SAPHY

Hermi starts swiping at my hair, and I'm surprised to see that the sun is low in the sky. I'm stiff, sore, and the beanbag turns out to have been a bad idea: getting up from it is a bitch. Hermi looks impressed at my recent mastery of four-letter words.

'Dinner time, Hermi?' She dashes ahead down the stairs, then looks back impatiently when I'm still on the top few. Going down the stairs seems harder than going up them was a few hours ago.

My phone rings. It's Claire.

'Hi, Claire.'

'Hi, Saphy. How's it going?'

'Good, thanks. I've remembered my tablets, before you ask.'

'Excellent work. Have you had anything to eat?'

'Not yet, but I was about to forage in the fridge. My lovely neighbour has filled it – literally. And I've got your yummy cake as well.'

'I've found a friend who can bring your chair around to you in a van tomorrow.'

My chair? The old lady monstrosity.

'Are you sure? Let me pay you for it,' I say, but I know I can't, and so does she.

'Absolutely not.'

'Claire, I don't know what to say.' I owe her so much that I'll never be able to repay and I'm blinking back tears. 'Thank you.'

'Give me front row seats at your first book launch, and a trip up the red carpet when it gets made into a movie. That'll be perfect. Bye, Saphy.'

'Bye, Claire.'

And I do all that I said, more or less. My appetite has been poor since the surgery, probably from all the drugs. Perhaps I've got more used to them as it seems to be back in force. It takes willpower to only have one small piece of cake after dinner. I'm in bed by ten, Hermi purring along my back – not sleeping with pets is one recommendation I'm going to flout – but I'm not ready to sleep just yet.

I'm curious about this Dr Charles Clifford, his family. He said he wants to meet. Would it be just him or would his wife and other daughter be there, too? What would they make of me? I'm even more curious about Flora. There is so much about her that I want to know, need to know. Every fact I can fill in will make her seem closer.

Before any of this happened, there were so many images of her online at events, often on the arm of different men. If they went through all her ex-boyfriends as suspects, it would have taken a while.

There are photos from much longer ago, also. There are several taken at the Chelsea Flower Show, alongside her mum, who had just won a gold. Checking the dates, Flora would have been eleven. She was blonde back then. The red was too bright to be natural so of course she was dying it, but why would she? Her hair was beautiful: blonde like her mum's, with natural-looking streaks. Even though the vibrant red suited her, now

I've seen her as a blonde, maybe the red was, I don't know, too much.

I'm transfixed, absorbing snippets of Flora's life, but all the time wanting more.

Why am I doing this? I can't even begin to answer. Maybe if I can meet her family, I'll get closer to Flora, to who she was. Which reminds me to check my emails in case Charles has answered.

And... he has. It was sent almost as soon as I emailed and it's been sitting there, patiently waiting, in my inbox. It takes me a moment to gather myself enough to read it.

Dear Saphy,

I'm so pleased to hear from you. This may seem soon, but are you free for lunch on Sunday? You mentioned you live in London – we're in Oxford. I'd book a car here and back again for you; I'm sure you'd rather avoid trains so soon after your transplant. Let me know what you think.

Best wishes,

Charles

Lunch – on Sunday? That really is very soon. But I want to meet him, don't I? So there's no point in delaying it.

Answer now or stay awake all night thinking about it.

I reply *yes*.

I need to sleep, but my phone is still in my hand. A different image of Flora – one that I found earlier, of when she was in a coma – fills my lock screen now. She looks like she is sleeping. I try to imagine that I am her parent, her sister, a friend. That the doctors all say she is brain stem dead, that there is no hope. That

I see her like this. Would I believe them, or fight to keep her this way as long as possible?

I want to hold her, protect her. Keep her safe. But it's too late.

When my eyes finally close, I'm pretending that Flora is here with me, now. Her arms are around me and mine are around her. She's whispering in my ear as the phone slips from my hand.

I drift to uneasy dreams. Of Flora, being taken to surgery, aware – silent screams that no one could hear. Her heart ripped out and stolen.

THIRTY-ONE

FERN

I'm rushing for the Tube when my phone rings. I'm almost at the entrance and think of ignoring it, but ever since I missed the first call about Flora, I get this uneasy feeling if I let a call go to message. It's not like getting the news earlier could have changed anything, but I scramble to get my phone out before it's too late.

It's Dad. I walk away from the stairs to the side, and answer.

'Hi.'

'Glad I caught you. I've had an email back from Flora's heart recipient. She'd like to meet us.'

'Really? It's so soon.'

'I'll forward her email to you. I've put it on the family calendar for Sunday lunch.'

'How's Mum – is she up to doing this?'

'She'll be fine.'

'Have you asked her?'

'Less warning works better, you know that. I have to go. I'll see you then.' Click – call ended.

Less warning so Mum has less time to get stressed. But I'm not sure that's fair with this.

Do I want to go? I sigh. Our family synched calendar includes both mine and Dad's work shifts to avoid conflicts; scheduling something there is pretty much a marching order.

I go to my inbox. The email he said he'd forward is there already and I scan it quickly before heading down the stairs.

So that's why she needed a transplant. Too many families have been torn apart by the pandemic. She lives in London; she or her dad could have been my patients. I don't recognise her name, but there were so many.

OK. I am curious to meet her – I admit it – but uneasy at the same time. I'm a doctor; it shouldn't bother me to think when I meet her that she's got Flora's heart beating inside of her. Saying 'Flora's heart' is emotive, but we know the heart isn't the centre of thought or emotion as the ancients believed. It is an organ with four chambers, made up of cells, tissues, like any other organ. It pumps blood around the body, and that's all.

Even though I know these things, I still feel almost queasy to think of meeting her recipient. How will this be for Mum?

I'm almost home when I realise that it's been a long time since Dad called me, without a Flora-shaped reason. But then, this is still about Flora. Isn't it?

THIRTY-TWO

SAPHY

Long dark strands of my hair fall to the floor with each assured snip of scissors. Dye is mixed in little pots; what is left of my hair is pulled this way and that. Soon there is enough tinfoil on my head to make a space helmet.

When the cut is finished and it's being dried, I'm trying not to watch in the mirror. Wanting to wait to see the finished look. There are a few final snips with scissors, hair spray.

'Well, now: all done. What do you think?'

I'm turning this way and that, in front of the mirror. The grin on my face is wide and getting wider.

Just past shoulder-length instead of halfway down my back, it's wavy without the weight pulling it down. Thick pale-blonde slices cut through a dark-blonde base, like white chocolate swirls in caramel. The way it frames my face, the warmer colours – I'm less drawn and pale. Even my brown eyes look lighter, more golden.

'I love it! Thank you, thank you, thank you!'

I add a tip and settle up, then text Zoe.

All done!!! See you there?

Ooh do lots of !!! mean you like it? Show me!

I love it! But will wait to surprise you.

Give me an hour.

Perfect: time for some clothes shopping. I wander into one shop, then another. Browsing without an idea what I am looking for – just wanting something different.

I'm drawn to a yellow jumper, take it off the bar and just hold it, looking at it. Three-quarter-length sleeves, square neckline, pretty details. It's so very soft, my hands are drawn to stroke it. But yellow? And is the neckline high enough to hide my scars? I hold it up in front of me in the mirror.

'That colour really suits you,' a sales assistant says. 'Try it?'

She finds me some grey jeggings and ankle boots to go with it. Pulling the jumper over my head hurts a bit but then when I straighten it, the softness – it's cashmere – against my skin is so soothing. And the neckline is just high enough. When I get the rest of it on and come out to look in the three-way mirror – she's right. The colour is just exactly right on me. She must know by my smile that she's got a sale.

'Can I wear this out?'

'Of course.' She finds scissors; tags are removed. When it's rung up and I see the total I almost faint, then hand my card across.

The pub is one Zoe picked and I follow my map app to it. By the time I get there, the shopping adrenalin is wearing off and I'm tired, sore.

I order a soft drink and sit at the bar while I wait. I feel eyes: I'm being checked out – the guy at the bar, another man there with a girlfriend, who gives him a tug on the hand and a sharp look to get his attention back to her. I feel like a different person.

A few minutes later, Zoe comes in the door. She looks

around, right past me, and then her eyes reverse. Stop on me, widen, and I smile.

'Oh my God, Saphy, you look amazing! I didn't recognise you at first. Wow!' I get up and she gives me a gentle hug, then gets me to spin around and I'm laughing, blushing.

'We're going to celebrate, aren't we?' she says. 'Wine?'

'I think I fancy some bubbles. How about Prosecco?' I say. The guy behind the bar tells us to sit, brings over a bottle, glasses. Opens it for us.

'What are you celebrating?' he says, his eyes on mine.

'Every day is a celebration.'

'I like the way you think. Let me know if you need anything else,' he says, and he's smiling and I'm smiling back.

'He was totally flirting with you,' Zoe says in a low voice, once he's gone.

'Thinking of his tip.'

'He was thinking of something else entirely, trust me.' She pours two glasses and I hold mine up, watch the bubbles. 'What should we drink to?'

'New beginnings.' Our glasses clink. It's been a while; my heart hasn't been up to even one glass of anything, for months before my surgery. I take a cautious sip. The bubbles fizz inside my mouth, tickle my nose. Leave a path of warmth through my body.

'Nice. And this is on me, by the way. I owe you some drinks.'

'Excellent news. But haven't you run out of money yet?'

'Not quite. I think.' A wide-eyed grimace. 'Actually, I'm afraid to find out.'

'Well, either jump on your banking app and make an assessment, or the drinks are on me,' Zoe says, and picks up my phone off the table to hand it to me. The case is open, and the movement brings the lock screen to life. I'd changed it again – back to the one of Flora in a red dress. I snatch it from her hand, snap it closed. Did she notice?

Her eyebrows are drawn together, puzzled. 'Why have you got Sleeping Beauty on your lock screen?'

I'm uneasy, like I've been caught at something I didn't want anyone to know.

'Saphy?'

'I've got some news.'

'Are you changing the subject?'

'News first, and the two things are related. I thought Flora – also known as Sleeping Beauty, as you said – might be my heart donor? It turns out that I was right.'

'Seriously? How did you find out?'

'When I got home, there was a letter from her dad in the post, the one the DFCS – the Donor Family Care Service – forwarded to me. He said he was a sixty-year-old doctor named Charles with two daughters, and that my donor was his younger daughter. I checked online, and that is all exactly the same as Flora's family.'

'That's a lot of similar details, but can you be sure?'

'There's more. He also said that he wanted to get in touch directly. I called the DFCS, got his details. And he *is* Dr Charles Clifford, father of Flora Hastings-Clifford. I emailed, he answered, and—' dramatic pause '—I'm having lunch with him, his wife and daughter on Sunday.' He'd emailed and confirmed that they will all be there.

'I need more Prosecco to process all of that.' She tops up our glasses. 'But that doesn't explain why you've got Flora on your lock screen.'

'I've been doing research – about her and her family – before I knew for sure that she was my donor.' I have another sip for courage. I wasn't sure I wanted to talk about this, but maybe I need to. 'I was just so convinced that it was Flora. But even though I felt sure, having it confirmed – well. It's a strange feeling. And I honestly don't know *why* I was so sure.'.

Her eyes on mine are serious. 'Have you ever had a strong feeling like that, and have it turn out to be wrong? I haven't.'

'I don't think so.'

'There are so many things we know – not us, I mean science, medicine and the rest – but there is still so much that we don't. Who's to say that there isn't a reasonable, logical explanation for how you feel, but we don't understand what it is yet?'

'Or maybe there isn't.'

'Or maybe there isn't. But you were right about Flora being your donor, weren't you? So, it's reasonable to keep an open mind. Trust your instincts – not without thought, but trust them.'

'Thank you, Zoe.'

'So, back to Sunday lunch. Are you nervous?'

'Very. And it's so soon since Flora died. I understand why I want to meet them; I'm less sure why they want to meet me.'

'Why do you want to meet them?'

'I want to know more about Flora – who she was, inside. Her family is the closest I can get. It's like there is this void I need to fill. I can't stop thinking about her.' I hesitate, not sure about saying the rest aloud. 'I've been dreaming about her, too.'

'What kind of dreams?'

'All sorts. Like I'm looking in a mirror and instead of seeing myself, I see her. And of Flora being taken in for surgery – to have her organs removed. And she was aware, knew what was happening. It was horrible.'

'That does sound horrible. But you know it can't be true, don't you? And it seems to me that we dream about things we think about, that we're worried about. Thinking about Flora and what was done to both of you must be natural in the circumstances. But it can't be healthy to be thinking about her all the time. You need to get some perspective. Maybe you need more things going on in your life, so she isn't so much the focus?'

'Such as?'

'Flirting with the guy at the bar was a good start. Meeting friends – like we are now. Getting back to something more like a normal life.'

'I'm not sure I know how.'

'I'll help you. And I've got one immediate suggestion. You can't physically do a lot just now, so what can you do? Get back to your writing. There was a Saphy I knew who never left the house without a notebook. Find her again, and I bet the rest will follow.'

I'm blinking back tears. I want to be that girl again – the one who dreamed and wrote and didn't think about dying. With Dad gone and all the things I've been through since, how can I ever be who I was before?

'No, no crying! Red eyes make flirting difficult. And now, we need to preserve this moment. Selfie?' she says, and I get control, push the tears away. She holds her phone out and we smile, hold up our glasses. 'I'll post it to the WhatsApp group I set up for our night out.'

'Show me first?'

She hands her phone across, and I look, then look again. Not light next to darkness, not anymore – we're both golden. My tears are back. Can changing the outside change me on the inside, too?

'Is that really me?'

Zoe gives me a hug. 'Yes, it is. Two babes about town.'

One with a lot of hidden scars.

By the time I get home that evening, the Prosecco buzz is gone, leaving a headache behind. I'm thinking through what Zoe said, what she didn't. I could tell she was worried.

She didn't come right out and say that it was weird having Flora on my lock screen – and thinking and dreaming about her – but that's what she thought.

I can't help myself. I go back online, find more photos of Flora. I can't stop thinking about her, looking at her images. Wanting to understand her, be inside her, but instead it is she who is inside me.

Images of Flora on my phone aren't enough. I use the colour printer in Dad's study, enlarge and print out images in A4 size. The one in the red dress. In a bikini on a beach somewhere tropical. At parties. In a coma, too. I crop them before printing, so if anyone is on her arm or next to her, they can't be seen. I tape them up in my bedroom until the walls are full, then in the hall.

Bit by bit, I'm piecing together her life, places she went. I study how she holds herself, try to emulate it. I'm starting to feel like I'm getting to know her, but there is still so much to fill in.

I love the way she does her eye make-up and want to try for the same effect. Mum's dressing table, in Dad's room – I can sit by the mirror. I fetch my make-up bag. Hesitate by the door.

I've avoided coming in here for so long. When I finally manage to open the door, Hermi dashes in so fast she almost trips me up. She jumps up on the bed as if to claim it.

The room is just as Dad left it, but dustier. There are all of his things, but also some of Mum's. A mum I can't remember, other than a few fragments that I'm not even sure are real. With Dad gone, there is no one to remember for me, to remind me things about her.

I pick up the framed photo of the three of us from his bedside table. He said it'd been taken soon after they brought me home. Mum has this smile of complete joy, gazing at baby-me in her arms. Her freckles and light brown curly hair are nothing like me. I know I was adopted. I can't remember a day when I was told – I just always knew. I was so special, I was chosen, Dad used to say.

I go to her dressing table, put down my make-up bag. Sit on Mum's chair, as I have done many times before. Brush my hair with her hairbrush – an engraved silver handle, a wedding present, Dad had said. Put on some of her favourite perfume. I use it very rarely, but it's almost gone.

In the top drawer of her dressing table are small boxes with jewellery, mostly the costume sort, some silver pieces. The next drawer has odds and ends – name badges from jobs she'd had, bookmarks. Hair clips. The bottom drawer has postcards and letters. Some of them are from when she went on a gap year, travelled the world. I've read all the postcards she sent Dad, but not the letters; when I was younger, he said not to. Love letters? I take them out, hold them in my hands. One day I'll read them, see her as she was, then – younger than I am now. But not just yet.

When I go to replace them, I see an unaddressed envelope that was underneath her letters. I don't remember noticing it before. Inside are three folded sheets of paper – they look like photocopies of handwritten letters. Each begins with 'Dear J' – just an initial? The first one is dated my first birthday.

Dear J,

Thank you, a million times over, for the joy that is our S. She is the happiest, most wanted and loved baby that ever was, and I hope that hearing about her will ease being parted from her as much as it can.

I scan through the rest of it. It's like a one-page snapshot of the first year of my life. The other two letters are dated my second and third birthdays and appear to be much the same. Mum's love for me, for Dad, is in every word.

Now I'm crying.

Do these letters mean that J is my birth mother?

Some adopted kids set out to find their birth parents as soon as they turn eighteen. I never felt any need to do this: to me, my family was complete. But it feels different now I've read these letters – they are a connection to someone real.

Did Dad take over writing to J after Mum died, or did the letters just stop?

Dad always kept everything – every bill, every statement, every document. Filed meticulously in alphabetical order in the cabinets in his study. Maybe there's something there.

Hermi follows by my feet, sniffing at dusty corners and then looks startled when she sneezes. She jumps neatly onto his desk to watch.

First, under J: nothing.

Then under my name: Saphira Logan. There are files full of things like childish drawings and school reports. But one file, thinner than the others, has the letters I'm looking for.

Dad's are computer printed instead of handwritten; he must have printed extras to keep copies. The first is dated my fourth birthday, just months after Mum died. Explaining why he's taken over writing them. Telling J that being two parents in one and making me as happy as I could be were the most important things in the world to him. Now I'm crying again.

The letters go up to my eighteenth birthday and I read them all. There are so many memories tied up in these pages. They are a record of my childhood, my family.

Holding them in my hands, I'm thinking maybe I can do this – sell this house. I can take with me the things that mean the most. The snapshots of my life in these letters will be on the list.

What about J though?

I still feel as always: Mum and Dad may have adopted me, but they are my true parents. But maybe it is time to think about whether I want to try to find my birth mother.

THIRTY-THREE

FERN

Dad collects me from the station. 'Thanks for coming early,' he says.

'No problem,' I say, even though I've barely slept for days. The fallout from a major pile up on the M25 meant extra shifts as patients were diverted from other hospitals; this Sunday was my first day off in ten. But when I finally crawled into bed late last night, all I did was lie awake, stare at the ceiling, and think about today.

'What time is she coming?' I say.

'About one. For lunch at one-thirty.'

'Did you tell Mum who is coming? In advance?'

'Yes and no; I told her this morning. I was waiting for back-up.' Backup: that's what he always called me in relation to problems with Flora. Now it seems that I'm my mother's keeper, too, even though we both know how badly that went with Flora.

'I think it may be best not to mention Marley and the possible interview around your mother today,' Dad says.

'Until we meet Saphy, it's hard to know if we even want to ask her about that. We should leave it for now.'

'Though I've arranged a car to take her back to London after lunch. You could go with her, feel her out about it?'

'I don't know. Maybe.'

I haven't been home since I came here with Marley, and before that, the wake. We go through the gates and all the memories of the funeral and wake are flooding back. I force myself to focus on here, now, to push them away. The sloping drive. The sprawling house. It was too big when there were four of us; how is it rattling around in there now? The windows sparkle in the sun, reflecting in my eyes when we get closer. I'm dazzled in the shadows on the side of the house where we park.

The door opens before we get to it. Mum is dressed carefully, make-up and hair just so. She's smiling, and the knot of worry eases a little inside of me.

'Fern. Lovely to see you,' she says. Double air kisses. 'Dorothy is setting out tea in the conservatory. Isn't this exciting?'

That's one way to put it.

THIRTY-FOUR

SAPHY

Having lunch with Flora's family seemed like a good idea when I agreed. But now that the day is here, I'm jumpy with nerves. I have so many questions about Flora clamouring inside me, but I can't quiz them about her – it'd be the surest way to find out nothing at all. It's got to come from them. But what if they don't want to talk about her?

My nightmares have been getting worse. Last night I had another where Flora was being taken in for surgery, completely aware, but this time it went further. Flora/Me in the dream could feel a surgical blade cutting deep inside. I shudder and try to push the memory away.

And I'm ready way too early. The car to take me to Oxford isn't coming for over an hour.

Needing distraction, I reread the letters to J. Should I try to find her? I'm still not sure. But just in case, I'll have a hunt through Dad's files. Maybe there's something there that will help.

Not sure where to look, I start going through the alphabet from the beginning, looking for anything that might be relevant. There's a file labelled Hatkin and Pearce that I almost go past, then backtrack for a closer look. It's a law firm. There are copies of letters dated over twenty-eight years ago, and reference to the adoption agency that handled my adoption! Bingo. I take the file to Dad's desk and read through. Mum and Dad had agreed to write once a year until I was eighteen – the address to send the letters was the adoption agency address.

If the agency knew where to send the letters, they must know who they were being sent to. Will they tell me?

The car comes right on time. The closer I get to meeting Flora's family, the more I'm confronting what was done to me, to her, in a real physical sense – not the hypothetical way I considered the process before it happened. The whole idea of taking a heart from one person and putting it in someone else – how am I supposed to feel? How are her family supposed to feel? And how do we actually feel, because that's not necessarily the same thing, at all.

When Charles insisted he send a car for me, I was relieved. I'm not through the first three months where they say to keep away from crowds and haven't been back on buses and trains much yet. But this car must have cost a mint. It's not a taxi, it's more like some sort of limo service. The driver is even wearing a hat.

Though if I were on a train, I could get off at the next station. Turn around. Email or message to apologise – say, *I'm not ready to take this step. Not yet.* Instead, I'm trapped, and my mind is going around in circles as the miles tick slowly down.

Finally, the driver pulls up to a gate. He opens his window, pushes a button and says who we are. The gates open. We go through to a long sloping drive, beautiful lawns and gardens all around. Is it a gated community or something? But when the house comes into view – it's the only one. And it's... wow. Massive, and beautiful. Imagine growing up in a place like this, like Flora did. This house isn't just doctor-rich, it's some sort of mansion. I wasn't sure what to wear; seeing the grandness of the place makes me nervous that I'm underdressed. I have so little that fits well so went with making another appearance in my new yellow jumper, hand-washed and dried just in time.

We pull in, and the front doors open. A man steps out. It's Charles – Flora's father – and seeing him in person is making my nerves even worse. My gut is churning and I'm trembling.

The driver gets out and opens my door just as Charles reaches us.

He takes my hand to help me out of the car, which makes my arms and legs feel muddled about how to get out of a car when someone is holding one hand. He steadies me, then lets go.

'Saphira? Welcome. I'm Charles.'

'Hi. Please, call me Saphy.'

'Of course. Saphy. Thank you for coming.'

THIRTY-FIVE

FERN

I stay with Mum, just inside the doors, when Dad goes out to the car. Saphy somehow loses her balance getting out of the car – almost falls – then she is saying something to Dad. They're walking towards us.

Her blonde hair is so like Flora's before her red phase. She's a similar height, slender, wearing yellow, too, and I'm blinking back the weird feeling that my sister is walking towards us.

'Oh.' A soft sound from Mum, next to me, as if she is thinking the same. I know Saphy is older than Flora was but she looks younger, uncertain and shy. She's pale; her face seems all eyes that just now are a bit rabbit-headlights.

'Saphy, this is my wife, Margot.'

'It's a pleasure to meet you,' Mum says, and air kisses one cheek, goes for the other but Saphy has moved the wrong way and they almost bump noses. Colour rises in Saphy's cheeks.

'And our daughter, Fern,' Dad says.

'Hi,' I say, and take pity on her and offer my hand to shake instead.

'Welcome to our home,' Mum says, and gestures. We step inside.

'The gardens are beautiful. Did you design them?'

'I did. You know that I am a garden designer?' Saphy nods. 'Well, I was, I suppose.'

'You're not designing anymore?'

'No. Are you a gardener?'

'Not really, but I need to do something with our garden at home. It was my dad's thing. I'd hate him to see the mess it's in now.'

'Would you like to see the main gardens?'

'Oh yes, please.'

'Fern, could you let Dorothy know we'll be ready for lunch at half past one? Thank you.'

I go to the kitchen and do as Mum asked. I should join them outside now, but instead hesitate by the open bifold doors. Mum is taking Saphy around, gesturing at plants, talking more than I've seen her do in a while. Dad is hanging back – he has even less interest in gardening than I do. The only one of us who shared this passion with Mum was Flora, and only when she was younger.

Observing them at this distance, there is a curious sense of displaced time. Years disappear. I was about to go away to medical school. Flora was upset, distraught that I could leave her. She ran outside. Mum went after her and I watched the two of them from these doors. Giving them a moment before I joined them. Flora threw her arms around me when I did. She was only twelve when I left. We were never as close after that.

But she's the one who has left all of us now.

I blink and I'm back to here, now. They're heading for the conservatory, where lunch will be soon. I take a deep breath and go to join them.

Mum settles Saphy facing the garden, Mum and Dad next to her and me across. Dad is offering wine and pours Mum and me a half glass of red, more for himself.

Saphy declines and asks for water. 'There's something I need to say,' she says.

All of our eyes are on her and I sense how difficult she is finding this.

'I can't begin to know how to thank all of you. At what must have been one of the worst moments of your lives, you thought about helping other people you didn't even know. Thank you, from the bottom of my—' She stops short. Horror crosses her face at what she almost said – and I have to apply control to not laugh. And it's not even that funny – it's this whole situation. It all feels so fraught that even saying the word *heart*, who it belonged to or belongs to now can't be mentioned.

'I have a knack for saying the wrong thing. Sorry,' she says.

'It's fine, Saphy. Don't apologise,' Dad says. 'And you're very welcome. It was the right thing to do, and I'm sure Flora would have agreed.'

'And now there's something I need to say.' It's Mum now. 'It was hard for me. Easier for a couple of doctors, I think. But I struggled, with thinking about Flora, what they were going to do to her – well. It was difficult to deal with on top of everything else. And when Charles told us that he'd written to you, I wasn't sure how I felt about it. But what I'm trying to say is that I'm glad I've met you, Saphy. It's made it clear to me that we did the right thing.'

Saphy's eyes are filling with tears. Mum's are, too. And Mum is holding out her hands – they both get up and Mum is hugging Saphy now. A proper hug, not one of those polite, distant ones she usually gives her friends.

I'm blinking, too. It was all hypothetical before, wasn't it? Despite all the medical details I know and understand, until I actually met someone whose life had been saved by one of Flora's organs, it wasn't real. And now it is. And it's a pretty amazing thing.

THIRTY-SIX

SAPHY

I get through lunch without any more heart-related gaffes or other mishaps. I was worried when I let slip that I knew Margot was a garden designer that they'd realise I've been finding out all I can about them online, but if that registered it didn't seem to be a problem. I still can't believe I'm here, in Flora's child-hood home, with her family. I'm trying to absorb every detail and nuance of emotion.

'I'm curious about your name,' Margot says. 'Were you named after a family member?'

'Not so far as I know.'

'It's an unusual, beautiful name,' she says. 'Saphira is also the name of a flower, native to Australia.'

'Really? I didn't know that.'

'What is next for you, Saphy?' Charles says. 'Study? Work?'

'I've got a few months more before I'm allowed to work. I need some thinking time so that is a good thing.'

'Have you been to university?'

'Yes. I read English Literature at University College London.'

'Flora went to UCL, too,' Fern says. 'For a while, that is. Psychology. She dropped out in second year.'

'Would we have overlapped?' I ask. We compare years and she would have been first year when I was final. 'We could have walked past each other, even met,' I say, and I guess it's true, but it's hard to believe I could have met Flora and not remembered her.

'And after your English degree?' Charles says.

'I started teacher training, but it wasn't for me. Then I was working in Daunts – the bookshop. In Marylebone. And writing. That's what I wanted to be – want to be, I mean. A writer.'

'A grand ambition. Have you made any headway?' Charles says.

'There was some interest from agents, but then I got sick.'

'And your dad did, also,' Margot says. 'I'm so sorry for your loss.'

I've struggled with people saying things like this to me. So often it feels like something they feel they should say and there's no real feeling behind it, or any idea what it was like, losing not only the only parent that I had, but one I was so close to. But Margot knows – she understands, doesn't she? Having lost her daughter, she gets it.

'Thank you.'

'Do you have any other family?' Margot says.

'Only distant cousins. My mum died when I was three. I don't really remember her.'

'So, being a writer is what you wanted – and want – to be,' Charles says. 'What is your plan to achieve this?'

'I'm not sure I have one just now. It's kind of like I have to work out who I am again.' I don't like talking about myself – this is starting to feel like a job interview, one where the chance of success feels small. There is also something – someone – else I'm desperate to talk about, and I can't hold back any longer.

'Could you tell me about Flora?' I say. 'I mean, only if you're OK to talk about her. If you'd rather not, that's fine.'

Charles and Fern both look to Margot, who tilts her head to one side, holds my eyes. 'What would you like to know?'

THIRTY-SEVEN

FERN

We spend most of the afternoon doing something together we haven't done since Flora died: talking about her, and going through photo albums, too. Doing so should be cathartic, and for Mum, I think it is. Other than when she's been drinking, she's been held in so tight since Flora was hurt, and even worse after she died. Now she's more or less sober, after just two small glasses of wine at lunch, and it's like something is unravelling inside of her – in a good way. With Dad, I'm not sure. He's not as, I don't know, *present*, somehow, and I sense that he's trying to hide some mixture of pain and what almost feels like impatience. He's never been a great listener, has he? And he seems reluctant to guide the conversation like he usually would.

And me? Listening to my parents talk about Flora is almost like they're talking about someone else, an acquaintance, someone only met once or twice. It's all the superficial things that everyone knows about her and none of the difficult stuff. Which makes me wonder if I feel that way because I knew her better, and they didn't really, at all. Or maybe, none of us did.

Mum closes the album from last Christmas. We're up to date.

'Would you like to see Flora's room?' Mum says. 'Well, her room until she was eighteen, that is.'

'If you're sure it's OK?' Saphy says.

'If it wasn't, I wouldn't have asked. It's this way.' Mum, me and Saphy troop up the stairs; Dad stays behind.

The door is ajar and Mum pushes it open.

'I haven't been in here in ages,' I say. 'It was never this tidy when she lived in it. And it was redecorated when Flora was sixteen, wasn't it?'

'The summer before. And she picked everything. She liked colour, didn't she?'

The walls are a vivid red – a bit much, maybe, but it kind of works with the light wood of the desk and bookshelves, the red and blue patchwork quilt. But it's not her childhood room – nothing is as it was when we both lived here – and I don't feel a sense of her here.

Saphy goes across to the bookshelves. There are memories for me here – all her books from age dot are on display. I'm surprised she didn't hide them away from her friends when she was a teenager. Maybe she did and Mum put them back after Flora left.

'I used to read to her,' I say. 'She loved being read to, even once she could do it herself.'

Mum's phone rings in her pocket. She glances at the screen. 'Just a moment, I need to take this,' she says, and goes into the hall.

'How many years older were you?' Saphy says.

'Six.'

'I'd always wished I had a sister or brother. But mostly a sister.' She hesitates. 'My mum couldn't have children, so I was adopted when I was a baby. They were planning to adopt again, but then she died.'

'It was just you and your dad for so long.'

She nods, and I feel like I'm beginning to get a sense of Saphy, who she is. How strong she must be to still be standing here. Yes, with the ultimate in medical interventions, but to go through that, alone?

Now it's my phone that is vibrating – a message from Dad. 'Dad says the car he's booked to take us back to London will be here soon, and to come down for tea.' We walk to the door of Flora's room and Saphy pauses, looking around as if she's memorising it. There is a flush in her cheeks that wasn't there before. Then we head down the stairs. Mum follows us, off her phone now. Dad meets us below. Dorothy is bringing in tea, biscuits, to the front room.

'I just want to thank all of you again, so much,' Saphy says.

'From the bottom of your heart,' I tease, and we are all smiling now.

'And also for today. Welcoming me to your home, telling me about Flora. Just, thank you.'

'Saphy, there's something I want to ask you,' Dad says. 'There has been so much negativity in the press recently about organ donation – I'm sure you've seen – even going so far as suggesting that was what actually killed Flora. It is hugely upsetting to all of us that Flora's name is being associated with a campaign to end the opt-out when organs are so desperately needed to save lives. Would you consider waiving anonymity and, along with us, talking to a friend of Flora's – a reporter – to show the other side?'

Saphy's eyes are wide – surprise? Dismay?

Before she can say anything, I interject. 'Don't answer, Saphy – you need to think this over carefully. And don't feel under any obligation if it's not right for you to do this. You're completely entitled to keep your medical history private.'

She hesitates. 'Fern's right,' she finally says. 'I'm not sure what to say. I need to think this through.'

'Of course. Take all the time that you need,' Dad says. 'But you could make a difference. Save more lives, like yours has been saved. Think about that, also.'

THIRTY-EIGHT

SAPHY

The driver holds a door open; Fern gestures for me to get in first. Then he goes round the other side to let her in. It felt a short drive on the way here as I was nervous and wanted it to take longer. Somehow, I'm sure that it'll feel longer going back. I'm suddenly exhausted, want to be alone. I wish Fern wasn't coming back with me.

There is so much to think through but one thing especially is making me squirm inside. They were so welcoming and lovely to me, and how did I repay them? By stealing from Flora's bookshelves – a seashell and a silver bookmark. It was an impulse – no planning or thought – I just palmed them both when Fern was reading the message on her phone, slipped them into my pocket. I was sure she'd seen the movement and felt the colour rise in my cheeks. But she didn't say anything about it, so she must not have noticed.

I can't believe I did that. I can feel them in the pocket of my jeans, digging into my side, and want to take them out, touch them, hold them – things that Flora touched and held. Wait, I tell myself. Wait until you're alone.

'I'm sorry that Dad dumped that on you,' Fern says. 'Don't

feel pressured – please. Take your time to decide what is right for you.'

'Thank you, I appreciate that. I'm so tired. I might close my eyes now if that's OK?'

'Of course it is. I might join you. I've been on nights all week.'

This car has comfy seats. I settle myself, take my jacket, roll it up and put it between my head and shoulders like a neck pillow and lean back. Close my eyes. Despite wanting to sift through everything that was done and said today, the fatigue is all-encompassing. Not so much physical tiredness, more from being nervous to begin with, and the emotional tension of the whole experience.

Margot had to thaw, warm to me, didn't she? Fern, too, in a different way. Charles – what he asked of me. I can't think what it might mean. But most of all, Flora.

Her images from her mum's albums flit in and out of aware-ness as I drift to sleep. A gap-toothed toddler. Teenage glares. Baby smiles, adult masking, and all in between.

THIRTY-NINE

FERN

When I wake up, the car is slowing. We're pulling in front of a three floor mid-terrace, a quiet street in Islington.

Saphy's eyes are closed, she's so pale, so still, and there's a moment of unreasoning panic.

'Saphy?' I say, my voice sharp, alarmed. She stirs, opens her eyes and the pinched worry inside subsides. 'I think we've arrived.'

Her eyes – they're wide – confused? She looks at me, then out the window. She nods. 'Home sweet home.'

'How are you feeling?'

'I'm fine. Just tired,' she says. She pulls at the seat belt, taking a moment to undo it as if pushing the release on it is hard work.

I'm not sure she's all right, at all, and make a decision. 'I'll come in with you.'

She turns to me. 'It's not necessary—'

'Yes, it is. Don't argue.'

I tell the driver he can leave us both here and Saphy to wait for me in her seat. The driver opens her door. I offer an arm and she leans on me as she gets up and out of the car. Then her legs give way, her body goes limp and I only just manage to stop her from falling to the pavement.

The driver helps me ease her onto the grass verge.

'Call an ambulance,' I tell him. 'Tell them a recent heart transplant patient has collapsed. There is a doctor on scene.' He's on his phone as I'm checking her breathing, her pulse – it's rapid. Heart recipients always have an elevated pulse but it is more than it should be. I say her name again, and her eyelashes flutter, eyes open – full of confusion, as to what is happening, maybe even who I am.

There's rushing footsteps – a woman coming towards us, panic on her face.

'Saphy? I saw through the window,' she says. 'What's happened?'

'She lost consciousness for a moment. I'm a doctor – paramedics are coming.'

Saphy's colour is improving, her pulse rate slowing.

The woman kneels next to her other side. 'I'm Neeha, Saphy's neighbour,' she says.

'I'm Fern.'

Saphy's eyes find mine. 'So, what happened?'

'I think you probably fainted.'

'Only probably? You're the doctor.'

'I haven't got all the usual kit, so it's kind of a guess.'

Other people are coming over, looking concerned.

'Can we go inside?' Saphy says.

'What we need you to do is to sit up and then stand, very slowly.' Neeha takes one arm and I take the other while the driver hovers, looking anxious. 'Was that OK?' I ask Saphy, once she's upright.

'I think so, my head is spinning a little.'

'Where are your keys?'

'Handbag.'

The driver gets it from the back seat, hands it to Neeha.

'Thanks for your help,' I say to the driver. 'We'll take it from here.'

Neeha finds Saphy's keys, unlocks the door and we go in, Saphy still leaning on me but less than she was before. A cat is winding around our feet making the highest decibel meows I think I've ever heard.

'I think I'm OK now,' Saphy says. 'You should call off the ambulance.'

'No.'

'You're rather bossy.'

'It's a doctor thing,' I say and bite back the words that almost followed, without thought: *and a sister thing*. Where did that come from?

I help Saphy towards the recliner in her front room.

'I never thought I'd be so glad for such an ugly chair,' she says. I use the control to raise then lower the chair as Saphy sinks into it. The cat jumps up onto her lap the moment it's back far enough.

'Now she needs fluids,' I say.

'Tea?' Neeha says.

'Water first, then tea.'

Neeha fetches water, makes tea, and the three of us are halfway through mugs of the stuff when there is a knock on the door – the paramedics are here.

They come in with their kit. I introduce myself as an emergency doctor. They check the usual things. Her blood pressure is a little low. Saphy says she's on blood pressure medication since the transplant – perhaps the dose needs adjusting. Everything else is fine.

'Should we take her in?' one of them asks me.

Saphy shakes her head. 'I've got my appointment tomorrow, heart biopsy and everything else. Can't it wait until then?'

'They can deal with this if it is the case, but sometimes fatigue and low blood pressure can mean rejection,' I say.

Saphy takes that in for a moment.

'As far as fatigue goes, I had trouble sleeping last night. Now that I've had a nap, I feel fine. I probably just got up too fast after being asleep and that made me faint.'

'That seems most likely. I think you can wait for your appointment tomorrow if you want to. But if any symptoms return or worsen, you'll need to go straight in.'

The paramedics take their leave, but I don't think Saphy should be alone.

'You need to have someone with you overnight, to check on you,' I say. 'I can stay if you like.'

'I don't want to impose on you any more than I already have.'

'It's fine.'

'I can stay if you want,' Neeha says.

'Don't be ridiculous,' Saphy says. 'Neeha has five children who run amok if she's gone more than an hour. What might they have got up to by now?'

'Seriously, I can stay,' I say. 'Unless there is a friend you'd prefer? I'm not on shift until Tuesday – it's fine.'

'I really should check if the house is still standing,' Neeha says. 'Call me if you need anything? Don't get up.' She leans down, hugs Saphy. Says goodbye and lets herself out.

'This is so embarrassing,' Saphy says. 'I'm sorry.'

'Don't apologise. You need to take care, don't you? And let people take care of you. Everything has gone well so far, from what you've said. But you need to stay vigilant, especially these first months. Don't dismiss things; tell your transplant team.'

'OK. I get what you're saying. I will be careful, I promise.'

My phone is ringing – it's Marley. With all this going on I'd forgotten she'd asked me for dinner tonight. Wanting to hear about Saphy.

'Sorry, I've got to take this.' I get up, wander into the hall to answer. 'Hi, Marley.'

'So, how did it go?'

'It was fine. Better than that, really. Until Saphy fainted.'

'Is she OK?'

'I think so. But I'm going to stay with her tonight and make sure.'

'So, no dinner?'

'No. Sorry. Although – hang on a sec.' I go back through to Saphy. 'I was meant to have dinner tonight with a friend – actually, she was Flora's best friend.'

'Don't cancel on my account – please.'

'I'm not going out and leaving you alone. But she could come here if you're up to it? We can get a takeaway or something.'

'Of course – if you're sure that's OK.'

I go back to Marley. 'Did you hear?'

'Yes. Sounds great. There's that thing we could talk about?'

'Let's see how we go.'

When the tap-tap of the door knocker comes a while later I start to lower my chair.

'Don't get up,' Fern says.

She goes to the hall to answer the door, but I keep the downward movement of the footrest going, then start to raise the back of the chair to help me stand. It's one thing to not answer the door but entirely another to stay reclined when you meet someone, and this isn't just anyone: she was Flora's best friend. I feel a flutter of nerves. There are low voices by the door, footsteps.

Marley is striking rather than beautiful – high cheekbones, short dark hair, clothes that are just right in that 'I don't care' effortless kind of way that says they cost a fortune – and she is totally cool. In short, the opposite of me, and just how I'd expect Flora's best friend to be. And there is also something about her that I recognise, but I'm not sure why. She's got a bottle of red wine in one hand.

'You must be Saphy, keeper-of-Flora's-heart? I'm Marley.' She extends her other hand and I take it.

'I should have warned you,' Fern says. 'Marley takes blunt to a whole new level.'

'It's fine,' I say. 'Sorry, have we met? You look familiar.'

'I don't think so, but I appear now and then on Sky News.' Of course. She's often the one sent to the scene when something is happening.

Then something else falls into place. 'Are you the friend Fern's dad mentioned? Who wants to interview us about organ donation?'

'The one and only. What do you think – do you want to do it?'

'She's taking some time to think about it,' Fern answers for me, and I nod.

'No matter what you decide – I'm really glad to meet you,' Marley says, and the cool facade is gone, replaced by raw pain. 'I miss Flora so much. It feels like you are a connection to her. I'm sorry if that's weird.'

I shake my head. 'It isn't – I promise.'

'Now on to important matters. Where's the corkscrew?'

They follow me to the kitchen. 'There's one somewhere – my dad used it now and then.'

'You don't drink?' Marley says, her face much like I'd said I came from a distant galaxy.

'Before the surgery, I wasn't able to have any alcohol for a long time. I can again now, in moderation.'

I start going through drawers, finding dusty odds and ends I haven't seen in a while. Dad loved to cook, which meant I mostly didn't.

'Here it is.' I pass it over to Marley, find glasses and we go back to the front room.

She looks at the corkscrew dubiously. 'It's one of those use-brute-force kind of ones. I'll give it a bash.'

'As far as dinner goes, do you think that since I fainted and got rather freaked out by paramedics – not to mention having a fairly stressful lunch beforehand – I should be allowed to eat my body weight in pizza and maybe even have a drink or two?'

'Are you asking me as a doctor?' Fern says.

'Definitely not.'

'Then of course you are.'

'Lunch was only fairly stressful?' Marley says, glancing up from wrestling with the resisting cork.

'It was great, actually,' I say. 'It was more thinking about it ahead of time, then arriving and meeting everyone that was stressful.' I turn to Fern. 'Your parents – especially your mum – were lovely.'

'First time for everything,' Marley says, and I must look shocked. 'It's just they're generally not very lovely to me.'

'Fair comment,' Fern says.

'Why?'

'My guess is that they think I led their previously well-behaved teenage daughter astray and turned her into a woman who could think for herself and do what she liked,' Marley says. 'Actually, I think she did that all by herself, and I just came along now and then to keep an eye on her. Which you'd think they'd appreciate. But it's also possible Fern's dad isn't a fan because I'm gay. He's a bit uptight about stuff like that, particularly in the vicinity of his daughters.'

'He hasn't quite joined the current century in some ways,' Fern says. 'Leaving Dad-analysis aside for a moment and stepping back to doctor mode, Saphy, aren't you supposed to be fasting before your heart biopsy?'

'Nil by mouth from midnight. We've got hours until then.'

Marley shudders. 'A heart biopsy? That sounds awful.'

'Believe me, with what I've had done lately, it barely registers on the scale. I'll be in and out a few hours later.'

'Sorry.'

'It's fine. Now, back to pizza. There's a good independent Italian restaurant that delivers not far from here. I'll get the menu up.' I find it on my phone to show them. 'There's also pasta. Tell me what you want and I'll order – my treat. I've hijacked your evening so it's the least I can do.'

I note what they want and make the call. On impulse, I add a bottle of Prosecco, then make it two. I give my card details, worrying it will be declined but it goes through. It's not until it's too late that I ask myself, what am I doing? How close am I to my credit limit? But even though there's a sensible part of me that knows I need to be careful what I spend, most of me doesn't care.

Cork finally extracted, Marley is pouring and then notices I only brought two glasses. 'Don't you want any?' she asks.

I shake my head. 'I'll wait until dinner arrives, thanks. I've ordered some Prosecco to come with it.'

Marley exchanges a glance with Fern. 'Why Prosecco?'

'I don't know, just fancied it. I never used to like it much but had some out with my friend recently and loved it. Why?'

'Flora always had Prosecco,' Marley says.

'She said it was better than champagne,' Fern adds. 'Which annoyed Mum, who said, "Darling, if you must have sparkling, at least get the real thing."' The way she said it so closely mimicked Margot's voice that we're laughing.

'You could say that Flora had Prosecco tastes on a champagne budget,' Marley said. 'Which wasn't very Flora in most areas. With clothes and everything else she'd never even look at how much something cost, would she? If her card got rejected in the middle of a particularly intense spending spree, she'd look so startled.'

'True. Mum was always bailing her out.'

They're soon on to a second glass – well, Marley is. Fern hasn't made much inroads into her first. I'm fascinated, listening to them, hearing things about Flora that I hadn't before. And Fern said it was her mum who bailed Flora out: was she the one with the money that explained the mansion-sized home?

When the pizza and Prosecco arrive, I find plates, some

dusty champagne glasses – rinse them out. Try to get the cork out, fail, and Fern does it for me.

'Still feeling tired?' she says.

'Not really. Honest,' I say, and fill the glasses.

'To Flora,' Fern says, and we clink glasses.

I take a sip. The bubbles tickle and it tastes delicious: what's not to like? We get pizza on plates and tuck in.

'Tell us about you, Saphy,' Marley says, between mouthfuls.

'There's not a lot to tell. My life has been on hold for what felt like forever. Waiting to die.' Marley must be rubbing off on me – saying just what you think without analysing it in advance feels good.

'Fuck. That must have been terrible.'

'Yeah. It really was. But that's all over now.' *For how long I don't know*, I add, silently.

'Did you have a bucket list?'

'Well, the day I found out that a donor heart was available, I'd just done a tandem bungee jump with my best friend, Zoe.'

'You didn't,' Fern says, shocked. 'I'm guessing you didn't clear that with your consultant?'

'Er... no. Or any other responsible adult.' I hesitate. Is it the Prosecco that makes me want to explain? 'It wasn't like me to do stuff like that. I've always been cautious. But I think when you are looking at dying soon, you just think, fuck it. You've got less to risk so why not?'

'I like the way you think, Saphy,' Marley says, holds up her glass and I clink mine against hers. 'Here's to having adventures! What will be next?'

'I don't know. Now I'm looking to hang around for longer, I should probably do some sensible stuff. Like get a job.'

Marley is shaking her head. 'You've got a lot to live up to, with that ticker inside of you.'

'You wouldn't believe all the stuff I'm not allowed to eat or do, like, forever! I bet when they weigh me tomorrow, I'll get told off.'

'No!' Marley says. 'Refuse to stand on the scales of the patriarchy!'

'It's medication she's taking that can promote weight gain,' Fern says. 'And that can lead to increasing likelihood of cardiac complications.'

'Thank you, Dr Fern. Now, Saphy. Back to the Prosecco.'

I hold up my mysteriously empty glass, she tops it up and hers; Fern holds a hand over her glass.

'Best make it your last,' Fern says to me. 'Being hungover at the hospital tomorrow wouldn't be fun.'

I sigh. But she's probably right. 'OK – last glass.'

'Back to the Prosecco,' Marley says again. 'You said you fancied it, that you'd had it with a friend recently and liked it.'

'Yes – shared a bottle with Zoe a few weeks ago.'

'When you had it with Zoe, whose idea was it?'

'Mine, but—'

'You said you never used to like it. Why did you choose to have it, then?' Marley seemed half drunk a moment ago, but she's remembered every word I've said.

'It was kind of a celebration, so it seemed the way to go. I'd just had my hair done, bought some clothes and was having a drink for the first time in over a year.' I shrug. 'I don't know why I chose Prosecco.'

'I do. Flora loved it. You have her heart. She desired Prosecco and you delivered.' There are goosebumps on my arms, the back of my neck.

'Honestly, Marley, from a medical point of view, that just isn't possible,' Fern says.

'I'm not finished, hear me out. You said you'd just had your hair done. How was it before?'

'Really long and heavy, like halfway down my back. Dark brown.' I find a photo on my phone, show them.

'Wow – what a difference it has made. But why did you go for the blonde look?'

'I needed a change – I hadn't done anything with my hair in a long time. I thought the dark hair was making me look too pale.'

'But just some streaks around your face and a decent cut would have dealt with that.'

'I guess. But it was an all-new me – a new beginning. I wanted to look different. I don't understand where you're going with this,' I say. But I do know. Don't I? From stalking Flora online, I knew she used to be blonde. If you can stalk a dead person. Then I remind myself I also saw photos of Flora today in Margot's albums from year dot, so I should know this. 'Oh – Flora was blonde when she was a child, wasn't she? I saw some photos this afternoon.'

'Not just as a child.' Now Marley has her phone out; she's looking for something. While she does so Fern excuses herself, heads for the loo. 'OK. Here you go.'

She hands her phone across. It's a selfie of a much younger Flora and Marley, the Eiffel Tower in the background. Flora's hair is wavy, blonde-streaked: almost exactly like mine is now. Even the cut looks similar. Their faces, so close to each other. A selfie like Zoe always wants to take but there is something different in this image. That flushed, happy look isn't just from the sun or wine.

'You were lovers, weren't you?' I say, without thinking whether I should. Marley's eyes open wide just as Fern is coming back down the stairs. Marley shakes her head, eyes on mine. Saying, *don't tell Fern*, or *no, that isn't so*? I think the former. Fern comes and looks at the photo but doesn't seem to see what I did.

'I must admit, I preferred Flora blonde like that,' Fern says, sits down again.

'You can see how much your hair looks like Flora's did then,' Marley says.

'As far as I knew – before this afternoon, that is – Flora had red hair.'

'She has dyed it red, for years – this was just after her eighteenth – we went away to celebrate. It wasn't long after that she went red and stayed that way.'

'If she liked it better red and was weirdly influencing me somehow, surely I'd have gone for red?'

'I'm not done yet. Why are you wearing a yellow jumper?'

'Marley, enough of this,' Fern says, looking at me with a concerned doctor face.

'It's OK,' I say. 'The same day, after I got my hair done, I was meeting Zoe at Covent Garden for lunch. She wasn't going to be there for an hour, so I went shopping. That's when I bought it. And with the blonde hair, I guess I was drawn to it – the colour just works with my hair.'

'You're right – it does,' Marley says. 'But have you worn yellow much before?'

'Not that I can recall,' I say. But I know I haven't.

'Yellow was Flora's favourite colour. Between that and your hair, I'm surprised Margot didn't faint when she saw you. Why did you decide to wear it today?'

I'd thought there was something there, from when Fern and Margot first saw me. Something in their reactions. Maybe that explains it. 'To be honest, I've hardly got anything half decent that fits, so I didn't have many options. Clothes from when I was sick are getting too tight.'

'Shopping ahoy!' Marley says.

'I wish. My savings are gone and universal credit only goes so far. This shopping splurge was a one-off.' Why did I tell them that? I flush with embarrassment.

'Let us cover the pizza,' Fern says, and Marley nods.

'No, please – it was my treat. It's fine.'

Fern changes the subject then, but even as we're talking, then loading the dishwasher, I'm still puzzling things over in my mind. Was Marley asking me all those questions because she's somehow worked out that I've been finding out everything I can about Flora, and thinks that I'm trying to be like her? Or maybe she actually thinks that Flora's heart, beating in my chest, is influencing things that I do, choices that I make. Or – perhaps most likely – she just can't accept all these things are random coincidences and she's trying to figure it out. She's a reporter and asking questions when she doesn't understand something is just what she does.

Marley calls a taxi soon afterwards. She's gone quiet now. I want her to like me – I want to be her friend. She's nothing like anyone I know and I'm afraid I won't see her again.

The taxi driver knocks and she's grabbing her phone, saying goodbye to Fern, then turns to me but I jump in before she can say anything.

'Marley? I want to do it. The interview.' The words are out before I even knew I was going to say them.

She grins. 'That's brilliant, Saphy.'

'Does it count as an adventure?'

'With Fern's parents involved? Absolutely.'

She gives me a hug before she goes.

Later I'm tucked into bed, Hermi curled along my side. Flora's seashell is on my bedside table. Did she keep it because it was found on a special day, or was it a gift from someone she cared about? The bookmark – thin silver, a cat engraved on its surface – is in my hand. It's smooth as if Flora often held it in her hand like I am now.

Fern is down the hall in Dad's room. She said she'd call Marley tomorrow and tell her to confirm the interview with me when I've sobered up, but I'm not going to change my mind. I don't even know why I feel so strongly that I should do it now – if it's just to see Marley again or for any other reason. Marley knew Flora in a way her family never did – that much is clear. I'm sure I can learn things about Flora from her that I wouldn't find elsewhere.

All the other things Marley said earlier have got me thinking. Could the Prosecco, my hair and wearing yellow just be weird coincidences, or is Flora's heart actually having some sort of influence on me and the choices I make? Fern obviously thinks that isn't possible, and she's the doctor.

It could be that without consciously meaning to I changed my hair and bought that yellow jumper because of Flora. Her life was like some kind of fantasy. Who wouldn't want to be more like her?

There's another thing Marley couldn't bring up because she didn't know. I've always been sensible with money. I've never had the kind of unlimited funds it sounds like Flora could tap into; I've had to be careful. But lately I've been spending without even stopping to think. I didn't look at the price tag when I bought this insanely expensive jumper, and I don't think I've ever done that before.

Maybe there really is something of Flora inside of me, beyond just the physical functions of her heart beating, moving blood around my body. Maybe it really is her visiting my dreams, not just my twisted imagination.

I want to have adventures – like Marley said. Not be safe, sensible, poorly Saphy.

I want to be Flora.

FORTY-ONE

FERN

There's a knock on the door the next morning. I go to answer as Saphy is in the shower.

It is a woman, in her fifties or so, looking very surprised to see me instead of Saphy. 'You must be Claire?' She nods. 'I'm Fern. Come in. Saphy should be down shortly.'

'I'm early,' she says, following me in and closing the door. 'How do you know Saphy?'

'Long story,' I answer, not sure what to say. If Saphy hasn't told her that she was meeting her donor's family, then I shouldn't. Though if she goes through with that interview, everyone will know. 'Would you like some tea?'

'Coffee. I know where it is.' We go into the kitchen together, and her eyes widen when she sees the empty wine and Prosecco bottles on the side as she fills the kettle.

Saphy comes down the stairs and joins us. 'Good morning, Claire.' She gives her a hug. 'Have you introduced yourselves?'

'Just first names,' Claire says, curiosity stamped on her face like a question mark.

'Ah. Well, Fern is the sister of my heart donor.'

'Oh! You've met them, then?'

'Yes – Fern and her parents. It all went well.'

'Very well, by the look of things,' she says, and gestures at the three empty bottles.

'Well, that was kind of unplanned. Fern is a doctor. She ended up staying over because I fainted when we got here.'

'You *fainted*? Why didn't you call me? I'd have come straight over. Are you all right? It's not rejection, is it?'

'I'm pretty sure the answers are yes and no. Paramedics checked me out and—'

'There was an ambulance called? Why didn't you go to the hospital?'

I answer this time, using my best reassuring doctor voice. 'Everything checked out fine, just her blood pressure was a little low – probably the dosage of her blood pressure medication needs adjusting. And Saphy said she was having a heart biopsy today. They wouldn't have moved that up any sooner if she'd gone in. I stayed out of an abundance of caution.'

She looks maybe a fraction reassured. Then she frowns at the bottles. 'No more than fourteen units a week,' she says to Saphy.

'I didn't have any of the wine and only a few glasses of Prosecco. Fern's friend who came over had most of it, I promise.'

Claire looks to me, as if wanting confirmation.

'That's exactly right,' I say, even though I think Saphy's Prosecco consumption was a bit more than that.

Claire glances at the clock, forgets about the kettle. 'We'd best get going in case there's traffic.'

'Can we drop Fern at the station on the way?' Saphy says.

'Of course.'

Once I'm home, I message Saphy.

I hope everything goes well at the hospital with the biopsy etc
– you'll let me know? And I think I understand now I've met
Claire why you didn't call her last night.

She answers a moment later.

Of course I'll let you know. And yeah, sorry – I probably
should have so you could have gone home. But I'm glad
you didn't. Last night was the most fun I've had in a long
time.

I'm glad. But please think some more about doing the
interview. You're not bound to go ahead with it at all.

Thank you – I know – but I won't change my mind. Can
you give me Marley's number?

I hesitate. I'm not sure doing the interview is in Saphy's best interests, but I'm not her doctor. I won't be like Claire, either, and tell her what to do. She's an adult; she can and should make her own decisions.

I copy and paste the number, press send.

FORTY-TWO

SAPHY

Back at home, two pieces of cold pizza later, my phone rings. There's a flutter of nerves in my stomach to see Marley's name on the screen.

'Hi,' I answer.

'Hello, Saphy! I'm so pleased you still want to do the interview. Even sober, as mandated by Fern.'

'Well, to be fair, I'm just back from the pub. Though I only had the one.'

'Sober enough, then.'

'I don't change my mind once I've made a decision.'

There's a pause. 'That is such a Flora thing to say. Anyway, this is what I think we should do.' She runs through where it would take place – a studio at Sky – to allow for a few hours there, but that she'd be looking at getting about half an hour actual interview, which will probably be edited back. Listening to her, I'm starting to get nervous. Will I be OK in front of cameras?

'When are you free?' she asks.

'Apart from hospital appointments on Mondays and going out next Saturday night, any day or time is fine with me.'

'I'll check with Charles and Margot and get back to you. I'm not sure if Fern is going to take part, but I expect she'll want to come along, either way, so I'll check with her also. Do you have any questions?'

'I'm a bit nervous about what we might end up talking about. Will you tell us ahead?'

'Absolutely. And it won't be live so it can be edited if anything goes wrong or you need a break. We can meet up to talk it through if you like?'

'That'd be great.'

'Hang on, let me check my diary... I could do lunch tomorrow if you're free. About one?'

'Sounds good. Where?'

'You don't drive, do you?'

'No.'

'I'll come and get you and we can decide where to go.'

'Thanks.'

Afterwards, I think about all the things that are coming up. Lunch tomorrow. The night out with Zoe and friends. And then there is the interview, on *television*. I'm going to have to go shopping again, despite my credit card balance. No real choice.

My phone vibrates with a message: it's Fern.

We've been thinking about what to do with Flora's things. You look about her size and height. I've spoken to Mum about it and we agree – if there are any of her clothes you can make use of, you're welcome to do so. Let me know what you think. Take care.

I stare at the words. Talk about synchronicity.

Flora's clothes – the clothes of a dead woman. A dead woman who, going by photos that appeared on my internet searches, had the most amazing wardrobe.

Her hair, her clothes – her drink of choice – her friends and family. Her favourite colour, too. I'm becoming Flora. I want her life.

FORTY-THREE

FERN

There's a message from Saphy the next morning.

Hi Fern, thank you so much for your message, and thank you to your mum, too, for thinking of me. Are you sure it's OK for me to go through Flora's clothes?

Once I'd thought of it, I was completely sure: it just felt the right thing to do. And the thought of taking Flora's things to a charity shop – having people I don't know trying them on, wearing them – no. I know they're just things and it shouldn't matter, but somehow, it does. Having Saphy make use of them just feels better. And once I'd told Mum that Saphy was living on benefits, she was right behind it, too.

Absolutely. And honestly, it solves a problem for us because we couldn't work out what we wanted to do with it all.

If you're sure, I'd love to. Any chance I could come by this morning? Then I'm having lunch with Marley to

talk about the interview – I'm sure you could come if
                                              you like?

I definitely don't want to take part in the interview. Apart from reasonable things like not wanting to be recognised by random patients at the hospital who will then want to talk about it, and not liking having cameras in my face – there was enough of that when Flora was first hurt – there is just a feeling in my gut that says, no. Don't do this.

I message her back:

Of course, come along this morning – I'm in Kensington. I'll ping the address. Give me an idea what time you'll arrive. But I'll give lunch a miss.

FORTY-FOUR

SAPHY

I check the address again: could this really be Fern's front door? It's in the middle of a narrow, cobbled lane of quirky mews houses, a part of Kensington that manages to feel villagey and apart from London despite its location. It might be small in comparison but probably cost more than Fern's family home in Oxford. I'm uneasy. I don't belong here and I'm too tired to fake it. Nightmares kept me up most of the night.

But I'm here now. Besides, I already told Marley to collect me here instead of at home for lunch later.

I make myself ring the bell and Fern comes to the door a moment later.

'Hi, Saphy, come in. I've just put the kettle on – tea?'

'Oh yes, please.' I follow her in, to a beautifully decorated open space – gorgeous sofas with masses of cushions, stunning kitchen, table and chairs – gleaming hardwood floors throughout, works of art on the walls that look the real deal. This place could be in a magazine with a famous actor or pop star in residence. But at the same time, it feels comfy, cosy. 'This place – it's so lovely.'

'I've been lucky to live here, especially as it's close to work. It's Mum's, actually.' She gets out mugs, teabags, puts the already boiled kettle back on and pours it a moment later. She hesitates. 'Though I've been thinking of moving. After living here with Flora, it feels too empty now.'

We've both lost someone, and we're linked forever by Flora. Reminding myself of these things makes me feel more at ease.

She hands me a mug of tea. I follow her up the stairs, to the first door. It's ajar. We go in and she shows me the Aladdin's cave that is Flora's built-in wardrobes, then says she's going for a shower.

Flora's room. Her bed. I sit on it, stroke the duvet.

I hear the shower begin down the hall. I'm never going to get a better chance than this to find out more about Flora. I close the door, grab some random clothes out of the wardrobe and drape them on the bed. Then turn to her dressing table.

Top drawer – make-up. I've tried to get my eye make-up like Flora's and haven't quite got there. I only hesitate a second before slipping her eyeliner into my bag.

Her second drawer is a mess of paperwork. Bank statements. To do lists scrawled on scraps of paper, receipts. A few small notebooks. She was a doodler, too – scribbles and drawings are everywhere. It's all a mess; there is no organisation. I can't resist a peek at a credit card statement. Her limit was twenty thousand pounds, and Marley said she often went over.

There are elaborate doodles around the edges of the statement – leaves and flowers with heart-shaped blossoms. Not just doodles – she was quite talented. I look closer. There are winding leaves that wrap around each other, and they contain calligraphy letters, F and B. Flora and Benji? The statement is dated November.

I'm sure I'd read that Flora dumped Benjamin months before she was strangled. This is only the month before. If she'd already dumped him, why was she doodling their initials together?

The bottom drawer looks to be mostly full of cards, letters, and I'm about to look through them, but then the water stops down the hall. I close the drawer and turn back to the clothes I'd put on the bed. Quickly choose a red dress, slip out of my clothes and pull it on over my head. It's silky, body hugging without being tight. It's easily the most gorgeous dress I've ever had on and that's not all: I recognise it. It's the same dress Flora wore in that first photo of her I put on my lock screen – the one she wore when Charles got an OBE. I love it, but where would I ever wear something like this? Anyway, it's too low-cut. The top of my scar is visible.

There's a tap at the door.

'Come in.'

Fern peers in, dressed in trackies and a T-shirt, wet hair. 'That fits you perfectly.'

I turn towards her, indicate the scar on my chest, mostly healed now but still red and angry. 'I think my days of low-cut are over.'

'I understand why you say that, but your scars are a badge of courage; you should wear them with pride.'

I spend the next two hours trying things on, getting Fern's input on some. Making piles of yes please and probably not. Sneaking peeks now and then into the cards and letters in the bottom drawer of Flora's dressing table. There's nothing from Benji, though that could be because the police took anything from him. I have a look at the F&B doodle again. It wasn't the work of minutes – it was elaborate. Were they still together – did the police get that wrong? If they got that wrong, who knows what else they could have got wrong.

I end with blue trousers, a beautiful, tailored blue and yellow blouse. I come out of Flora's room, go downstairs.

Fern is at the breakfast bar. She looks up from her laptop. 'That's a yes for sure.'

'I might wear it to lunch if that's OK?'

'Of course it is. It's yours now, if you want it.'

There's a lump in my throat and I swallow, a rush of emotion coming through me.

'Fern – just thank you. Thank you so much. You have no idea how much I appreciate everything you've done for me.' And I'm across to her and she's standing up now and hugging me, and I'm not sure which of us is more surprised.

'It's just stuff – it's emotive because it's Flora's stuff. But really, you're very welcome. I promise.' She looks at me searchingly. 'Saphy, are you feeling all right? You look, well, not quite yourself.'

'I had trouble sleeping last night.'

'Were you in discomfort or pain?'

I shake my head. 'No, it's not that.' And I don't know if I should tell her, but maybe it's a way to ask about Flora and Benji. 'It's... well... I've been having nightmares, about what happened to Flora. As if I'm her.'

A mixture of pain and sympathy crosses Fern's face. 'I've had dreams about that, too – except in mine I'm standing there, watching. Not helping her.'

'Oh Fern. How awful.'

'I guess that, in the circumstances, it's natural for you to think about it – as it is for me. And dreams take hold of things in your mind, replay them for you.'

'Is it OK to talk about what happened to Flora? It's just that there's something I want to ask you.'

She hesitates. 'Ask. And then I'll see.'

'I've read about it online. I remember hearing the news about it when it happened as well. It's this Benjamin Lawrence who has been charged with her murder. I gather he's a doctor. Did you know him?'

She turns, putting spoons in the dishwasher, teabags in a countertop compost bin – avoiding eye contact? 'I worked with him. So yes, I knew him.'

'The stuff I read said he was an ex-boyfriend. Were they together for long?'

'I think about six months. It ended late summer.' *Late summer*: that doodle was on a November bill. Something doesn't add up.

'Do you know why they broke up?'

She shakes her head. 'Flora wouldn't say. Why are you asking about Benji?' Benji, not Benjamin or Lawrence: Benji.

'I'd struggle to tell you why, but there's this conviction, in my gut – that he didn't do it. That they've arrested the wrong person.' That isn't really true. Despite finding it hard to believe what he'd done when I'd first looked into his eyes on a photo online, I know that people can hide and mask; anything could lurk inside of him. But that doodle of Flora's has me unsure enough to want to know what Fern thinks.

'Actually, I find I'm not able to talk about this after all. I'm sorry, Saphy.'

'I'm sorry if I've upset you.'

'It's – well, it's fine. Though I am concerned if dreams like that are interfering with your sleep. Talk to your medical team about it.' She is retreating, pulling away from me – hiding behind her doctor-mask. She hesitates. 'Also, if you feel that you know things – like about Benji – that could only come from Flora, I'm concerned about how you're coping, mentally. I hope it wasn't Marley the other day that got you thinking this way. But you need to talk to your team about that, also.'

'I will. Thank you,' I say. Though I'm fairly sure that I won't. I don't want to be told that this connection I feel with Flora isn't real, but I can't say that to Fern because I don't want to upset her further. I'd felt we were becoming friends. I hope asking her about Benji hasn't damaged this.

Fern doesn't believe Benji is guilty, I'm sure of it. If she did, that would have been an easy thing to say – far more difficult to admit that she thinks the police are wrong, that Flora's attacker is still out there. And she knew Benji, even though she seemed to find that hard to say, even turning away when she answered. Was there something going on between Fern and Benji?

FORTY-FIVE

FERN

Marley sweeps in, whistles. 'You look fabulous,' she says to Saphy. Then she turns to me and clocks what I'm wearing. 'Aren't you coming?'

I shake my head.

'Because you don't want me to talk you into taking part in the interview.'

I raise an eyebrow and we both know she's right, though that isn't the only reason. 'Actually, I'm on night shift tonight. I need to get some sleep.'

'I hope I haven't been keeping you up,' Saphy says.

'Not at all, it's fine. First shift of the week, it's always hard to sleep during the day.'

'I've got some news,' Marley says. 'If it works for you, Saphy, we're looking at Thursday afternoon at two for the interview. All being well it will go to air next week. I'll get back about what day.'

'Fine with me,' Saphy says. 'Are you going to come to the interview, Fern?'

'I'll come. But not on camera. Deal?'

'Deal,' Marley says.

I help Marley cram bags of Flora's clothes into her boot that she'll drop back at Saphy's later. I watch through the window as they go.

What is it about Saphy? Being around her... unsettles me. Seems to make me feel things I don't want to feel, think about things I don't want to think about. Picks at the scab over the Flora-sized wound, makes it bleed again. When she hugged me, I was almost in tears and could tell that she was, too. And when she asked me about Benji, I had this sense that she could see through me, knew what I wasn't saying.

I'd suggested Saphy have Flora's clothes for all the right reasons, but I'm not as sure now that it was a good idea. Saphy seems too in tune with Flora and her life – and how it ended. If she is developing an unhealthy fixation with Flora, wearing her clothes could make her obsession worse. There was something in Saphy's eyes when she spoke about Flora and Benji that felt disturbing, strange. She was making me feel nervous and I'm not sure why. And even though she said she would talk to her medical team about these matters, I doubt she will.

I go to Flora's room. I'd insisted Saphy leave it as it was, that I'd deal with the rest of the mess. Clothes are piled up on her chair, the bed; the wardrobes are almost empty now.

I won't put things back in the wardrobes, I decide. It'll just be harder to get them back out again. I should try to sleep but instead make a start on folding things, filling more bags. I'll need to do a charity shop run at some point.

Her dressing table I've looked through, before. There is loads of make-up, paperwork. That'll be for the bin and the shredder, I suppose. The bottom drawer is mostly full of greetings cards – birthday, Christmas, others. Unsure what to do with them, I have a look through. Many have had the Flora doodling treatment. She could have been an artist if she'd applied herself, couldn't she?

There are cards from me, Mum and Dad, Leo, Marley, and

a host of other names I don't recognise. There are several from Imogen, her boss – more of a friend than just someone she worked for, though she must have been something like twenty years older. I wonder again why Imogen didn't come to the wake.

There's a Christmas card from her – a kitten climbing a Christmas tree on the front, the usual season's greetings printed inside, and then written underneath, *you are stronger than you know*. Nothing else, just *love Imogen*. That isn't a usual senti-ment added to a Christmas card. No one who knew her would say Flora was weak, though that is what the words imply. Flora had doodled next to Imogen's words: an hourglass, sands trick-ling through and almost gone. Time running out.

Goosebumps prickle on my neck. Imogen's words imply that Flora had a problem she was struggling to deal with. If so, maybe it has something to do with what happened to Flora. Does Imogen know anything about it?

I'm being ridiculous. It's Saphy saying what she did about Benji that has me thinking like this – looking for someone else, some other reason that Flora was taken away.

I put the cards back in the drawer. I'll decide their fate another time.

There are people I should let know about the interview. I start with Leo. It rings four times and just as I'm trying to decide if I should or shouldn't leave a message, he answers.

'Hey, Fern.'

'Hi, Leo. How are you doing?'

A pause. 'Meh,' he says. 'You?'

'I like that word – meh. Me, too. I'm calling to let you know that my parents and one of Flora's organ recipients are doing an interview, with Marley, for Sky.'

'Seriously? To get a big pat on the shoulder for all the good they've done?'

'It's because of all the press against organ donation. To show what a difference it can make. I didn't want it to come as a shock.' There's a pause. 'Leo?'

'I'm still here. Thanks for letting me know. When is it?'

'It's happening on Thursday afternoon – it should air next week.'

'Are you taking part?'

'No, I decided not to. But I'm going along to watch.'

Another pause. 'Gotta go. Bye, Fern. And thanks.'

Should I call Imogen?

We've never really spoken, past hellos – even at that dinner party with Flora, Leo, Marley, Owen, Benji and me. I don't have her number. But I know the name of the art gallery she runs, where Flora worked. I find it online.

She answers on the second ring. 'Good afternoon. Sunset Gallery.'

'Hi, is that Imogen? It's Fern, Flora's sister.'

'Yes, it's me. Hi, Fern, how are you?'

'A bit meh.' I've decided to adopt Leo's term; I like it.

'Aw, I get that. Me, too. Anything I can do for you?'

'Well, I'm letting a few people who were close to Flora know about an interview that's coming up.' I explain it to her.

'Thanks for letting me know.'

'I saw you at the funeral. I meant to speak to you, but there were so many people.'

'I know.'

'Unless I missed you in the crowd – you didn't come to the wake?'

'No. I'd had enough by then.'

Me, too. But I didn't have a choice. 'There's something else I was wondering about.'

'What's that?'

'There was a card you'd given Flora, that I found in her things – a Christmas card.'

'Oh?'

'You'd written something inside that had me puzzled.'

'What's that?'

'You are stronger than you know.' She doesn't say anything; I wait a beat, two. 'Was there something happening with Flora? Something I didn't know about?'

'Maybe it's too late to care now, Fern. I've got to go.' It clicks and she's gone.

FORTY-SIX

SAPHY

I'm looking at the menu in the fancy gastropub Marley picked for our lunch. Despite feeling nervous at being with her, everything sounds so good.

'I should have salad,' I say, and sigh.

'Did the scales of the patriarchy chase you down and make you step on their evil surface?'

'Kind of. I gained two kilos in a week.'

She whistles. 'That's an impressive effort.'

'I spent months with no appetite and suddenly everything tastes delicious. But I'm feeling inspired to be sensible by clothes, like these, that fit nicely. I want to keep on being able to wear them.'

'You really do look amazing. Even since the few days I saw you last – your colour is so much better.'

'Thank you.' I hesitate. 'Are you OK with me having Flora's clothes?'

She shrugs. 'It was a sensible idea and it's fine. To be honest, she had so many clothes that I'm unlikely to recognise anything.

The waiter comes with our drinks, takes our food order, and

Marley starts going through her plans for the interview. Even just thinking about it makes me queasy.

'What if I freeze?'

'Just ignore the camera and talk to me – that's all you have to do. And we can edit things out if there are any glitches.'

'What happens if I don't like the way I answer something, but you do? Who decides if we edit it out and try again?'

'Ultimately, the producer. But if there is anything you're uncomfortable with talking about, just say so.'

I hesitate. 'There is, actually. Can we not talk about my dad? Because I might cry. I really don't want to ugly cry on TV.'

'That's fine. We'll want to have a little information about you so viewers have a sense of who you are and what you've been through, but we don't have to discuss it – I can put it in an introduction that I'll record before or after.'

'OK. How about you, Marley? Are you going to find it diffi-cult, talking about Flora?'

She takes a moment to answer. 'I will. But I think what we're doing is important. Also, I've had years of reporting on things where I have to hide my personal feelings. I'm good at it.'

'But this is Flora. That photo I saw of the two of you – I just knew how you felt about her.'

She blinks back tears. 'Look what you're doing to me.'

'I was right, wasn't I? That you had a relationship?'

'Years ago, we had kind of a fling. Not recently. She really was my best friend, and that's it.'

'That's everything.'

'Yes. It is. I don't know how you worked that out from one photo of the two of us. You should be the reporter. You haven't mentioned this to Fern?'

I shake my head. 'Of course not. It's not my story to tell.'

'It's just that I promised Flora. She didn't want her parents to know she was bi.'

'That doesn't sound like Flora. I mean, everything I've heard about her is that she was fearless.'

'She mostly was. But underneath it all, in some ways she was still her daddy's little girl,' she says, with a disparaging tone. Marley didn't like it that Flora wouldn't acknowledge her publicly when they were together. Is that what tore them apart? If so, how could they stay friends after that?

'Speaking of best friends, can I bring Zoe along? For moral support.'

She looks relieved to move on to another subject. 'Sure. Actually, I could ask her a few questions about you and your dad. For context. Would she be up for that?'

'I don't know. I'll check and get back to you.'

'Any other questions?' Marley says.

'There's something else I'm wondering about, but it has nothing to do with the interview.'

'What's that?'

'Flora and Benji. Fern said earlier that they were together about six months and broke up in the summer.'

'That sounds about right. I'm surprised you got her to talk about Benji.' A head tilted, sceptical look. She must know that Fern wouldn't broach it voluntarily.

'I got the feeling she is finding it hard to accept that he was responsible for what happened to Flora.'

'That wouldn't entirely surprise me.'

'Was there something between Fern and Benji?'

A raised eyebrow. 'Like I said, you should be the reporter.'

'So, there was, then.'

'I don't think so. Fern liked him, though – not that she admitted it, but it was there to see. I'm not sure if he ever worked it out.'

'Then it would've been hard for her when he got together with Flora.'

'For sure. But Flora was oblivious to things like that. Not that she didn't care – she just wouldn't notice.'

'Fern said she introduced them?'

'That's right. I was there at the time.'

'Do you agree with Fern, that Benji wasn't the one who strangled Flora?'

There's a pause. Her eyes, narrowed, lips in a line. I've pushed her too far.

'I doubt Fern said anything of the sort. Finding it hard to accept and thinking someone else was responsible are not the same thing.'

'Well, no, but—'

'Let's look at the facts, shall we? He and Fern were the only ones who knew that Flora had gone to the family cottage in Dorset, and Fern was at work. It was late December; no one expected Flora to be there.'

'But you still haven't said what *you* think.' The words are out before I can filter.

'I'll tell you what I think. I'm sick of well brought up white boys who went to the right schools getting away with things because no one can believe they'd ever do wrong. This trial is going to drag Flora through the mud when she can't defend herself, and Benji was just another privileged git who couldn't accept that the beautiful girl didn't want him anymore.'

'OK. I'm really sorry if I've upset you.'

She nods, gathers herself. A smile is back but less genuine, I think, and it hurts inside. I want Marley to like me – which sounds pathetic.

'It's fine,' she says. 'I understand the curiosity – I really do. Especially coming from you, with the connection you have to Flora. But I'm sick of her life being examined now that it is over. And it won't end until after the trial.'

'I'm sorry. That must be really hard for you.'

She's looking at her watch. 'We've got to get going if I'm to drop you home before an appointment I have this afternoon.' She's signalling to the waiter to bring the bill. 'Anything else you need to know for the interview?'

By the time we've reached my street we've exhausted the superficial stuff and don't seem to have anything else to talk about. It feels wrong, falling out with Marley. I'm really tired now, too. Hours of trying on clothes and difficult conversations have worn me out.

She pulls in. I get out of the car and for a moment everything spins and I have to hold on to the car to stop from falling to the ground.

She rushes around the car. 'Are you all right?'

'I think so. Just got up too fast.'

She helps me to the front door. I find the keys and we go through.

'Have a seat,' she says. 'I'll bring in the stuff from the boot.' I sit on the sofa, head in my hands. I hear her making a few trips to bring the bags in to the hall.

'Do you want them upstairs?'

'It's OK, leave them there.'

'I've got a few minutes.' She lugs them upstairs and my eyes are prickling with tears that won't go away. A few slip down my cheeks.

She comes in. 'Saphy?' She kneels on the floor next to me. 'What's wrong?'

I shake my head, not sure if I can even try to explain what I don't understand myself, and now the tears are coming faster.

'Hey. Whatever it is, it'll be all right.' And she's close now; my head is on her shoulder. One of her hands awkwardly patting my back. 'Look. It's not too late to stop or delay the interview if you're not up to it.'

I'm shaking my head. 'It's not that.'

I pull away, look into her eyes, and then – does she move, do I? Or maybe it is both of us. We're kissing. Her lips, so soft, and I'm breathing her in and kissing her at the same time and now I'm dizzy again, falling back on the sofa and pulling her with me, and then—

She's moving away.

'What was that?' she says.

'I – I don't know.'

'Neither do I. Until we do, let's stop this.'

'All right.' I sit up, breathless, still looking at her lips and wanting to kiss them again, when she says goodbye. The door closes a moment later.

I just sit there, stunned. The rush of blood through my body – my lips – tongue – was nothing like anything I've ever experienced before.

What the fuck was that? I've never kissed a girl before; I've never wanted to. But then, all at once, it was the only thing I wanted to do.

And it was amazing.

FORTY-SEVEN

FERN

Maybe it's too late to care now, Fern.

Imogen's words go over and over in my mind that night at work, an ear worm that won't be banished. What did she mean?

There was something about Imogen I didn't like when we first met, though I could never quite work out why I felt that way. So why can't I just leave this alone? It's not like I care what she thinks.

I care because it's all tied up with Flora. What if it has something to do with what happened to her? I have to know.

I won't phone – she could just hang up again. I'll go to her, instead.

I've been to Imogen's gallery on the South Bank a few times – when Flora was helping with an exhibition of an artist I liked; when I met Flora there before we went out for dinner. At the end of a busy and tiring night shift, I walk across the park to home – have a fast shower – change. Look longingly at my bed, then head out to the Tube.

When I get to the South Bank, my footsteps get slower the closer I get to Imogen's gallery. Maybe this was a mistake. But I'm here now.

I go in, hesitate near the door.

There's a young woman I haven't seen before at the desk – maybe Imogen isn't even here. If not, I can file this away as a bad idea and move on. But just as I'm about to turn and go, Imogen steps through from a back room. She walks towards me.

'Good morning, Fern. Is there something I can help you with?' Her words, the tone, are pleasant enough, but there is cold hostility underneath. Why?

'I was hoping we could talk for a moment.'

'I'm a little busy.'

I glance around the empty gallery, too tired to be anything but blunt. 'Imogen, I don't know what's behind your rudeness. I know you were close to Flora. I hoped if there was something going on with her I didn't know about that you could explain it, but instead you accused me of not caring and hung up. What is that about?'

'You must know.'

'I really don't.'

'Fine, let's pretend I believe you. I'll spell it out for you. Flora was in love with Benji. Despite all she'd been through, they were making it work. And then what happened? She dumped him, Fern, because you fancied you were in love with him, too. She did it for you, and what have you ever done for her when she needed you?'

'What? That's not true – I mean, I never told Flora anything like that about Benji.'

'You expect me to believe you?'

I'm bewildered. 'I never said anything to Flora about Benji. Did she tell you that I did?'

'Unlike with you today, sometimes you don't have to spell things out.'

Maybe Flora worked it out, without me saying a word? I thought I was a champion at hiding my feelings – a protective mechanism that became stronger the more years I practised medicine – but maybe I let something slip. Would she really have done that for me? Tears are threatening and I blink them away.

'Flora never told me why they stopped seeing each other,' I say. 'If that was the reason, I didn't know it.'

'You haven't denied how you felt about Benji.'

'No.' I sigh. 'No matter what you seem to think, I'm not a liar, Imogen.'

She's studying me, then shakes her head. 'There's no point to this, is there? Whether I believe you or not, Flora is still gone.' And I can hear the pain in her voice. 'Just go.'

It isn't until I'm almost home that more of the words Imogen used come back – *despite all she'd been through.* Put together with what she'd written in her card, *you are stronger than you know.* What did she mean?

The Flora most people saw smiled and partied her way through life, doing pretty much what she wanted when she wanted. She only lasted at the job with Imogen because she liked it – late starts, schmoozing artists and buyers with wine and bubbly. She didn't need a proper job when Mum's money was always there to bail her out when she needed it.

Imogen's words hint at a darker side. Flora was unsettled and moody at Christmas – even more so when she left for Dorset. She threw things into a bag and almost ran out the door, as if she was running away from something. Or someone.

What was wrong, Flora?

The question I should have asked her then haunts me now.

FORTY-EIGHT

SAPHY

The next afternoon, a message pings on my phone – it's Marley.

*I can't stop thinking about you. But this isn't right, not for me.
Can we stay friends?*

Are we friends? I'm not sure.

My instincts are telling me to be careful, and it's one of those strong gut instincts like I was telling Zoe about. Somehow, I'm certain that crossing Marley in any way would be a mistake. Did I kiss her or did she kiss me? I don't even know if it was one or the other or both of us. But *why* did it happen? It was like this wave of attraction that came from nowhere.

Or maybe it came from someone else: Flora. And now I'm verging into the fantasist realm that'd make my medical team and friends completely freak if I told them. Which is why I won't.

I think a bit longer, then message her back:

I'm so relieved you said that, I completely agree.

All OK for the interview tomorrow?

Absolutely. See you there.

That's one problem dealt with – or so I tell myself, since I have a feeling this thing with Marley isn't over just because we both say that it is.

Now to go back to another problem: the mysterious J.

There have been too many things going on to focus on whether I should or shouldn't try to find her, but it has been niggling away inside. What clinches it in the end is that I owe J. Because of her, my parents wrote these letters that I now treasure. I can at least say thank you for that.

The file with the lawyers and adoption agency is still on Dad's desk. I'll try calling the adoption agency, see if they can help.

My hands are shaking as I enter the numbers.

'Good morning, Adoption First, London. How may I help you?'

'Hi. I was adopted through your agency over twenty-eight years ago. I was wondering if I can be put into contact with my birth mother?'

She confirms my identity and then checks their records. Tells me that it was a semi-open adoption.

'What does that mean, exactly?'

'All contact was mediated through us. You could write to your birth mother and we could forward that to her. Alternatively, we can contact your birth mother and ask her if she wants direct contact with you. If she says yes, then we could facilitate an exchange of details between the two of you.'

'If she says no, what happens then?'

'Unfortunately, then we can't give you any of her details. What would you like to do?'

If I just write to her and she never writes back, what would that achieve? If they ask her, whether she says yes or no will tell me all I need to know. If it's a no, it might hurt. But at least I'll have tried.

'I'd like you to ask her if she wants direct contact. And then we'll see what happens.'

She takes my number, email address.

Now all I can do is wait.

FORTY-NINE

FERN

Just as I'm wondering if I should message Mum to get an idea of how late they'll be, she and Dad are shown to our table.

'Darling. So good to see you.' Air kisses. Mum is looking well – like she's started eating a bit more, might even have some colour in her cheeks that isn't just blusher.

'Fern.'

'Hi, Dad.'

'Isn't this exciting?' Mum says.

'Aren't you nervous at all?'

'Not really. I've been on TV before, you know.' Of course – Chelsea Flower Show interviews, though that was years ago now.

'Well, this is a bit more personal.'

'Of course. But I've been assured any gaffes can be edited out.'

A waiter comes to take the drinks order. I'm so glad I'm not going to be part of the interview this afternoon – I wouldn't be able to eat. Mum doesn't fool me; she *is* nervous. As far as Dad goes, I can't say I've ever seen any sign of nerves in him, about, well, anything. He's got unflappable surgeon face perfected.

And while I try for a similar facade at work, it isn't that much a part of me that it is always there.

'We have some news,' Mum says. 'We've heard from two more of Flora's recipients.'

'Really?'

'A woman in her forties who had her corneas,' Dad says. 'A young man who had one of her kidneys.'

'Are you going to meet them?'

'We've emailed. I've told them about this interview as I expect they'll want to watch it when it airs.'

'Have you suggested meeting either of them? Invited them for lunch?'

'Not just at the moment,' Dad says. He looks vaguely uncomfortable for a nanosecond – only someone who knew him well would notice. Then he changes the subject to the road-works out of Oxford that delayed their journey.

Interesting. He wanted to meet Saphy as soon as possible – pushed it a bit early for her, really, so soon after her surgery. Two more get in touch and he's less interested. Why?

Dad has always been ruled by logic, facts – the quin-tessential scientist and doctor, who finds the messy emotions of the rest of us mere mortals difficult to navigate. Could it be that he actually had some romantic notion about Flora's heart being that much more significant?

FIFTY

SAPHY

In Zoe's car I check my email while she sets her satnav for Sky Central.

'Woah. There's an email from the adoption agency.' I'd told her earlier about the call I'd made to them. Seeing it there in my inbox – my stomach lurches.

'Ooh exciting! What do they say?'

'I'm afraid to find out.' I didn't even know J existed just days ago – well, obviously I knew I had a birth mother, somewhere – but not any details that made her feel real. 'OK, here goes.' I read through it quickly, first relieved and then nervous again. 'They've got in touch with her – my birth mother. It turns out that J is Jenny Turner, she lives in London, and she wants to hear from me. They've given me her email address.'

'What are you going to do?'

'Well, email her. I guess. I never thought this would happen so fast, if at all. Maybe we can get through today first, and then I'll think about what to say?'

'Sounds like a good plan.'

We crawl along in London traffic. So much has changed in such a short time. My life before was so narrow – doctors, drugs, hospitals. Zoe and Claire, Neeha, Hermi. The Saphy I was before wouldn't have done what I'm doing now – both going to be interviewed on TV and having reached out to find my birth mother.

And it isn't just improvements in my health and having – hopefully – years more to look forward to that I didn't have before. It's like I'm someone different, inside, too.

It's all Flora: her family, her friends. Her clothes. I'm getting closer to her, to living her life. Today is another step, a way of becoming more of a part of her family. I need them to see – to feel – that I belong.

FIFTY-ONE

FERN

Our names have been left at the desk at Sky Central and an assistant comes to take us up to the studio. Saphy and her friend, Zoe, are already here.

When I first see Saphy across the room, talking to Marley, I'm struck by how different she looks – so much stronger, healthier, than she did, even just days ago. The dress she is wearing – I assume one of Flora's, though I don't recognise it – really suits her. And it's not just that her health is improving. When I first met her, she was so uncertain, shy. I'd felt a sort of kindred introvert connection with her. And now? She is somehow more poised, confident. Was the awkward shyness an act, or is this?

Marley waves us over. Soon she is discussing with Saphy and my parents what they'll be doing, talking about. I'm in the background, watching – so glad I insisted it be this way. Even Zoe is taking part. An assistant offers me coffee, finds me a chair out of the way. Soon they begin.

'I'm Marley Jansen. Usually, I'm a roving London correspondent with Sky News, though we're in the studio today. I'm also grieving my best friend, Flora Hastings-Clifford. You might have known her as Sleeping Beauty, after she was assaulted and left in a coma for months.' Images of Flora, before and after, in a coma, appear on the screen. 'But to me she was the girl who always laughed at my jokes. Who couldn't pass a fountain without making a wish. Who held me when I cried after my mother died. Today, we'll be examining the recent furore over organ donation – so-called living donors – but it's not just a hypothetical subject to me or my guests. We have Flora's parents, her mother, Margot Hastings, and her father, Dr Charles Clifford. And we also have Saphira Logan, whose life has been saved by a heart transplant – with Flora's heart. Her best friend, Zoe Hendricks, has also joined us.'

Marley excels at this, achieving a balance between her own pain and the professionalism and warmth she conveys with her questions. Zoe is holding Saphy's hand. She's the one who explains about Saphy's health, the loss of her father. Why she needed a transplant and what she was like before she had it. Tears shine in Saphy's eyes and Mum, on her other side, takes Saphy's other hand. With prompting from Marley, Mum tells how Flora's condition had worsened – explains how it felt to make the decision they had to make for Flora to be an organ donor, knowing she would never recover. How she struggled with it. And then how, when she met Saphy, she knew what an amazing thing they had done. Dad comes in next, explaining the medical situation in more detail. What it means to be brain stem dead. That the heart would stop beating was a definite thing, no matter what was done – what made the person who they were was gone and could never return.

Finally, it is Saphy's turn. She talks about what it felt like, being so young and told you're going to die, that your only hope was a heart transplant that wasn't likely to happen. So few organ donors are available generally, and families are particularly reluctant to agree to heart donation. How it felt when she was contacted that a heart that was a good match for her was available, knowing that what saved her life meant some other family was grieving and in pain. And then Marley asks her why she agreed to come on air and tell her story.

'It was a really hard decision to make – to be here today. Talking about such personal things. I've always been a private person. But it is so important that I had to speak out. People like me die, every day, waiting for a transplant.'

Marley sums up, thanks her guests for coming. I feel a sense of pride in what my parents have done today – in Marley, too. Changing the narrative, from Flora's story making people shy away from organ donation to the opposite. It could make a difference. It could save lives.

No one could listen to Saphy's story and not be moved. And although each of them did well, it was Saphy who shone most of all.

FIFTY-TWO

SAPHY

When the cameras are off at last, I relax back in my seat. The relief that it is over is intense, but now the worry begins.

'Give it to me straight. Did I talk nonsense?'

'Not a bit,' Zoe says. 'I promise.'

'You – all of you – did brilliantly,' Marley says.

'Well done all around,' Fern says.

'Shall we go for a drink?' Margot says, but Zoe had already made me promise we'd go for one on our own to dissect it all afterwards.

'Any other time – I'd love to. But I'm so tired now, I need to go home.'

'Of course, should have realised,' Margot says, concern in her eyes. 'Go and rest.'

After we say our goodbyes, she draws me to one side, hands me an envelope. 'I've got a card for you – don't open it now, leave it for later when you're on your own.'

'Thank you.' I slip it into my handbag.

FIFTY-THREE

FERN

Zoe and Saphy say goodbye, head for the lift.

'How about you, Fern? Marley?' Mum says. 'Shall we go out for a drink? Flora's favourite cocktail bar isn't far from here.'

'Thank you, but sorry, I can't. I've got to do a few things here now,' Marley says. She'd already asked if I could stay after, said she needed to speak to me.

'I've got night shift tonight, so likewise. You go – I'll get the Tube back.'

Mum and Dad take their leave. Marley is speaking to an assistant, then turns to me.

'Come up. I'll find us a room to talk.' We go to another level. It's busy – almost frantic – people, desks, monitors everywhere. She speaks to someone and draws me into a small conference room. Shuts the door.

'This looks serious.'

'It is. It's about Saphy. I'm not buying her act anymore – the whole sweet, shy thing. She's been inveigling herself into your family. Your parents – your mum, especially – seem besotted with her, and your mum is particularly vulnerable just now. And with Saphy wearing Flora's favourite colour when we met her, changing her hair, somehow convincing you to give her Flora's clothes – it's like she is manoeuvring herself in to be Flora's replacement.'

I'm surprised – shocked, even – at Marley's words, but can tell that she means what she says. 'Is that fair? It wasn't Saphy's idea about the clothes.'

'Really? Didn't she plant that in your mind by talking about having nothing to wear that night at hers?'

'I don't think so,' I say, but now I'm wondering if Marley is right. 'Though she didn't know about the colour yellow and the rest of it.'

'That's what she said. But it would have been easy enough to find online – what about all the photos from the vigil?'

I'm uneasy, uncertain. 'It had occurred to me that maybe Saphy was too focused on Flora, but I don't think that's unusual from a psychological point of view in the circumstances. What you're suggesting goes far beyond that, though.'

'Trust me. I've interviewed enough criminals and politicians to recognise the manipulative mind. I almost pulled the plug on today, but thought it was too important to do that. But keep your guard up. And an eye on your mum and her purse strings.'

FIFTY-FOUR

SAPHY

Finally, we're in Zoe's car. I sit back in the seat, exhausted.

'When I said I was too tired to go out, it wasn't just an excuse. I meant it. Can we skip going for drinks and just go back to mine?'

'We can do that. Unless you'd rather just call it a day?'

'No, a drink sounds good, if mine can be tea.' She pulls out from the car park to the road and into rush hour traffic.

'What did you think of Flora's family?'

'Honestly? I'm not completely sure. Margot is so posh. Everything she did or said felt a bit, well, contrived – and then, all at once, it wasn't. You could see the pain in her eyes. How genuinely happy she was to have met you, that they helped you.'

'And Charles?'

'He seemed to reduce everything he said to the medical question. There was nothing about how he felt.'

'In a typical man kind of way?'

'Maybe. But it felt more than that to me – he was almost too detached, as if he were talking about a patient rather than his own daughter.'

'I get why you say that. Maybe the doctor persona is so ingrained he doesn't know how to switch it off. Or maybe it's a protective mechanism – a way to stay detached enough to hold it together.'

'Maybe. As far as Fern goes, I don't know – she was quiet, we didn't get a chance to talk.'

'I got the impression that Fern really lived in her sister's shadow, which doesn't make sense to me. I mean, Fern is the one who went to medical school and works in emergency medicine at a major London hospital – she's accomplished such a lot – and Flora didn't even finish university. And Fern has got this, I don't know, quiet strength about her. But with her parents, it felt like Flora was their golden child.'

'Much as in all areas of life – the pretty one always wins, don't they?'

Not Flora. At least, not anymore.

After Zoe is gone, I nap. Get up a few hours later and potter around in the kitchen. Feed Hermi and make eggs on toast.

Check my emails. There's one from Charles, thanking me again for taking part in the interview today. And he says if I ever need help with anything at all, he's there – just ask. There you go, Zoe – he is human, after all. I email a quick thank you.

A message pings from Zoe with a selfie, her and Claire holding up glasses of wine – looks like the pub around the corner from Claire's.

Mum is having your glass and hearing all about today. Sleep well.

Even though Zoe complains about Claire, they've got such a close relationship – something I always wished I'd had. No matter how great Dad was, sometimes a girl needs a mum.

Claire has always been there for me but it's not quite the same.

Hang on – J. The email. With everything going on since it came, I completely forgot. I said I'd get back to it once I got through today, and the day has been officially survived. A nap, food, and I'm good to face it.

I reread the email from the adoption agency.

So, Jenny Turner of London: who are you? Why did you give me up? Do you really want to hear from me now, after over twenty-eight years?

The adoption agency said she did. Butterflies begin an elaborate, choreographed dance in my stomach.

The Saphy of years gone by would have agonised for weeks over contacting her, if not months. But now I know that time isn't always there when you need it. Don't waste it.

How do I want to come across? Neither desperate for her attention, nor completely uninterested – go for somewhere in between.

Dear Jenny,

My name is Saphira Logan. Adoption First in London gave me your email address. They tell me you're my birth mother.

Perhaps we could meet up and talk? They said you're based in London, and so am I. Let me know what you think.

Best wishes,

Saphy

I hit send: done. Then head for bed. I'm about to turn out the bedside light when I remember Margot's card, the one she said to open when I was alone.

I find it in my handbag. Open the envelope.

Inside is a card with a photo of a lovely garden on the front. I don't immediately read what she's written, because when I open the card, there is a cheque inside. For... *oh my God.* Ten thousand pounds.

I focus on her words:

Dear Saphy,

Meeting you has been an uplifting experience at the darkest of times. So please, please, allow me to do something for you? It's a small gesture to help you out until you've written your best-selling novel.

Best wishes,

Margot x

Ten. Thousand. Pounds.

I look and look again to see that I got the numbers right: I have.

The breathing space this could give me. I could put off selling the house, see if there is another solution. It would make everything easier. But why is she doing this?

I'm remembering Flora's twenty-thousand-pound credit card limit, that Fern had said Margot was always bailing Flora out financially. This doesn't feel right, but maybe it's not a lot to Margot. I mean, I wouldn't accept a loan from Zoe or Claire. But I'd let Zoe, say, buy me a drink, knowing she can afford it more than I can, and that I'd do the same for her if situations were reversed. This is a huge sum of money to me, but is Margot so well off that it is her equivalent of buying me a drink?

But I need to look past *now*, think about what would happen next and after that. What does this cheque represent to Margot?

Even though her life is so different to mine, I think I can understand. I'm sure she supports charities, gives them money to take away distress she feels when confronted with the pain of others. Giving money to starving children or mistreated animals or climate victims to make herself feel better, and in doing so they are dealt with – othered, pushed away. But I don't want to go away. I want to be part of her life, like Flora was – a part she can't do without.

I'll give it back, I decide. See where that leads.

I put the card up on my bedside table, the cheque in the drawer. And close my eyes.

* * *

Mum's hairbrush – the engraved silver handle – the cool weight of it in my hand. I draw it through my hair, watching in the mirror of Mum's dressing table. I'm wearing Flora's red dress – the one I wasn't sure about because my scar showed at the top, still raw and red. But Fern said to be proud – it's a badge of courage.

How would my hair look up? Gather it into a ponytail, twist it around, look down for a hair clasp I know I've seen in the second drawer. I find it, look back to the mirror, let go of my hair and almost scream. The hair clasp clatters to the floor.

Other eyes are looking back into mine from the mirror. It's Flora. She's found me.

You can never get away from me, Saphy. I'll never leave you alone – not when you've stolen my life.

I haven't – I'm not –

You're a thief: it's plain to see.

She's out of the mirror now, standing behind me – both of us reflected in its surface, her cold hands on my shoulders.

My dress, she says, tugging lightly at a shoulder strap. My heart. She touches the top of my scar, lightly. I'm shaking, scared, and she laughs. She knows.

Then her hand slips down the scar and her fingers are claws, digging into skin and bone, rivers of red blood flowing down her dress.

* * *

I'm screaming, thrashing in the blankets. There's a sudden sharp pain on my arm. I knock the bedside light over when I try to turn it on. Hermi's eyes glow in the dark.

I feel blindly for my phone, turn on its light and the familiar room around me begins to bring me back to myself. There's a scratch on the inside of my arm – must be courtesy of Hermi. I probably scared her. I'm otherwise intact.

It was just a dream, right? A dream. That's all. But when I eventually try to get back to sleep, I leave the light on.

FIFTY-FIVE

FERN

That night at work, Marley's words keep replaying in my mind. Could she be right about Saphy? Enough of what she said strikes a chord to make me question everything Saphy has said and done since we met. Marley is perhaps right about how Mum, in particular, feels about Saphy. The way Mum reached to hold Saphy's hand during the interview, the hug she gave her when they said goodbye. It's like the pain of losing Flora has shifted focus, as if Saphy gives her something else to think about. Someone she can save when she couldn't save Flora. But is that all coming from Mum, or has Saphy deliberately manipulated Mum's feelings for her?

Have I felt that way also? Perhaps, to a degree. Saphy makes me feel protective, like she needs looking after.

Is Saphy playing on our emotions, trying to get what she can from us? Just Flora's clothes are worth more than I can probably guess. She could sell them online and probably make quite a bit of money. But I doubt she'd do that, not if wearing her things made her feel closer to Flora.

So, the question is this: is Saphy vulnerable and confused, in need of help; or is she the calculating schemer that Marley sees? I can't be sure. But if she does need help, I can do something about that.

The next morning, I call her hospital and ask to speak to someone on Saphy's medical team. Eventually get put through to a transplant nurse.

'Good afternoon, I'm Dr Fern Hastings-Clifford at St Mary's. I'm calling about Saphira Logan because I'm concerned about her mental health.' I run through how she met her donor family, the interview that will air next week. Her apparent fixation on her donor. My connection with the situation.

Saphy had said she'd discuss the interview with her medical team, but from the note of surprise it seems that she hasn't. Apart from considering her own care, she should have done so. It will resonate with families of possible donors, those on lists waiting for transplants. Others, like Saphy, who have already had surgery. It's better for the doctors and nurses involved to be aware of what is coming.

They'll talk to Saphy about the interview and her feelings about her donor, assess if she needs assistance in dealing with all of this. I've done what I can to help her.

But do we need help?

FIFTY-SIX

SAPHY

The nightmare casts a cold shadow over my morning that is hard to shake off. The sun is shining – it's warm, a sunny June day. Spring is here and summer will be soon, but I'm shivering inside.

What if... it wasn't a dream? What if Flora has followed me here – is haunting me – will never go?

But *why*? Because I'm a thief. Not of her heart – that wasn't taken, it was given, and, OK, it wasn't Flora's decision, but it was her family behind it. She can hardly blame me for that. But what of the rest of it?

Saphy – get a grip. You're losing it if you think any of that could actually be true.

I make myself go into Mum and Dad's room, walk across to the dressing table, look around. It's as always, ordinary, reassuring. I step back towards the door and step on something hard and sharp. Look down. It's Mum's hairclip. The one I dropped on the floor in my dream.

I pick it up – it's broken. If it was just a dream, why was the clip on the floor? Maybe it fell out when I was going through the drawers the other day and I didn't notice; it might have been out of sight and then Hermi batted it about on the floor to where I trod on it.

It was a dream. Probably brought on by that cheque Margot gave me. Now I'm even more certain that I have to give it back.

I don't have Margot's number. I could email or call Charles, but I don't know if he knows about the cheque. The way she slipped it to me and asked me to open it later suggests maybe he doesn't. I'll give it to Fern, I decide. She'll know how to handle her parents. Decision made.

I go downstairs, make tea, toast. It's time to stop avoiding the other worry and check my emails.

The butterflies are back: there's a reply from Jenny in my inbox, sent late last night.

Dear Saphira – or do you prefer Saphy, as you signed?

I was so happy to see your message. There are so many things I want to tell you, like how long I've been on the Adoption Contact Register, hoping you'd register and want to find me, too. When I got the call from the adoption agency – they actually called my mother, as her phone and address were the details they had for me, and she gave them my current number – I said yes, yes, yes! I didn't know that they could facilitate this or I'd have been on to them years ago.

I'm pleased, too, that we're both in London. This may be too soon or not convenient, but are you free tomorrow night for dinner? Or any other night next week or after if that suits better?

If you'd rather talk first, my mobile number is below.

All my best wishes now and always,

Jenny

Wow. I mean, just, wow. She's been trying to find me, so this isn't something that has been thrust upon her that she is unsure of; she really wants to meet me.

But tonight? I'm still trying to avoid crowded places. Also – boring but true – I get tired so easily, and Zoe wouldn't forgive me if I bowed out of tomorrow night because I needed rest.

So, what should my next move be? Do I want to call Jenny? I shy away from that. It's hard talking to someone I don't know on the phone. I'd rather first hellos to be in person.

I'll reply by email:

Hi Jenny, could we perhaps make it tea this afternoon instead? If not, then next week sometime.

A reply comes almost instantly, like she's been waiting, watching her inbox:

That'd be lovely. Could you come to the South Bank? About two?

She suggests the Green Room, a place I've been to before, busy at lunch and dinner but hopefully not mid-afternoon.

Sounds good. I'll meet you there.

FIFTY-SEVEN

FERN

There's a knock at my door after lunch – a light tap I only just hear, as if whoever it is knows I might be asleep during the day with night shifts. I glance out the window: it's Saphy. She has something in her hand. I get downstairs and to the door just as she is pushing it through the letterbox.

'Hi, Saphy.'

'Hi. I wasn't sure if you'd be here or awake, so I wrote you a note just in case, but I'm glad to have caught you.' She pauses. 'Can I come in?'

'Of course. I'll put the kettle on.'

I fill the kettle. I'm feeling uneasy after Marley's words, and that I called Saphy's hospital – it felt kind of like I was telling on her, a childish concept. Saphy looks ill at ease also.

'What brings you by?'

'I want to return this.'

She opens the envelope she'd retrieved from the door as she came in. There is a note inside and what looks like a cheque. She hands the latter to me now – a cheque from Mum, made out to Saphy, for ten thousand pounds.

'She gave me a card with this in it after the interview. It

was so kind of her, but it doesn't feel right to keep it.' She hesitates. 'I'm worried how she is coping with things. I don't want to offend her, either. Can you give it back to her, try to explain how much I appreciate the thought, but I can't accept it?'

'Of course,' I say, relieved. Marley was wrong about Saphy, and here is the proof. As happy as I am about that, this money would probably make a big difference to Saphy. 'Are you sure? It's not a lot of money to Mum, quite honestly. She wouldn't miss it.'

'I'd guessed that, but I need to stand on my own two feet.'

'I understand. I'll take care of it.'

'Thank you.'

'So, what are you up to today?'

She hesitates. 'I think I told you I was adopted?' I nod. 'Well, going through some of my parents' things, I found a bunch of letters that had been written to my birth mother – about me. One thing led to another, and I'm meeting her this afternoon.'

'Really? That's such a huge thing to deal with, on top of everything else. How are you feeling about it?'

'I don't know, exactly. I'm curious. I want to know her story, even though it might be difficult to hear. I'm nervous, too. What if I don't like her? What if I do, but she doesn't like me? What if, what if. You know.' Even as she says these things, she's looking bright about taking this step.

'I have a feeling you'll cope, no matter what.'

'Thanks.'

She reaches for her cup of tea and that is when I notice a red mark on the inside of her arm. 'What have you done to yourself?'

'It's just a scratch. From my cat.'

'Let me see.'

She turns her arm, extends it to me. As she said, it's just a scratch, but on anti-rejection drugs these things can easily go wrong.

'It looks OK at the moment, but it could get infected, Saphy. You need to get some prophylactic antibiotics.'

'Really?'

'You need to be careful about things like a scratch from an animal.'

'I know. I guess I've been too distracted with all the stuff.'

'Understandable.'

She looks at her watch. 'I think I've got just enough time to take care of that. I'd better get going.'

A few quick sips of tea and she's gone, with a wave and goodbyes.

FIFTY-EIGHT

SAPHY

I lied. I don't have enough time. I dash into a chemist on the way, get some antibiotic cream for my arm and hope that will do.

I won't lie to myself – I felt a real pang handing that cheque to Fern. She even seemed to think it'd be OK to keep it, though I could tell she was pleased when I said I couldn't. Imagine having so much that you wouldn't miss ten thousand pounds? But this isn't just about the money, is it? I hope I'm right that giving it back will allow me to get closer to Margot.

On the Tube, I reread Jenny's email. *My mother*: I try the words on for size, but they don't feel real.

I get to the Green Room at exactly two, wondering now if she's booked or if I should call her number.

A waiter approaches.

'I'm meeting someone, not sure if she's here yet. Her name is Jenny Turner?' He starts to check a screen but there is a woman at a table looking our way – neat dark hair pulled back, dark trousers and a gorgeous multi-coloured jacket. But she must be too young? She gets up, walks towards us.

'Is that Saphy?'

'Yes. Hi.' We're staring at each other. Is she doing what I was thinking earlier – looking for resemblance? We're similar heights – her hair colour is similar to what mine would be naturally – there is something about her eyes—

She smiles. Holds out her hand and I take it. A firm grip. 'I'm so happy to meet you. Come – have a seat.' We walk to her table.

'Tea? Coffee?' she says.

'Tea, please.'

She turns towards the waiter. 'Tea for two please.' He nods, disappears.

'I don't know what to say, where to begin,' she says. She's smiling still and it takes over her face. 'I'm just so happy to finally meet you.'

'I don't know what to say, either.'

'There are so many things I want to know about you, your life. But you must be curious, too, and maybe it's a shorter tale to tell you how it started. Mostly with stupidity – mine. I thought I was in love but I was wrong. He was gorgeous, older than me, and had me convinced he'd be there forever. But I got pregnant and that ended that. You were born just before my sixteenth birthday.'

Pregnant at fifteen – she was so very young. 'I'm glad that when you made me, you thought you were in love. Even if it went wrong. Do you have any contact with him now?'

'No. I don't. I wouldn't cross the road to see him – more the opposite.' She pauses, as if weighing her words, whether to shield me or not wanting to go there herself. 'It's so long ago now that it's a part of myself I've compartmentalised, closed off. I'm not that girl anymore; I'm not even straight. To drop another bombshell.'

'That's not a bombshell – that's totally cool. And I'm sorry to make you revisit things that hurt.'

'Don't apologise. If anyone has a right to know, it's you.'

The tea arrives now; there's a pause – milk to be added – stirring. Biscuits on the side. I wrap my fingers around a teacup, the heat of it soothing when inside everything is whirling with what she's said. She was so young.

'When you were born, I held you, and cried. I knew I couldn't give you the life you deserved, but I've never stopped thinking about you. Every year on your birthday and at Christmas I've bought gifts for you, then gave them to a women's shelter.' There are tears in her eyes now, mine too. There is a wealth of pain and loss behind buying gifts for a daughter she never knew. She hesitates. 'There is one question I have for you that is more important than any other: did your parents that adopted you love you? Did they make you happy?'

'That's two questions. But both get a yes. I couldn't have felt any more wanted or loved.'

'I'm so glad. But is there something you're not saying?' She must read it in my eyes.

'My mum – you know this, don't you? – died when I was three. My dad was the best parent he could be, which was pretty amazing. I loved him so much.'

'Past tense?'

'He died of Covid.'

'Oh no, Saphy. I'm so sad to hear that.' Her eyes – I can see it now, the resemblance. A reflection of my own, and they echo my pain. Then puzzlement. 'I didn't know about your mother, though?'

'It was in the letters.'

'What letters?'

I frown, confused. 'That's why I contacted the adoption agency – I found these letters that first my mum and then my dad wrote to someone, initial J, my birth mother. They were sent every year to the adoption agency until I was eighteen, then forwarded on to J.'

'I would have loved to read them, but I've never received any letters.'

She never got the letters? What does this mean?

I've met who I thought was my birth mother – liked her – felt we had some rapport. But if she didn't get the letters, then where is the mix-up? Is the mistake that she didn't receive letters she should have, or that she's the wrong J and isn't my birth mother at all?

FIFTY-NINE

FERN

'I've got something to show you,' I say, and open the kitchen drawer where I'd stashed the cheque earlier, and hand it to Marley.

'Your mum has written a cheque to Saphy, for – wow. That's a hefty sum. What did I tell you? Next thing you know she'll be moving in with them.'

I shake my head. 'Mum gave it to her after the interview, in a card – told her to open it later. When she did last night and saw what it was, she came straight over here today and gave it to me, asked me to return it. Said she couldn't accept it.'

She nods her head slowly. 'Oh well done, Saphy. I've got to give her credit. She's very clever.'

'What do you mean?'

'She's playing the long game. This will make them trust her even more.'

'Marley, I think you're being unreasonably suspicious.'

'And you're too trusting,' she says.

What made Marley question Saphy like this? There must be a reason. 'What happened between you and Saphy?'

'Nothing happened.' She's shaking her head but there is something she's not saying. Some way in which Saphy over-stepped with Marley, unwittingly or otherwise?

'She did or said something that upset you. What was it?'

'Can't you see it? She's trying to be Flora. Isn't that enough?'

'If you really felt that way, why did you go ahead with the interview? There might be another of Flora's recipients who would agree to it – they had two more get in touch.'

'It was too late to call it off.' Not, it was too important – what she said the other day.

'Why too late? It must happen all the time, someone changes their mind or an emergency comes up.'

She's looking at her phone – at the time? 'I've got to go.'

'Don't you want the cards? The ones you sent to Flora.' She'd forgotten them – the reason she came over. 'I've got them together for you.'

They're on the worktop. I hand them across to Marley. There are tears in her eyes now. 'Thank you, Fern.' She gives me a hug and then rushes for the door.

Something weird is going on with Marley and Saphy. Whatever it is, I don't buy that Marley couldn't have cancelled or delayed the interview, if she was concerned about Saphy's motives. But Saphy gave such a good interview. And Marley knew she would, didn't she? Saphy is the perfect, sympathetic poster child for organ donation. And the whole thing – the pathos of it – that Marley set up and conducted like a symphony. I've no doubt that once it airs next week it'll be much watched and talked about. It'll raise her profile, maybe lead to a promotion. And that was what she was after – what she wouldn't risk losing.

So, she used Saphy to get what she wanted, and now she's undermining her.

Marley said I was too trusting – she's wrong about that. But I do trust my instincts on people, and they're telling me that

Saphy is for real. She might need both time and help to work out how Flora and her family – my family – do or don't fit in her life, but I've never felt she's been dishonest in anything she's said or done.

Marley, on the other hand, is definitely hiding something.

SIXTY

SAPHY

'I'm sorry,' I say, struggling to control the tears in my eyes. I can't seem to banish them and I don't even know why. I only just met Jenny, so why does it matter so much that she is my mother?

'We'll find out what has gone on with these letters. OK?' A calm, reassuring gaze.

'OK.' I nod, swallow. Blink them back.

'And I don't think there could be any mistake as far as me being your birth mother. I'm sure of it.'

'How?'

'You look so much like my younger sister, Emily. I'll show you a photo.' Phone out, she finds a photo of a teenage girl, and Jenny is right. It's almost like looking at one of myself. 'This was taken quite a few years ago. Emily sadly died not long after.'

'I'm so sorry.' I look again, then hand her phone back. 'We could be sisters – twins, even.'

'Except for the hair.'

'Mine is dyed – dark brown is my natural colour. Like yours.'

'See? There you go. Where I work is close by. Come back there with me and we can go into the back office, call the adoption agency on speaker phone together. Let's see if we can get to the bottom of this.'

'OK.' She waves at the waiter to bring our bill. 'I'm not usually such an emotional wreck. I've had a hell of a year.'

'Losing your dad.'

'That was a big part of it. I've also been very unwell. I had heart surgery – well, a transplant – weeks ago. I'm still recovering.'

Her eyes open wide. 'My sister Emily died waiting for a transplant. Congenital heart defect.'

'I had congenital heart problems too. I was doing OK but my heart was further damaged by Covid.'

'I'm so sorry you had to go through that. Dodgy genes from my side, I guess.'

The waiter comes over now and she taps a card to cover our teas.

'It's just a few minutes from here,' she says, and we head out the door, walking in the sunshine towards the river and then right.

'Here we are,' she says, gestures to the open doors of a shop, and we go in.

'I know this place. I've come by here, looked in the windows – we might have even seen each other.'

A half smile. 'I often used to play a game of pretend in my mind. I'd see someone go by and think, she could be my daughter.'

'Maybe one of them was me.'

'Maybe.'

There is a young woman at a desk, smiling at us now.

'Hi, Kay. We're going to the office – don't disturb us unless essential.' We go through a stock room to an office.

She shuts the door, gestures at chairs next to a desk and we sit down.

'OK. Let's give them a call.' She gets her phone out, finds the number.

'Hi, this is Jenny Turner. Also here is Saphira Logan – I'm just putting you on speaker. Saphira is my biological daughter, she was adopted through your agency and you've recently put us back in touch. But there's something we're confused about.' She gestures to me.

'Hi, this is Saphira.' I explain about the letters I'd found which led me to calling them; Jenny then tells them she didn't know anything about letters and never received any. 'What I want to know is if Jenny is definitely my mother, or has there been a mistake?'

'That must be so upsetting. Let me go through some details with you.' She gets us to give our full names, dates of birth. Current addresses and Jenny's address way back when. Gets us to hold a moment, then comes back. 'All of your details and our records match.'

'So, what about the letters?' I say. 'What happened to them?'

'We've noted receipt, yearly. Then they were forwarded on to an address supplied by Jenny's representative – a post office box.'

'I've never had a post office box,' Jenny says. 'And who was this representative – my mother?'

There is a pause. 'No, it was your lawyer.'

'My lawyer? I didn't have one.'

'Perhaps that was arranged by your mother?'

'Not that I know of. I'll check with her.'

'And we'll look into this further at our end as well.'

We say our goodbyes and Jenny puts her phone done. 'So, Saphy, going by their records, I am your birth mother. You are my daughter. Not that we had any doubt, given the family resemblance. The letters are a mystery, but we'll get to the bottom of it.'

'If it wasn't for the letters, I wouldn't have called them. We wouldn't have met.'

'Can you tell me about them?'

'The first few were written by my mum. After she died, by my dad. Once a year on my birthday, describing all the big things that happened with me that year: first words, first steps. Starting school.' Remembering reading them that first time has tears pricking in my eyes again. 'I wanted to meet you to thank you. I treasure them. It's like this written record of my family and childhood, going back to before I can remember.'

'I would have treasured them, too – if I'd read them. The more I think about it, I'm angry that somebody messed up. They'd have meant so much to me.'

'It's years late. But would you like to read them now?'

'I'd love to.'

We arrange for Jenny to come over to see them on Sunday. Soon after, I head for home, pleading tiredness – which was true – but I also needed some time alone with my thoughts.

I'd been so nervous to meet Jenny. Then when I did and I liked her but found out she hadn't had the letters – the uncertainty and confusion that brought.

And finding out that Jenny's sister, Emily, died waiting for a transplant. She looked so much like me. It's the toss of a coin, isn't it? Who lives, who dies.

It could have been me.

SIXTY-ONE

FERN

I get a taxi from the station to home. I'd checked the family calendar so know Dad is at work; Dorothy confirmed that Mum was in, but I asked her not to mention I was on my way.

I go through to the garden. Mum is sitting on a bench, knees drawn up. Statue-still. Staring into the distance and not turning to the sound of my footsteps.

'Hi, Mum.'

She turns her head slowly. Focuses on my face and smiles. 'Fern? Now, this is a lovely surprise, darling.' I sit next to her. 'You should have said you were coming. I would have arranged lunch.'

'Dorothy has offered just that. You looked lost in thought just now. What were you thinking about?'

She shrugs. 'Nothing and everything. Come. Let's go in and have a glass of something together.' And I'm not working tonight, so why not?

I follow her back in; there is an open bottle of white wine she extracts from the wine fridge in the conservatory. She pours, hands me a glass. Notices then that the table in the conservatory is already set.

'Dorothy knew you were coming, didn't she? You two are sneaky.'

'Guilty as charged.'

'So why have you come today?'

'Do I need a reason?' She raises an eyebrow. 'Well, there is one thing I need to talk to you about. It's Saphy, and this very generous cheque you wrote to her.'

'I was afraid of this. Has she sent it back?'

I nod, take it out of my bag and put it on the table.

Mum sighs. 'I just really wanted to help her, and how else can I?'

'That's really kind of you.'

'It's selfish. It would make me feel good for a moment, and it's all I have to give. Can we call her? Have you got her number?'

'I do, but I don't think she'll change her mind. Do you want to call her now?'

Mum nods. I find Saphy's number on my phone, hit call.

'Let me,' she says, holds out her hand and I hand it across. She puts it on speaker.

'Hello?'

'Hi, Saphy. It's not Fern – I'm sure you can tell. It's Margot. I'm on speaker with Fern.'

'Hi, Saphy,' I say.

'I'm calling about this cheque that Fern has brought back to me. Are you sure I can't persuade you to reconsider?'

'It's a lovely gesture,' Saphy says. 'I can't tell you how much I appreciate the thought. But I need to get on with things, look after myself. I'm going to have to put the house on the market – downsize. It'll make everything easier.'

'This is your family home?'

'Yes. It's crammed full of memories, but I need to find my own space somewhere to start again.'

'Are you sure I can't help you in the meantime?'

'Can I interrupt a moment?' I say. 'I just had a thought. Mum would really like to help you, Saphy. You don't want to accept money and we must respect your decision. But how about this: if you're putting your house on the market, you'll want to have it looking its best. Perhaps Mum could help with the garden?'

Mum's face – first surprised, then thinking. 'What a wonderful idea. Do say yes, Saphy,' she says. 'Or at least let me come over and we can talk about what we can do with the space.' Her face – it's more animated than it was before.

'Really? Are you sure?' Saphy says.

'Completely.'

'Then – thank you! That would be wonderful.'

SIXTY-TWO

SAPHY

Zoe knocks at six. I open the door, and whistle. 'You look amazing,' I say. She's in Flora's little black dress and looks stunning.

'Love the make-up but not so sure about your wardrobe choice,' she says. I'm in a dressing gown but have finally managed to perfect the cat's eye flicks with Flora's eyeliner.

'I'm having trouble deciding. I mean, I know what I want to wear, I just keep changing my mind about whether I should or I shouldn't. Come and have a look.'

Upstairs, I put on the red dress and call Zoe in, nervous she'll recognise the dress from the photo she saw on my lock screen.

Zoe's jaw actually drops. 'You have to wear that. It's stunning.' If she recognises it, she doesn't say.

'But – the neckline. Look. If I move or breathe in at not exactly the right angle – my scar. See? I'd be weird all night, checking it all the time and worrying people were staring at me for the wrong reasons.'

'The solution is obvious: you need a scarf.'

'A scarf? Like a pretty one? I haven't really got anything like that,' I say, but then remember where I've seen a few. 'But I think Mum had some.' At the bottom of a chest of drawers are some odds and ends of Mum's, and I go there now. Dad didn't keep much of her clothes, just the odd pretty thing he thought I might like one day.

There's a filmy black scarf. I try it and look in the mirror, but I don't know. Too much contrast, just red and black?

Zoe shakes her head. Has a look through the others.

'Wear this one!' she says, draws it out. It's a striking animal print in rainbow colours. Lovely and silky, but the colours? The pattern?

'Seriously?'

'Try it.'

I drape it around my neck, then Zoe reaches for it, loops it around, adjusts it. I slip on flat sandals. They don't do this dress justice, but I'm still too nervous about tripping over to wear heels. Half-healed bones in my chest are too fragile to risk it.

We go down the stairs and Zoe checks out the front window. 'Perfect timing, our ride is just pulling in.' We head out the front door just as someone from the car approaches. She introduces him as Tim, husband of school friend Charlotte.

We get in the car, head off. Soon we reach the promised outdoor area of a pub, reserved for us. A warm summer evening makes it perfect. Faces, names – some I know, many more I don't. The compliments that would normally make me squirm with embarrassment but somehow don't, tonight. It's the dress. Isn't it? And the Prosecco. A glass and another and the sun is low in the sky when dinner comes. Pub food but the best sort. Another glass after, and if I was giddy before I am more so, now.

'Don't look now, but a very fit someone is checking you out,' Charlotte says.

'Who?' I glance across, and she's right. A wicked smile. Long dark hair. He's standing, coming towards us now.

'Hi,' he says, eyes on mine.

'Hi yourself.'

Charlotte melts away to the side. She said he was fit – he really is – and seriously sexy with that grin. I wouldn't have thought he was my type – tattoos on his neck, forearms – a pierced eyebrow. But being close to him is doing something to me.

'I've been watching you,' he says.

'Have you?'

'Oh, yes. That scarf – it's wild. I needed to meet the girl who wears that scarf with this dress.' His eyes travel up and down me slowly.

'It's just to cover a scar,' I say then wish my words back.

He sits next to me. His raises his hand – his fingers brush my neck, my throat, as he straightens the scarf. Then a feather-light touch to the top of my scar makes me shiver. 'That's a good one. Knife fight?'

'Sure. Let's go with that.' And I'm smiling and laughing and he's smiling back. There is something about him – what is it? I don't even know. I'm drawn to him, and it's all I can do to not reach up and touch his cheek. Push his hair out of his eyes.

'I'm Jack. What's your name?'

'Saphy.'

'I'm very pleased to meet you, Saphy.' He takes my hand as if to shake it but then holds on to it. He leans in close, his lips so near my ear that I can feel his warm breath. 'Let's slip away together. Go somewhere we can be alone.'

I don't do that sort of thing. But the wearer of this dress does, doesn't she? But I have just enough sense left to shake my head.

Now Zoe is here, clocking how close he is, that he's holding my hand. She introduces herself and then hovers uncertainly, as if unsure if the right friend thing to do at this moment is leave us alone or the opposite. I smile at her to let her know I want her to stay; she sits with us. After a while Jack writes his name and number on a coaster, slips it into my hand and says goodbye.

'You've got a few more weeks to wait, you know. He looked like he was about to carry you off over his shoulder.'

'Mmmm,' I say. She shakes her head but then her phone is ringing, she's getting it out to answer. 'Loo,' I say, and get up, go inside to go to the ladies, but Jack is just inside the door and curves a hand against my back, draws me closer and then he's kissing me, lips soft then more and more urgent, a touch of his tongue on mine and I'm gone, lost. So in this moment that I don't know where I am – who I am.

He pulls away. He doesn't say anything but his eyes are asking mine a question, and then he takes my hand and starts to lead me towards the front door.

This is insane. I pull back at his hand. Point at the ladies room door with my other hand. He lets go and I go in.

I breathe in, out, slowly, try to steady myself. Go into a cubicle for the usual, then come out, wash my hands. I look in the mirror to straighten my hair, trying not to think who is waiting for me, who probably thinks I'm leaving with him when I step back through that door. Am I? I can't think straight and it takes me a moment to notice – Mum's scarf. It's not around my neck. Did it fall off? Where is it?

My vision, it's blurred – the surface of the mirror wavers. Something – someone – is there, staring back at me. Is it Flora? *No.* Not here – not now—

The world around me is closing in, to a tunnel – everything shifting, moving – drawing me forwards, towards the mirror. I push against the sink to stop the headlong rush, leaning over it now, holding on.

'Are you all right?' A woman is here now whose name I forget. She works with Zoe.

I shake my head. 'Can you get Zoe – please?'

Zoe is there a moment later, just as my legs buckle. She supports me but I slide to the floor.

'Too much Prosecco,' I say, but her hand is on my forehead.

'You're burning up,' she says, but she's wrong. I'm cold, shaking. Someone else is here now – an off-duty nurse, she says. Her face and Zoe's fade in and out.

Is that sirens?

Paramedics arrive. As they bring me out on the stretcher, Jack is off to one side – the way he looked at me before replaced by shock.

SIXTY-THREE

FERN

A message vibrates my phone. It's late but I'm awake, turn it over – it's from Saphy.

You were right. I'm officially an idiot.

What about?

That scratch on my arm.

What's happened?

I've got an infection. Fever. Passed out at my first night out in forever and I'm back in hospital and on an IV etc.

Anything I can do? Do you need anything?

No, I'm good. Zoe is here. Feeling better already. Could you let your mum know might have to reschedule garden stuff, not sure when they'll let me leave.

Will do.

Gnite.

Take care x

SIXTY-FOUR

SAPHY

This is where I belong. Isn't it? In a hospital bed. Not out in the wild world, full of possibility. The kiss of a stranger. That's not me. Red dress gone, probably wrecked as I'd started vomiting before we got to hospital, replaced by a hospital gown. Zoe in a chair next to me, asleep now. Make-up smudged on her face and heels kicked off.

They said this was from a cat scratch – from Hermi. They're wrong. I know what caused this, or rather, who: Flora. The nightmares. In my waking hours now, too. I saw her in that mirror tonight.

That's ridiculous – the fever had me imagining things, that's all. It made me see things that weren't there.

Maybe that instant attraction to Jack was part of the fever, too. I don't know what happened to that coaster he wrote his number on and that is probably just as well. Being close to him felt like being on the top of a cliff, vertigo pulling me closer to the edge.

Doesn't matter anyhow. After what happened, he won't want to see me again without paramedics on standby.

My thoughts aren't as scattered as before. Whatever cocktail of drugs is in that IV must be doing its magic. I'm safe here. Nothing can happen to me. I'm safe here. I tell myself this over and over again and finally my eyes close.

SIXTY-FIVE

FERN

I juggle the huge bunch of flowers in my arms to knock on Saphy's front door.

She opens it a moment later. She is pale, dark smudges under her eyes and hair all over the place, but upright and steady on her feet. A delighted smile transforms her.

'Oh, Fern! They're beautiful – you shouldn't have.'

'They're from Mum, I'm just delivering.'

'Thanks to both of you, then. Come in. Sorry I'm such a mess.'

'Don't apologise. I'll put these in a vase for you.' I follow her into the kitchen.

'There might be one in that top cupboard?' I have a look in the one she indicated, then open a few more cupboard doors until I find the right one. Water in, plant food and then flowers.

'Thank you,' Saphy says. 'Tea?'

'I'll make it.'

'I'm not a complete invalid,' she snaps, then apologises straight away. 'Sorry. It's frustrating, that's all. I was feeling so well and now I've taken a step back.'

'I told you so.' I can't resist. Unlike Flora would have, she doesn't roll her eyes.

'You did. I will always listen to you in future.'

'Excellent. Then I'll make the tea.' I fill the kettle while she finds cups, milk, then I shoo her into the front room to sit down. I'm startled by a sudden banging noise in the kitchen – it's just her cat, coming through the cat flap. She eyes me suspiciously, then goes through, meowing all the way. When I bring the tea in a moment later, Saphy is in the recliner with the cat on her lap.

'Is this the source of the scratch that landed you in hospital?'

'The one and only. Hermi doesn't scratch – it was a one-off, I promise. I'd had a nightmare and was flailing about. Probably scared her.'

'Perhaps she shouldn't sleep in your room?'

'You have a point, but I'd be lonely. Plus, it'd be hard to sleep with her yowling on the other side of the door.'

'Hmm. Well, any future scratches, what do you do?'

'Seek medical advice.'

'I should go, you need to rest. Don't get up, I'll let myself out.' She holds out a hand, I go over and lean down, give her a gentle hug. 'Bye, Saphy. Take care.'

'I will. And thanks again.'

SIXTY-SIX

SAPHY

I fall asleep in the chair, almost as soon as the door closed behind Fern. It's hours later when I wake, hungry.

I convince Hermi to jump down with a promise of dinner. Pad into the kitchen behind her and find her food. She gulps it down, then exits through the cat flap for her evening patrol of the neighbourhood. I'd had to tell Neeha I was in the hospital again so she'd feed Hermi, and when I got home this morning, I found several big pieces of her home-made lasagne in my fridge, which she knows I love. Once I sell this place and have some actual money, I'm going to take her out for dinner somewhere amazing.

I heat it in the microwave because the oven is too time-consuming. Eat but don't manage more than half, even though it's delicious. Put stuff in the dishwasher and after that degree of effort, I'm ready for the chair again. But this time I retrieve the coaster with the numbers scrawled across it, put it next to my phone.

Should I, or shouldn't I?

It's been a few days since we met. Jack has probably found

some other girl in a red dress who didn't need an ambulance after just one kiss.

I sigh. Even Hermi is out – she has more of a life than I do. It's quiet; all I can hear is distant traffic, the clock over the mantel ticking, each second there and then gone forever. How much time do I have? I don't know. But do I want to waste it, being afraid?

I'll message – less frightening than a phone call.

Hi Jack, it's Saphy. Zoe said you'd asked her friend to check on me, so thanks for that. Thought I should let you know I'm OK.

I read it over and again. There is nothing flirty in that; he can take it how he will. It was right to say thanks, to let him know I'm OK. That will do for now. Press send.

Minutes later my phone vibrates with his reply.

I'm so glad to hear from you. I heard that your fetching scar wasn't from a knife fight, after all. Are you really OK? xx

So, he knows – Zoe or someone else told him. It wasn't a secret that could be kept for long, but I'm still annoyed. The night we met, I'd felt like I was any other woman – one he fancied. Not a walking medical miracle.

I think for a moment, then answer.

I am, or will be – had an infection, that's all, set to rights after a few days in hospital. Things like that are more of a problem for me.

I hesitate, then add one *x* for his two. Send.

Excellent. I mean, the kiss at the end. I'm hoping there are more on our horizon. When can I see you? xxx

Three kisses. Is this escalating? OK. So, he knows, and he still wants to see me. What do I want? Another message comes through while I'm trying to decide. Just *xxxx*. Four kisses, and now I'm giggling.

Is this childish? I don't care. It's fun.

I can see where this is going... xxxxx

> *Your place or mine? ;-) xxxxxx.*

Slow down, that isn't going to happen.

You forgot to add, not yet. What is the required number of dates these days? Three? And you forgot xxxxxxx.

At least five, possibly more. Dates, that is. I've lost count of the x's.

> *Best get started, then. Tomorrow?*

I pause, thinking. I'm not sure I'm strong enough to do much and there's no chance of me giving him my address just yet – even without Fern and Zoe's rules for modern dating, I'm not daft enough to do that.

Another message lands: *xxxxxxx*

I smile.

Are you free for lunch tomorrow?

> *With a little manoeuvring at work – yes.*

How about we meet at Granger & Co, behind King's Cross station. Say at one?

Perfect. I'll be there.

Later I'm just getting into bed when another message comes through:

Sleep well. think I missed a few: xxxxxxxxxxxxxxxx

I close my eyes with a smile on my face.

SIXTY-SEVEN

FERN

I'm walking across the parks to work when my phone rings, shattering the early morning calm of dog walkers and joggers. It's Mum.

I answer. 'Hi. You're up early. Is everything OK?'

'Just fine, thank you. Are you free tomorrow evening?'

'I think so. I'm on days this week, so if nothing goes wrong I'll be done about six.'

'I've been waiting to hear back from one of the other two of Flora's recipients that contacted us, and finally have this morning. We're going to meet up tomorrow night for a drink, in London. Do you want to come?'

Two more potential Saphys to worry about. But of course I do. 'Where?'

She gives me the details, time.

'Should we invite Saphy along?' Mum says. 'Assuming she is well enough to come.'

I've just reached the front of the hospital now. 'I have to go now, I'm at work. Why don't you check with her? I'll send you her number.'

'Will do, darling. Thank you. Have a good day.'

'You too. Bye.'

Marley wouldn't approve of Saphy having Mum's number. Even though I decided to ignore her suspicions, there is still a vague sense of unease as I copy it and press send.

SIXTY-EIGHT

SAPHY

I'm ten minutes early, but Jack is already out front of the restaurant.

He hasn't noticed me yet. There's an air of melancholy about him – the way he stands, his face. Then he looks across and sees me, watches me walk towards him. Smiles when I reach him.

'You came,' he says.

'Did you think I wouldn't?'

'Let's just say I've been stood up before.'

'No. Really?'

'Hard to believe, I know.'

He's reaching for me now – a hug, a kiss on the cheek – not an air kiss. His lips linger on my skin, send a shiver through my body. He takes my hand. We go in. It's busy but they find us a table by the window.

'I was so glad you messaged last night,' Jack says. 'I was worried.'

'Sorry. I take it someone told you about the origins of my fetching scar?' It's safely hidden away today. I'd decided against wearing anything like I was when we met – it's not me, not really, and seemed to do something to any degree of sense I should have. So I dressed simply in jeans and a lovely soft blue shirt of Flora's, buttoned up enough to hide.

'That you had a heart transplant? Yes. That's, well, amazing.'

'I'm alive, which is a plus.'

He reaches across for my hand, holds it in one of his, rests a light finger of his other hand on my wrist.

'I'm glad. And I can confirm that you are alive,' he says. 'I can feel blood pulsing under your skin.'

The nerves that were attached to my own heart were cut – they can't re-join them to the new one. It's meant to take longer for heart rate to increase or decrease without that feedback, but just now, I'm sure I can feel it: my heart beating faster in response to his touch. His eyes are holding mine.

Then a waiter comes over and he lets go of my hand. We order. We talk about normal stuff. Lunch arrives; we eat. I'm surprised I'm hungry again. He tells me he manages a gym; he's a personal trainer, too. That's why he's so fit. I manage to not say that out loud, though. I tell him I'm a writer and not just that I want to be one, like I usually do.

'Will you see me again?' Jack says. 'Say yes.'

His eyes hold mine. There is no thought and only one possible answer. 'Yes.'

'How about tonight?'

I can't. Fatigue is settling around me again. I shake my head. 'Sorry, no. Boring as it is, I'm still recovering.'

'Tomorrow night?'

'I've got something else booked then.'

'Cancel whatever it is. I cancelled two training sessions to meet you now.'

'Did you? I really can't.' I'm not sure I want to tell him why

– having left talk of all that behind at the beginning. But it is part of my life. 'I've met the family of my heart donor. Tomorrow night, I'm meeting with them and two other organ recipients from the same donor.'

'Not something you can cancel,' he says.

'No.'

'How about the night after?'

'I think I'm free.' I absolutely know that I am.

'Don't ask what we're doing. It'll be a surprise.'

'Where do I meet you?'

'I could come get you?'

'I'll meet you.'

He raises an eyebrow and his wicked grin is back. 'Four more dates to go, I promise I'll behave. But give me some time to work out details, and I'll message you where and when.'

'OK.'

'Unless I cancel another training session, I've got to go.' He waves the waiter over for the bill. 'My treat,' he says, taps the card machine.

'Thank you.'

We get up, walk to the door and my nerves are jangling inside. Scared he'll kiss me and it won't be like it was the other night – that it was just a Prosecco and fever-induced dream. Scared that he won't.

We go out through the door.

'Before I forget – I've got something of yours.' He reaches for the jacket over his shoulder, a pocket. Pulls out Mum's scarf.

Tears are welling up in my eyes. 'I thought it was lost. Thank you. It was my mum's.'

'Let me,' he says. Drapes it loosely around my neck, straightens it, leans down. I kiss him and he kisses me – both at once. We say goodbye.

My eyes follow him as he walks away. He turns just before

he's out of sight – catches me watching him. He raises one hand, then he's gone.

I'd say his kiss was as good as Saturday night, but I'd be lying. It was even better.

SIXTY-NINE

FERN

Mum is getting out of a chauffeured car out front just as I walk down from the Tube.

'Hello, darling,' she says.

'No Dad?'

'He's on call.'

He'd have known that when they picked the day and time – either he didn't want to come, or Mum didn't want him to. Which was it?

We go in, are shown through to a terrace overlooking the Thames at the back. There is a woman who has arrived already – she stands as we approach the table.

'Hello, is that Debra?' Mum says, and the woman smiles, nods. 'I'm Margot. My daughter, Fern.' Hands are shaken.

We're just settling ourselves when Saphy arrives, a young man with her also – could it be Jack? She'd messaged they'd had lunch yesterday, that it went well. If so, he's both younger and somehow not how I imagined him to be.

Mum is up, giving Saphy a hug. 'So glad you could come. How are you feeling?'

'Much better, thank you.'

'I'm Liam,' he says – shakes hands all around. So not Jack, I was right. 'I'm kidney.' He points in the approximately correct anatomical location. 'I met Saphy on the way in – heart – and you must be corneas,' he says, turning to Debra.

She glances at Mum and then gives him a disapproving look. 'Perhaps listing body parts is too much?'

'Apologies. I'm both lacking in tact and incredibly grateful to not be on dialysis.' He gives a dramatic bow to Mum, then kisses her hand – she raises an eyebrow at me, amused or charmed or both. Then he sits down between Saphy and me – Mum and Debra opposite.

'Thank you all for coming,' Mum says. 'We met Saphy a while back and it has been a tremendous comfort at a difficult time.'

The usual *so sorry for your loss* and *thank you so much* follows from Debra, and I settle into my customary social position – observer. Mum is looking better. Saphy is also, and not just healthier than when I last saw her – she is – but also there is somehow more of a sparkle about her. Is that due to Jack? Liam is a character. Irreverent, but in a cheeky way that endears him to Mum. He is a graduate student in economics so must be older than I initially thought. Debra is a secondary school teacher. No surprise there; the way she spoke to Liam she sounded like one. She teaches English, and she and Saphy are launching into a discussion of the lack of flexibility in the curriculum to choose the texts studied in school – that Debra could quote every word of *Never Let Me Go* in her sleep. A bottle of wine is gone, then another. Mum tells them about the interview we did with Marley.

'Do we know yet when it is going to be aired?' Mum asks me.

'Marley messaged earlier. It was supposed to be sooner, but with one thing and another in the news, it's going to be aired on

Sunday afternoon. She's going to message me the time when she knows – I'll pass that along.'

'To us, too?' Debra says. 'It sounds so interesting.'

'Of course.'

'I'm sorry – it's been a long day,' Debra says. 'I'm going to have to head home soon. It's been lovely to meet all of you.'

Soon we're all saying our goodbyes. Mum offers lifts in her car. She must have planned ahead; it's limo-sized, so we'll all fit. We work out that Debra is on the way to Saphy's and then Liam's, then mine. The driver calls when he's arrived.

At the first two stops, we say goodnight to Debra, then Saphy.

As we pull in at Liam's, he's looking behind. 'That's odd. That motorbike has been following us all along,' he says. I turn to look, but it speeds down the road and disappears.

SEVENTY

SAPHY

'Hi, come in.' It's a few days later than originally planned, but Jenny is here at last.

'This is such a lovely house,' she says.

'Thanks. It's in a bit of a state as I haven't been able to do much in the last year.'

'Understandable. Have you always lived here?'

'Yes. My parents already lived here when they adopted me. Would you like tea or a tour?'

'Both would be good.'

I take her through the lounge room, the kitchen and then up the stairs. Showing the place to someone I don't know well is making me cringe at the mess. I find myself saying sorry again.

'Stop apologising. You haven't been well – it's fine.'

We go down the hall to my bedroom. Hermi is curled up on the bed. I introduce them and Hermi allows Jenny to stroke her.

'I'm trying to imagine you here. As a toddler, then a little girl. A teenager. The beautiful young woman you are now. Do you have photo albums? If you don't mind showing me.'

'Of course I don't mind. They're downstairs,' I say, and I'm thinking how this echoes the day I had lunch with Flora's family

– both of us wanting to know the unknowable, the past that we didn't experience and want to imagine for ourselves.

Down the hall – Dad's office, then his room. We go up the stairs to the loft. I'd planned ahead – Flora's images are off the walls and tucked out of sight. 'This was always mine – a playroom, then teenage hangout. My place to read, to dream.'

We go down the stairs to the kitchen, put the kettle on.

'This place is going on the market soon. I'm going to have to do something about tidying things up,' I say, beginning to realise how much there is to do.

'Have to sell or want to?'

'A bit of both. Initially I was only considering it for financial reasons, and the thought of leaving behind the place with all my memories was hard. But memories will come with me, and more and more I'm thinking that downsizing and picking a place that is all my own could be a good thing for me, like a way of drawing a line: before, I was this. Now I am something different, new.'

'I get that. By the way, I chased up about the letters again with the adoption agency. I've also checked with my mum – she really wants to meet you, by the way – and she didn't know about them, either. She also confirmed that we didn't have a representative or lawyer. The adoption agency has tried writing to the post office box address asking for a reply, but that letter was returned – the post office box has been closed. Given the letters stopped when you were eighteen – ten years ago – that's not surprising, I suppose. Also, the lawyer who they thought was my representative is a dead end – the contact details they had are not for a current law practice. Which maybe sounds suspicious, but it was twenty-eight years ago.'

'That's so odd. If the letters were sent to a wrong address, surely they'd have returned them.' I hand her a mug of tea, take her to the dining table. 'But here they are, years late.' I hand Jenny the file. 'They're in date order of when they were written.

The first few were handwritten by my mum, later ones were written by Dad and printed out.'

'Thank you for letting me see them.'

'I'll give you some privacy. I'll be in the front room if you need anything.'

'OK. Thanks, Saphy.'

I go to the chair with my tea. Eighteen letters, a page each – sometimes double sided, sometimes not. There are passages I almost know by heart. Reading them might be difficult for Jenny. All the little details of the life of the daughter she never knew.

I glance at my phone. There is a message from Jack.

Don't forget about tonight xxxxxxxxxxxxx

> *I won't, I promise. I can't keep track of how many kisses we're up to? Why not call it a truce and stick to the usual message sign off of two or three. As I recollect there have only actually been three.*

Three? One was on the cheek and doesn't count. So two. We can do some catching up later – beginning at 8.45 p.m.

> *I know!*

Don't be late.

> *I won't be, Mr Bossy. I'm generally very punctual.*

It's the generally that worries me xxx

It's quite a while before Jenny emerges from reading the letters. Her eyes are red-rimmed.

'Thank you for sharing these letters with me. How much they loved you is in every word and page.'

My eyes are stinging with tears, too. 'They really did.'

'Is it OK if I take photos of them – to show my mum?'

'Of course. Then if you're up to it, we can look at some photo albums. Or would you rather save that for another day?'

'Let's do it now.' I show her where they are, on a bookshelf in the dining room and get her to move them to the table.

'There is an album a year – actually, they coincide with the letters. Maybe they used the albums to help write them?'

We open the first one. 'You were a beautiful baby. When you were born, I held you – just for a moment. It haunted me for so many years. I'd dream someone was stealing you from me and I was screaming, but someone was holding me back. I couldn't stop it from happening.'

'Why did you have me? Not have an abortion, I mean.'

'If I'd understood things more clearly at the time, I think I would have done. I'm so glad, now I've met you, that I didn't. But it was like I was in denial. I was hiding my shape in baggy clothes – hiding it not just from the rest of the world, but myself, too. By the time my mum worked out I was pregnant, it was too late.'

'And then, why did you give me up?'

'I was fifteen when you were born. I could barely look after myself, let alone anyone else. These were things I was told and I must have believed, because I went along with it.'

'Was it pressure from your mum?'

'Partly. And your birth father. Mum never knew about that, or who he was – I wouldn't tell her then and still haven't now.'

'After so many years?'

'It would upset her so much.' She hesitates. 'I've been thinking about how much to tell you about him. I'm not sure if it's better for you to know the whole story, or not.' I stay silent; she nods as if she's reached a decision. 'I think you deserve the truth. I told you he was older – not how much older. These days you'd probably say I was groomed. I was only fourteen when it started. My mother worked for him. It was wrong on his part in so many ways. But back then I thought I knew everything and didn't see it that way. You're shocked, aren't you? I'm sorry.'

I am. She was *fourteen* when it began? As her mum's employer, he was in a position of power – he was a predator. From what she's said, he didn't force her. But if she was under-age, it was still rape. And he was my biological father. I tell myself it doesn't matter, that it doesn't change who I am, but I'm still shaken.

'Are you OK, Saphy?'

'Yes. Or I will be. And I'm glad you're being honest with me. It must be hard to talk about.'

'I've only ever told one other person the truth. There was a friend, one I lost recently. We talked about it. She'd had a similar experience and hadn't been able to leave it behind. I was trying to help her. I failed.'

There's something she's not saying, but she's in pain and I don't press. She lost her friend – does she mean that this friend killed herself?

'I shouldn't have told you, should I? You didn't need to know that about your father. I'm sorry.'

'Don't apologise, and he wasn't my father – not in any way that counts. Also, I think no matter what it is, I'd always rather know the truth.' Now I'm the one who is hesitating. 'Feel free to ignore me – what do I know of your family and your life? But I'm guessing that no matter how much it hurts, your mother would still want to know the truth. And keeping secrets makes them fester. It's corrosive to you, and to your relationship with your mother.'

'How did you get to be so smart?'

'I don't know about that, but I've always been a good observer of people – wanting to know what makes them do and say the things they do. Maybe it was part of being unwell, having to be the quiet one in the corner.'

'I get what you're saying – about secrets. And you're probably right. But it's difficult with Mum. Your father helped her a lot when my sister was unwell. I'm not sure she'd be able to accept what he did – she thinks he's some kind of hero.'

'That must have been hard for you.'

'It's ancient history now.'

But is it? How do you get over something like that, especially when most of the time you pretend it never happened?

She says she has to go, gives me a hug goodbye. I go back to the loft. Retrieve Flora's images and instead of taping them up again, I've got a plan – an old roll of wallpaper. I unroll enough of it to tape the images on the backing. Now all I have to do is roll it up if someone is coming by, unroll it when they are gone.

There's an uneasy feeling in my gut. That I'm doing something I'm ashamed of, that I have to hide away.

* * *

I'm on the middle of Westminster Bridge at 8.40 p.m. Take that, Jack – five minutes early. I can't see him yet but there are people milling about all over the place. Then there is a light touch on my shoulder and I turn. His smile is as wide as mine.

'I told you – I'm very punctual.'

'Glad to see,' he says, slips his hands on either side of my waist. I tip my face up to his and a kiss that goes on and on. Somebody whistles as they walk past. He takes my hand, and we walk south.

'Any guesses?'

'Let's see. The aquarium? A river cruise?'

'Nice. No. Next guess?'

'The London Eye maybe?'

'You're good.'

'I love it. Haven't been on it for years, though, so it's a good choice.'

'That's not all.'

We go to a VIP queue, then on to a pod that we have all to ourselves. There is champagne on ice. Chocolate truffles. Jack pours me a glass as the doors close and we start the slow ascent. London is on show just for us as the sun sets. He kisses me again and the taste of the bubbles and chocolate is on his tongue. I'm lost, in this moment, wanting to be closer and closer to him.

He pulls away. 'This is only date two,' he says. 'Admire the view.'

Right.

We have another glass of champagne. Jack stands behind me, his arms around me. His lips are on my neck and my eyes close again. His hand creeps up under my jumper. Featherlight touch on my scar, then to the left. Over my breast.

'I can feel your heart beating,' he whispers in my ear.

Flora's heart.

Her face – I see it as clear as if she was in front of me and my eyes were open. I stiffen, move away.

SEVENTY-ONE

FERN

'Hi, Fern. Thanks for coming,' Imogen says. 'Let's get a coffee, we'll talk?'

'All right,' I say, still not entirely sure why I came after how she spoke to me the last time. Her message was cryptic – just said there was something she needed to tell me.

We go in, she waves at a waitress and we sit down at a table. The waitress takes our order: tea for me; some fancy coffee for Imogen.

'Let me go first,' Imogen says. 'I want to apologise. I shouldn't have said what I did the last time we spoke, or on the phone before that. It wasn't fair.' She's looking a combination of genuinely contrite and embarrassed. I believe her, but that isn't enough.

'I appreciate the apology. But I'd appreciate an explanation even more – of what you wrote on Flora's card. And why you reacted the way you did when I asked you.'

'Now that Flora is gone, it's really hard to know if talking about this will serve any purpose. It's too late to do anything about it, and it's painful.'

'I can't answer that when I don't know what this is about,' I say, but dread is building, acid in my stomach.

'I know. And I'm truly sorry about what I said the last time. My anger was misplaced.'

Our drinks are being brought now; there's a pause while I add milk to my tea, stir. I sense she's thinking and don't say anything.

'All right. This is going to be very personal to begin with.' There is a pause, as if she is gathering herself. 'When I was a young teenager, I was raped. And don't – no sympathy, I don't want that now. I'm a survivor. I've mostly dealt with it, as much as is possible. And moved on with my life. The thing is, I recognised my younger self in Flora.'

'What are you saying?'

'I'm saying, Flora was abused – also at a young age. You weren't there, you were at university.'

I want to close my ears, push her words away. 'She told you this?'

'Not in as clear a manner as I'm relating to you now, but, over time, yes.'

'But who?'

'She wouldn't say. She said she tried to tell you once – but I understand if you didn't work out what she meant. It was probably in an indirect way because she couldn't quite say it.'

'I don't remember anything like that.' I'm horrified, wanting to call Imogen a liar, get up and leave, so she can't say any more.

'It's true, Fern. If you think about it for a while, you might start to see how it shaped Flora as she grew older. That card I wrote her – it was about this. I was trying to convince her to face it, name whoever it was. Make them pay for their actions in a way I never did. I think I'd succeeded. She wouldn't tell me, but she said there was one person she trusted. She was going to tell them.'

'Who?'

'She didn't say, but I think she meant Benji.'

All at once I'm struggling to breathe. 'When... when was this?'

'A few days before she was strangled.'

SEVENTY-TWO

SAPHY

Margot arrives early. The front garden is small – it's a mess, but not much to do there, or so I thought. But she's in a flight of fancy immediately that goes even further when she looks in the back.

'This garden, its size, in Islington? It could make this house something unbelievably special.' The plans she outlines will probably cost way more than the cheque she tried to give me. And it'll bring us together, make us closer. Another step to living Flora's life. Becoming part of her family.

We stop for tea and chocolate biscuits that she brought – made by Dorothy, she says.

'Didn't Marley do well with the interview?' Margot says. 'So professional. I know how much she cared for Flora. It couldn't have been an easy thing for her.'

'They were friends for a long time.'

'Since Flora was, I think, seventeen – so eight years or so. I'm fairly sure they had a relationship, too. You know – that they were dating.'

'Really?' I'm surprised. From what Marley said, I didn't think her parents knew. 'Did Flora tell you?'

'She didn't have to. I'm rather good at picking up on those little signals between people.'

'Did Charles know?'

'I never mentioned it. I don't think so, though I was wondering if they could keep it a secret much longer. I was thinking of raising it with Flora, but then it was over – she was with Benji.'

Does that mean their relationship was a long-term thing? Up until Flora started dating Benji? That isn't what Marley said.

'Are you nervous about the interview airing?' she says.

'I've been trying not to think about it.' And between Flora, Jenny and Jack, mostly succeeding. 'I guess I wonder if people will recognise me from it. You know, if I get in a taxi and the driver says, hey, aren't you that girl who had a heart transplant? Or if people I know slightly will suddenly think it gives them licence to ask me all about it. After being ill for so long, there are things I'd rather talk about.'

'I understand that. I've been finding that since Flora died, I get one of two reactions. Either extravagant sympathy, or nothing at all. Neither are comfortable.'

'It was exactly like that with my dad. And now that some time has gone by, people forget. They think I should have got over it, but you don't get over it. You just get more used to it.'

'I'm not at that stage yet.'

'Of course not.'

'It still doesn't seem real. I wake up in the morning and, for just a small moment, I forget. And then I remember that Flora is gone, and the pain comes again. So much that I can't move or speak. But meeting you, Saphy, has made such a difference. Let me do your gardens for you. Please.'

I think Fern was right. Somehow Margot really needs to do this. She's suffered so much.

I can't deprive her of this. And it's a good beginning – to slipping into Flora's role in Margot's life.

'There is a yes on your face, I can see it.'

'OK, yes. But don't go overboard!'

'Thank you.' She gives me a hug.

SEVENTY-THREE

FERN

I somehow get through another night shift, without having slept more than a few hours since the last one. I can't stop thinking about what Imogen said. If it's true – did Flora try to tell me, and I either didn't listen or didn't understand?

Flora changed when I was away. That first time I came back from uni for Christmas, she clung to me – I remember that. Like she wanted me with her all the time. Then the next year, she almost ignored me. We were never as close as we had been, again.

If what Imogen said is true, was that why Flora changed? And if Flora thought I wouldn't listen, does that explain why she was different towards me?

If it's true, then who? She had started boarding school for secondary, just coming home some weekends. Was it someone at school?

When I have a moment, I search her school on my phone. Oh, God. There has been an abuse scandal there, only recently in the news – allegations that complaints by students against a teacher were not taken seriously, not referred to police. The years are about right.

And the rest of what Imogen said and implied: that Flora was going to tell someone, maybe Benji. But before she could, she was tied up and strangled. Did an abuser from all those years ago somehow find out what she was going to do, and then did that to her to keep her quiet? And let Benji take the blame? But from what she said, Imogen was the only one who had an inkling of what Flora had been through – the only who knew she had decided to name her abuser. How could someone from so many years ago have possibly known what Flora was planning to do?

In the morning I walk back across the park after my shift. Stop, sit on a bench. The sun is shining – the park is beautiful this time of day, peaceful – but there is grime around the edges, as there always is in a city. In leafy villages and expensive independent schools, too, if you know where to look.

I message Imogen.

Have you told the police what you told me about Flora?

No.

Why?

They won't believe me. There's no point.

I pause, weighing her words. Did she report abuse when she was a young girl and no one believed her? Then I can understand why she feels that way. But this isn't then, it is now.

I reply:

This isn't about what happened to you. It's about Flora. It's about Benji, too.

There's a long pause.

There is nothing to back up what I said. And I just can't.

When sleep finally comes for me that afternoon, it sends confused dreams, memories that unwind in my mind. Flora, my happy, beautiful trusting little sister. Flora, who became someone else. Flora, who wouldn't talk to me anymore.

I'd thought as Mum had said at the time – teenage moods. Was that all it was?

Flora's arms around me. *Don't go. Please don't leave me again...*

SEVENTY-FOUR

SAPHY

Date three: a picnic, brought by me. With leftover biscuits from Margot's visit – it was a complete battle to make myself save them for now – and a selection of delectable goodies from Neeha, who still seems convinced I'm unable to feed myself. A rug on a grassy slope near the Serpentine and this time I'm early enough to pick the spot of my choice, and to work out how to sit on a blanket in a sundress without flashing my knickers. My phone rings: it's Jack.

'Hi. Are you lost?'

'I know just where I am. Where you are, on the other hand, I'm not so sure about.'

I scan all around and think I spot him. 'Turn to your right,' I say, and wave. He walks towards me, glancing around as he goes – is it the sunbathing girls? No, he doesn't look their way any longer than any other. He almost looks nervous, which doesn't fit him somehow. But he smiles when he reaches me, sits next to me on the rug.

'Hi,' he says, and his eyes on mine feel warm.

'Hi yourself.'

'I've been looking forward to this picnic. I'm very hungry.'

'Just so there is no misunderstanding, there is one thing I need to make perfectly clear.'

'What's that?'

'I can't cook. The yummy things in this basket were all made by other people. I can even burn toast.'

'Luckily, I'm not after you for your cooking skills.'

'Oh? What are you after, then?'

He brushes my hair back, tips my face towards his. Kisses me thoroughly, and now I'm asking myself why I said five dates when three is a perfectly adequate number.

My phone rings in my pocket – brings me back to reality, to the fact that we're in a public park – people all around us. I pull away, glance at my phone – it's Fern. I motion to Jack that I need to take the call.

'Hi, Fern, how're things?'

'Fine, thanks,' she says, but even with just a few words she doesn't sound quite herself, as if there is some strain in her voice.

'Is something wrong?'

'Not at all. I've heard back from Marley – the interview is airing tomorrow, at five. Do you want to come over and watch it here? Mum and Dad are coming – Mum thought it'd be nice to watch it together, and to invite Zoe also.'

'That sounds lovely, thank you. What time?'

'Come an hour or so before it's on. We'll have some drinks.'

'Can I bring Jack?'

'Of course.' He's raising an eyebrow, wondering what I'm inviting him to.

'Thanks. See you then. Bye.'

'What's this?'

'Well, it's a long story. I need some sustenance, first.'

I'm getting things out of the basket – passing plates, cutlery – setting out all kinds of nibbles, plus cheese, bread from a bakery on the way, much of it between us now on the blanket so unless we want to wear lunch, we'll have to leave the kissing for a while.

'Looks delicious,' he says, but he's looking at me when he says it. We make a start on lunch and in between mouthfuls I tell him about the interview, and that my donor was Flora – Sleeping Beauty on the news.

'Seriously?' he says.

'Yes. And that's not all. I'd actually worked it out before Flora's dad contacted me. I mean, I saw on TV about this vigil they had for her, in Kensington Gardens. And she was the right age and died around the right time, and somehow, I just knew it was her. Do you think that's weird?'

He shakes his head. 'How do we know things sometimes? Like I knew when I first saw you that I had to meet you, know you. Kiss you.' He risks crumbs and reaches for me, kisses me again with half of lunch still in between us. Then there's a throat-clearing sound nearby: it's Zoe.

'Sorry to interrupt,' she says. 'I'm a little early.'

'Join us,' Jack says, and moves across to make room for Zoe on the blanket.

'You remember each other?' I say.

'Of course,' he says.

'I just heard from Fern. That's Flora's sister,' I say to Jack. 'The interview is going to be on at five tomorrow – come watch it at Fern's? Her parents are coming also. And Jack – if you're free?'

'That sounds good,' Zoe says. 'Do you think I could bring Mum?'

'I expect so, I'll message Fern to check.' I do so and a reply comes a moment later. 'That's a yes.'

We finish lunch with some help from Zoe. Jack has to go – just gives me a quick kiss goodbye, but there is something about the way his eyes hold mine for a moment that makes me want to pull him back down on the blanket.

'Bye. Nice to see you again, Zoe.' He walks off.

'Oh my,' she says. 'The air fairly sizzles between you two.'

'Mmm. Doesn't it?'

'That look on your face.' She's laughing. 'But isn't this all going a bit, well, fast? What do you even know about him?'

'Let's see. He's a brilliant kisser – totally the best.'

'A good point.'

'Ah, he manages a gym. And is a personal trainer.'

'Do you know which gym? Where it is? Any corroborating evidence of these claims?'

'Well, no.'

'Anything else?'

'I don't think so.'

'So overall, top scores on kissing and you don't know much else about him.'

'I suppose not. I'll try to do better.'

'If he comes tomorrow, Mum will likely make inroads.'

'Tell her to be nice!'

'She's always *nice*,' Zoe says, and winks. 'In a shades of questioning by MI5 kind of way.'

'Maybe I should rethink his invitation,' I say, and then realise he never actually said if he could make it.

SEVENTY-FIVE

FERN

Saphy, Zoe and Claire arrive together.

'Thanks for inviting us along,' Zoe says, and hands across a bottle of wine. Claire has another.

Saphy has some spring flowers. 'They're from my garden,' she says. 'Before it all gets ripped out and redone.'

'They're lovely. Thank you, all of you.'

'Is Marley coming?' Saphy says.

'Unfortunately not.' I don't add that I didn't invite her. Some forms of awkward I can do without. 'Where's Jack?'

'Sorry, I should have told you; he can't make it. He sends his apologies,' Saphy says.

Then there's another knock – Mum and Dad. Claire is introduced; we're finding places to sit around the TV. Glasses of wine. Prosecco. Tea for me as I'm on nights and will be back at work in a few hours.

'It's time – turn it up,' Mum says. I find the remote and do so.

'And now we have a special piece from our usually roving London correspondent, Marley Jansen.'

. . .

After the interview and goodbyes, I walk across the park to work. I knew the interview had gone well, but it was even better once it was edited. Seeing Mum and Saphy together, both on the screen and as we watched it, I can see what so worried Marley. Mum's feelings for Saphy were obvious, and I'm wondering if I was right to discount Saphy's motives, even though she gave the cheque back.

But once I get to work it's soon out of my mind. A&E is particularly frantic tonight – to the point where I can't think, only react. And it isn't the sort of busy where I know we are making a difference, helping people who really need help. Saving lives. Instead, it is the sort of busy where everyone is drunk or high, abusive, injured in fights, or, worse – attacked by someone who should protect them. Empty, blank eyes are one of the things I hate the most of all. Not that I'm angry at them. My rage is focused squarely on whoever made them like this. But that might get bumped down the most hated list after a call comes through – ambulance on the way, stabbing victim, a woman – bilateral penetrating eye injuries. A knife wound in each eye, through eyelids, corneas and conjunctiva. Images of the injuries taken by paramedics before dressings were applied come through.

London is really outdoing itself tonight, and it's not even midnight.

They bring her in. Despite the IV morphine they've instigated she's still writhing in fear, pain. She calms gradually as morphine takes better hold but her hand grips mine so tight it hurts.

It's hard to recognise someone with their face mostly obscured, blood over what isn't. But I do.

'Debra? It's Fern. Try to stay still. We'll do everything we can – you're in the best place now.' I say the words to comfort, but there is no chance of repairing this much damage. Even if she doesn't lose her eyes, she'll be blind.

We take her for a CT scan, and it gets worse. There is penetration through the back of the left eye socket, damage and swelling behind the eye. A brain injury like this could be life-threatening. When the on-call ophthalmologist arrives, along with everything else I also tell her that this patient has recently had bilateral corneal transplants. The gift of sight undone on the blade of a knife.

Debra is taken to be prepped for theatre. Now she's out of my hands, I'm shaking.

I lock myself in a staff loo. Flora's corneas, through which she saw the world for twenty-five years; Debra could have done so for decades more. Destroyed.

Can this be random? That someone stabbed a corneal graft recipient in both eyes?

It can't be. It has to be personal.

That leaves two possibilities I can think of. The attacker was someone in Debra's life. Or they were someone from Flora's.

SEVENTY-SIX

SAPHY

A message vibrates my phone – it's from Jack.

> *I know it's late, but I'd really like to see you tonight. Date four?*

I glance at the time, surprised to see it's gone midnight.

I should be asleep.

> *But you're not.*

No. What were you thinking?

> *I've got a few ideas...*

Ideas? Do you mean, naughty ideas?

> *Well, more like going to watch a late film – though we could sit in the back row.*

What's playing?

I don't know, I'll check.

*How about you come here, instead? I've got loads of
DVDs and can even make popcorn.*

Ooh. Are you going to give me your actual address?

I guess I am.

I message it next.

I'll be about half an hour.

A quick tidy up of me and the house is almost done when a
motorbike rumbles up our road, then stops out front. It's Jack.
He's taking off his helmet when I open the door.

'Hi,' he says, smiles. And then I'm kissing him, we're barely
through the door and he has me pinned against the wall.

What am I doing? And why do I keep asking myself questions when I know the answer?

Hermi miaowls near our feet. Startled, Jack stops kissing
me, looks at the tiny tabby cat staring up at him – fur completely
fluffed out – and hissing. She really doesn't like the look of him,
at all.

'You didn't tell me you have an attack cat.'

'I have an attack cat. Jack, meet Hermi – Hermi, this is Jack.'
He bends down as if to stroke her but she strikes out with a paw
– a streak of red wells up on his hand.

'Sorry. You should probably stay striking distance away
from her claws.' I shoo her into the kitchen and shut the door.

'Should I take this personally?'

'To be fair, she doesn't like men. Apart from my dad, and I think she only tolerated him because he gave her treats.' All true but, to be fair, she doesn't usually draw blood.

'Treats, check. I'll bring some next time.'

'Next time?'

'Well, this is only date four.'

'Good point. You'd better go.'

'What?' He's startled.

'I mean it – go.'

Confusion on his face as I open the door, push him back through it – close it. Then open it again. Reach a hand, pull him in back in.

'And now... this is date five.'

'I thought you wanted to watch a film, make popcorn.'

'Maybe later.'

'Later?'

He's coming closer, about to kiss me. I raise a hand – touch it to his lips and he kisses my fingertips.

I make myself say what I should, even though I don't want to. 'I've got bones that were broken, not yet fully healed.' I take his hand – touch it to the top of my scar, gently trail it to the bottom of my ribs. 'I can't have any pressure here at all. Think you can cope with that?'

'We'll find a way.'

I take his hand, lead him upstairs.

He turns the lights off and I'm surprised – he doesn't seem like an only-in-the-dark kind of guy. And he does find a way. Undresses me slowly, kissing every inch of me. Leaving a trail of fire that burns until that is all I am. He's the one who has to remind me to be careful. There is wave after wave through my body and it has never been like this for me before.

After, he holds me – spoons me so he's along the length of my back, legs. His lips on my neck. A hand over my heart.

. . .

When I wake up in the morning, Jack is gone.

SEVENTY-SEVEN

FERN

By morning, I've convinced myself to make the call, even though I'm not sure if I'm breaking any privacy laws by doing so without permission. Debra isn't in any state to ask for it. She's had surgery to remove both eyes just hours ago and is in an induced coma.

I find the card where I'd tucked it in my address book all those months ago. Call and leave a message for Harry Jennings, the DCI in charge of Flora's case.

My phone rings soon after.

'Hi, Fern, returning your call.'

'Something happened last night that may relate to Flora's case.'

'Go on.'

'A patient was brought to emergency. She was stabbed in both eyes.'

'I am aware of that incident.'

'The thing is, I recognised her – I know her. She was one of Flora's organ recipients. She'd had bilateral corneal transplants from Flora.' I leave a pause, for him to take that in. 'It can't be a coincidence – can it? That someone who had that specific surgery with Flora's corneas then got stabbed in both eyes?'

'Thank you for drawing this to our attention. We'll look into it.'

'I don't know how much you know about organ donation. Her identity as one of Flora's recipients would only have been known by a handful of people – it's subject to strict privacy requirements. I only know because she wrote back to my parents, agreed to meet them.'

'That attack likely has nothing to do with Flora. But if you could provide a list of those who knew, please do so. Do you have my email address?'

I glance at his card. 'Yes. I'll do it shortly. There are also two other recipients of Flora's organs that I know. Saphira Logan – she was on the interview on Sky with my parents about organ donation, if you caught it.'

'I did.'

'And another, Liam Flynn – he has one of Flora's kidneys. He's a graduate student at King's College. I'm worried about them. There must be other recipients, but I don't know who they are.'

We say our goodbyes and I start on his list. Me, Mum, Dad, Liam, Saphy. Did Marley know? She knew we were in touch with more of Flora's recipients, but I can't remember exactly what I told her. Then the Donor Family Care Service. Debra's medical team. Any family or friends that she told.

Apart from the fact that she's an English teacher and has had enough of Ishiguro, I don't know much about Debra, at all. But I'll never forget the way she held my hand, so tight.

SEVENTY-EIGHT

SAPHY

I'm staring at the ceiling, still in bed. Caught between this delicious feeling of warmth from last night, and the indisputable fact that Jack is gone.

Don't freak out, I tell myself. The way he held me – it *meant* something, I know it did. But what, exactly, do I think that is? I don't know. Be honest: right from the beginning, it's all been about this intense physical attraction. It's made me feel *alive*, beyond just surviving like I have for so long. Maybe that is all there is to it, but even if that is so, I still want to see him again. And if last night was as amazing as I thought, surely he'd want that, too?

Should I message him, either now or wait a while? If I do, what should I say? I don't know.

Finally, I get myself up, have a quick shower. Clean clothes. Then wonder if there is a note somewhere downstairs, but find nothing except an extremely indignant cat scratching at the closed kitchen door. I open it and she tells me off in a crescendo of miaowls.

'You didn't like him, did you? Tell me why.'

More miaowls ensue, but she didn't come with a translate button. She's soon appeased by breakfast.

The radio is on while I burn toast. I will message Jack, I decide. The key here is tone. Keep it light, flirty, just like how it was before last night.

Hi Jack, I'm thinking about date six... xxx

And I hit send. As soon as it goes, I want to call it back. Maybe I should have asked Zoe – she's better at this stuff than I am. I stare at my phone, willing Jack to answer.

I'm so focused on the absence of messages that the news on the radio takes a moment to register. A woman was attacked in London yesterday evening – stabbed in both eyes. How completely sickening is that? She has now been identified as Debra Hales.

The name is familiar. Was Hales the surname of Debra from drinks the other night? I rush to put on the TV news just in time for a brief image of her to flash across the screen. It *is* that Debra. She had bilateral corneal transplants from Flora, and now this?

My phone vibrates and I check the screen. It's not Jack, it's Fern.

Have you seen the news?

I hit call. She answers on the first ring. 'Hi.'

'It's her – Debra. From the other night. Isn't it?'

'Yes. She came in last night. To A&E. I recognised her.' What a shock that must have been.

'Is she going to be all right?'

'No.' She pauses. 'Her eyes had to be removed. There was some brain damage. She's in an induced coma now. The next day or two will be crucial.'

'Are you on your own?'

'Yes, but—'

'I'm coming over.'

She says she's got the day off and I convince her she can't talk me out of it. I remember to take tonight's tablets in my handbag in case I'm not back in time. Give Hermi a cuddle and some treats. Head out and walk to Angel. One last check of my phone for a message from Jack before I go below.

I can't stop thinking about Debra, which pushes Jack down the queue of things to be upset about. How terrified she must have been. The pain. And that she went through corneal surgery – not as involved as swapping a heart, I appreciate – only for this to happen.

Did someone target her because she was a recipient of Flora's? I start to feel nervous, looking around at the other passengers. No one seems to be paying me any attention, but then a woman across the carriage comes over.

'Excuse me, are you that girl who was on TV? The one who had a heart transplant?' I shake my head, deny it. She doesn't look convinced but goes back to her seat.

I'm not exactly anonymous. Everyone who saw that interview on Sky knows I was Flora's heart recipient.

SEVENTY-NINE

FERN

I'm nervy, pacing. Checking the street through the window now and then. When I see Saphy approaching, I put the kettle on, then open the door just as she reaches it.

'Thanks for coming,' I say and she gives me a hug.

'Are you OK?'

'I see horrible things most days at A&E. I should be OK.'

'But you knew this woman, even though briefly. And you knew she was a recipient of Flora's. Not the same thing, at all.'

'I suppose not.' I sigh. 'It felt like someone was attacking Flora all over again. I know that's insane.'

'Do the police know about the connection between Debra and Flora?'

'I told them. But it is unlikely what happened to Debra had anything to do with Flora. So few people knew she had Flora's corneas – us, my parents, Liam, those involved at the DFCS. Her medical team. But none of them or us would have any reason to do this.'

'Then who?'

'Someone in her family – perhaps a violent partner or ex-partner? I don't know. Or a psychopath with a thing for eyes, who just randomly happened to pick a victim who so recently had eye surgery? Which seems way too many coincidences to believe, but I suppose it's not completely impossible, either.'

'Do your parents know?'

I nod. 'I spoke to Mum earlier. She's in pieces.'

The sympathy on Saphy's face is instant, genuine. 'Should we go to her?'

'I was going to. But according to Dorothy, she'll soon be sleeping off rather a lot of whisky. Perhaps tomorrow.'

'How about Liam – has anyone checked in with him?'

'I've got his number from the other night and tried to call him after I spoke to you. There was no answer. I wasn't sure about leaving a message about this or what to say, so I didn't.'

'Should we try him again?'

'Let's.' It rings three times, goes to voicemail. This time I leave a message. 'Hi, Liam, it's Fern – Flora's sister. Could you give me a call please, on this number? Thank you.'

'It's making me nervous that he's not answering,' Saphy says. 'I get why you said it's unlikely that what happened to Debra has anything to do with Flora, but the whole time I was coming here, I kept looking around me on the Tube, thinking someone, anyone, might have a knife. Want to hurt me. What if the same person has done something to Liam?'

She's really frightened. Is there reason to be? I don't know.

'Liam could be doing any number of things that mean he can't answer his phone.'

'I know. I'd just feel better if we hear from him.'

Saphy's phone vibrates and she glances at it – a flash of disappointment and she rolls her eyes. 'Just some pizza place wanting to give me a discount.'

'Were you hoping to hear from someone else?'

'Well, Jack.' She sighs. 'If you want distraction – we slept together last night. He vanished when I was asleep and now I think he's ghosting me.'

It's pretty good distraction, as these things go. She tells me more about him, things they did together – that he surprised her with a private pod on the London Eye.

'Well, that sounds to me like he's way beyond interested in you. Maybe there's a completely reasonable explanation for why you haven't heard from him – just like why we haven't heard from Liam.'

'Such as?'

'I don't know, he could be insanely busy at work.'

'That's never stopped him from messaging before.'

'A family emergency, then.'

'Maybe,' she says, her face glum. 'But more likely he's with his other girlfriend. Or wife.'

'Don't go there unless you have a reason. Uh, perhaps he's been in a car accident?'

'Not car, he's a biker – he came on a motorbike. Oh. Do you think that could really be the case? That he's been in an accident and I've been getting annoyed at him when he could be hurt, injured? Or even worse.'

'It's always possible but not likely, so don't worry.'

'This speculation feels, not exactly trivial, because it's still important to me, but, you know. With what happened to Debra.'

A phone vibrates on the table between us, but it's mine. I glance at the screen. It's Owen.

Come to the Devonshire tonight? It'd be great to see you.

'You've got a smile – who is that for?'

'His name is Owen, but it's not like that. I mean, he's good-looking and single, as far as I know, and has just said come to the pub tonight.'

'And?'

'He was a friend of Flora's. He's just being kind, that's all.'

'Are you sure?'

'Well, mostly.'

'Do you want to go?'

'No,' I say, but do I? A night at the pub isn't usually my thing, though maybe being around other people just now sounds like a good idea – whether comforting or for distraction, I don't know. But they're Flora's friends, not mine.

'Are you sure?' Saphy says. 'I don't want to stop you.'

'You shouldn't be on your own,' I say, and she looks relieved.

'I know: how about we both go?' she says. 'Between us we can work out Owen's story.'

I think for a moment. Why not?

EIGHTY

SAPHY

We arrive early to be sure of getting a table. I need to unwind and might manage to, as there are no worries about getting the Tube back on my own – Fern has asked me to stay over.

The guy at the bar seems to know Fern, going by the look of sympathy he gives her when he brings our drinks – white wine for Fern, Prosecco for me.

Fern holds out her glass. 'To Debra. Hoping she recovers well.'

'To Debra.'

It's getting busy and we're on our second drink when Fern nudges me. 'Owen is just coming in,' she says, tells me what he's wearing – jeans, buttoned shirt – and I look to the door. He's cute. He's speaking to a woman who is holding hands with another man, the three of them heading towards the bar. Then he glances over, sees us and a smile crosses his face as he diverts to our table.

'Fern, so glad you could come.' A kiss on the cheek.

He glances at me; his eyes widen a little. 'Owen, this is—' Fern starts to say but he interrupts.

'No need for introductions. I saw you on TV – is it Saphy?'

'That's me.'

'This is just...' He pauses, searching for words.

'Weird? Creepy? Or a combination of that and some other difficult to describe emotion?'

He laughs. 'I was thinking more, amazing. I'm pleased to meet you. Can I get you both another?'

'Sauvignon blanc for me,' Fern says.

'A Prosecco, thank you.'

'Coming up,' he says, and walks back to the bar.

'So?' Fern says.

'He's easy on the eye. Seemed very pleased to see you and —' I stop mid-sentence. My phone is vibrating in my pocket. I take it out and glance at the screen.

'At long last – it's Jack.' I almost messaged him again this afternoon – got so far as tapping it in before I talked myself out of it and hit delete.

'And?'

'Just psyching myself up.' I open the message.

Hi Saphy, so sorry I haven't messaged before. If you're still speaking to me – can I come over tonight? Please say yes xxxxxxx

'You're smiling so it must be good?'

'I think so.' I show her, just as Owen returns with our drinks, a pint for himself. 'But tonight?' I shake my head. 'I have plans – with you! He made me wait all day and expects I'll be free. He's wrong.' I put my phone away but it vibrates again.

It's Jack.

I really am sorry.

I relent, answer.

Hi. It's good to hear from you – can't do tonight, I'm out with a friend. Tomorrow maybe...?

That'd be great. Sure it is just a friend?

Positive.

OK xxxxxxxxxxxxxxxx

We have that round, then I get another and everything is feeling better than it did earlier. I get some decidedly odd looks from a few of Flora's friends when they work out who I am, but once they say hello, they're all right. Fern and Owen are cosied up together, talking in low voices. How she didn't know that he likes her I have no idea. He goes back to the bar – another round – I decline. The room is spinning quite enough already.

'I think he's trying to get you drunk,' I say.

'I think he's succeeding. Uh oh. Here comes trouble.' I follow her eyes to the door: Marley is coming in.

'Trouble? How so?' I'm uncomfortable. Has Marley told Fern we kissed? I haven't thought of that at all lately, not since I met Jack.

'Don't ask.'

Marley is speaking to a few people near the door, makes her way towards the bar. It's crowded now but it's not long before her eyes wander across. A mixture of a surprised smile to see Fern, then something else as she sees me. But she comes over.

'Good to see you out again, Fern.' A nod to me. 'Saphy.'

'Saphy convinced me,' Fern says. 'I think I'm going to have a headache tomorrow.'

'All in a good cause.'

They start talking about the reaction to the interview – Marley not ignoring me, exactly, but not including me either.

'Excuse me,' I say, and head for the ladies. I don't need to go, just splash some water on my face, wash my hands. Marley comes in. Did she follow me?

'We need to have a word,' she says.

'About what?'

'I know what you're doing. You're trying to *be* Flora – to worm your way into her family, her friends – but I'm on to you. You're not going to get away with it. And when you worked out we'd had a relationship, you kissed me in some sort of twisted attempt to be more like Flora.'

'If you really think about what happened, that kiss wasn't just my idea.'

'Whatever.' She goes towards a cubicle. I should just get out of here, but there is something I want to know. Did she lie to me?

'Margot knew.'

She pauses. 'Margot knew what?'

'About you and Flora. I didn't tell her – she's the one who mentioned it. Only she thought you'd been together for much longer than what you said. She thought it continued right up until Flora started seeing Benji. I guess that means that she dumped you for Benji.'

'I don't give a damn what you think.' She goes into the cubicle, slams the door. I dry my hands; they're shaking. I leave the ladies and make my way through the crowd to our table. Wondering if Marley will come back to us, and wanting to leave, just in case.

Marley didn't deny that she and Flora were in a long-term relationship. Why does it even matter? Maybe I'm hurt. I liked Marley, wanted her to like me – not necessarily in a girlfriend kind of way. But she lied to me, and not just that – she's angry. She thinks I'm trying to be Flora. What was the word she used? That I'm worming my way into her family. Honesty compels me to admit, at least to myself – isn't that exactly what I've been doing? Fern is looking concerned when I sit next to her.

'Everything OK?'

I'm saved from answering by Owen's return, and don't remind him I'd said no to another drink when he puts one in front of me and Fern. He goes back to the bar to get the rest he'd bought for other friends. There is muffled ringing and Fern gets out her phone.

'It's Liam,' she says, and I feel a swell of relief. She answers. Motions that she'll go outside to speak to him. She's still gone when Owen brings everyone else's drinks.

'She had to take a call,' I say in answer to his unspoken question.

'Gives us a moment to talk. I'm really glad you came, Saphy. I just want to say how much respect and admiration I have for you. That surgery – all you must have gone through – and then, doing that interview? That took guts.'

'You sound like you know something about it. Are you a doctor, too?'

He shakes his head. 'Pharmacist. In a hospital – a different one to Fern's.' He's glancing at the door again.

'It's not a boyfriend she's speaking to, if that's what is worrying you. I promise.'

Fern is coming back in now. Her face, the way she holds herself: something is wrong. She gestures for me to go to her, draws me nearer the door where we can talk without ears all around us.

'Is Liam all right?'

'Absolutely fine. Distressed about Debra, of course. He's been busy all day, just got my message.'

'What is it? Is something else wrong?'

'I picked up another message after I spoke to Liam. I'd asked to be informed of any changes in Debra's condition. She – she's died.'

EIGHTY-ONE

FERN

We make excuses to Owen and the others. Get a taxi back to mine. Both suddenly sober, but there is a pounding headache starting behind my eyes. We don't talk on the way. Once home we put the kettle on without discussion.

Saphy is so pale. 'I just can't believe it,' she says. 'She was having drinks with us, just days ago. And now... she's gone.'

'I know. It's hard to take in. And the way she was attacked – so vicious. Senseless.'

I'm pouring tea, milk, keeping my hands busy but everything is whirling so much inside that I overpour, spill milk. Get a cloth and wipe it up.

'I can't stop thinking it has something to do with Flora,' Saphy says. 'Like someone is out to kill her all over again.'

I flinch and Saphy apologises.

'No, don't. I keep thinking the same thing. Maybe it is more likely to be someone in Debra's life – but what if it isn't? What does it mean if it isn't?'

We take cups of tea to the sofa. Pull a throw over both of us even though it's not cold, as if it'll keep the world away.

'What it might mean, is this: if the same person who

attacked Flora wants to kill all of her – all the parts of her that are still alive, in recipients, like me – then Liam and I could both be in danger.'

Tears are rising in my eyes and I'm blinking them back. I nod. 'I said as much to the police when I told them about Debra's connection to Flora. I don't know if they took it seriously, or if the fact that she's died now will make any difference.'

'If Debra was attacked because of Flora, surely that suggests the same person who attacked Flora is responsible. Benji is out on bail. Will the police question him about Debra?'

'Maybe. I don't know.'

'When I asked you about this before, you couldn't talk about it. But do you believe it was Benji who strangled Flora?'

'I don't know. It's been the worst nightmare, that not only was Flora hurt, but Benji was arrested. But it's like thinking versus feeling. I think that the police and prosecution wouldn't be doing this unless they have a strong case. I think if Flora rejected him again, he might have been driven to violence. But I *feel* that he couldn't have hurt her. And for me to even whisper that to myself feels like I am betraying Flora. And I was the one who introduced them. If it was him, it's my fault.' I pause a moment. 'Full disclosure? I loved Benji, too. He didn't know – nobody did, as far as I know. Except Marley. She worked it out somehow.' Saphy doesn't look surprised.

'Fern, listen to me. You've been looking at things through a prism, one where even questioning Benji's arrest made you feel disloyal to your sister. Put that aside. Maybe if we talk it all through, together, we'll see something you haven't?'

I sigh. 'I doubt there is anything that I haven't thought of before or that the police missed. But I guess it's worth a try.'

'How about I begin? This is what Marley told me the other day. She said the only ones who knew where Flora had gone were you and Benji. Is that right?'

'I think so. Flora had been upset about something – she said she had to get away for a few days. It wasn't planned – just spur of the moment. She took the keys to our family holiday cottage in Dorset. We don't use it much in winter, so no one would expect her to be there then. And soon after Benji asked me to switch shifts at work – said it was important. At the time, I wondered if he was going to meet her, but he didn't say.'

'No one else knew?'

'I don't think so. Though Flora could have told someone without me knowing. Well, and Marley of course – she knew. She drove Flora there.'

'She didn't mention that.'

'Maybe she didn't mention herself because she was telling you who else knew, if you see what I mean.'

'Maybe. But there have been a few other times she's been less than honest with me.'

'About?'

Saphy hesitates. 'I said I wouldn't discuss this – Marley said that Flora didn't want her parents to know. But your mum already knew, so maybe it's OK to tell you. She told me the other day when she came to see the garden.'

'What are you talking about?'

'About Flora and Marley – their relationship. They weren't just friends.'

I frown, taking in her words. Could they have been together like that and I didn't notice? I was around the two of them all the time. 'Seriously?'

'You didn't have any inkling?'

I shake my head, surprised – but then less so, the more I think about it. They were always very tactile with each other. I'd often come home from night shift and find Marley there in the morning.

'The thing is, Marley told me it was just a short-term fling, years ago – that they were best friends afterwards. But your mum thought it had gone on for a long time, until Flora and Benji got together. If that is so, then Marley was lying about their relationship and how important it was to her. Maybe she was jealous, angry.'

'I see where you're going, but there is no way Marley could have hurt Flora.'

'Are you as sure of that as you are of Benji?'

I think for a moment. 'No, I suppose not. Marley has... edges. She can be ruthless. But it's still a stretch to think anything like you're suggesting.'

'She more or less accosted me in the loo a few hours ago and accused me of trying to worm my way into Flora's life.' Saphy tilts her head, looking at me. 'You're not surprised – did she say that to you, also?'

'Pretty much. Warned me against you.'

'But you didn't listen.'

'No. I'm a good judge of people. Which is why I think you're wrong about Marley. She was always Flora's biggest defender. It's hard to imagine she could have harmed her.'

'For the sake of argument – Marley drove Flora to this cottage in Dorset. What if Flora told her on the way that Benji was meeting her there? Could Marley be the one who strangled Flora, left her there for Benji to discover?'

'Well, there are a few problems with that. Flora had been drugged – with a sedative similar to Rohypnol, the date rape drug. One available in hospitals but difficult to source elsewhere. Even if Marley could get her hands on some, having it with her means advance planning. Not a jealous rage.'

Saphy nods, thinking for a moment. 'That's a good point,' she finally says. 'OK, let's leave Marley aside for the moment. Were there any other suspects?'

'There was Leo, another ex of Flora's. He's troubled, has had problems with the police, drugs. Assault charges. Flora went out with him for a while a year or so ago. He took it very badly when she left him for Benji. But the police said he had an alibi that checked out. And I've known Leo since he was a little boy. He's got a fierce temper. I could believe he did something in a fit of rage, but drugging Flora, tying her up, strangling her? No.'

'OK. Anyone else?'

'Not a suspect, but there is something else I wondered about.'

'What's that?'

'The police and everyone seemed to assume that whoever it was meant to kill Flora. But I'm not sure about that.'

'What do you mean?'

'She was strangled in a very specific way. Blood was cut off to her brain from pressure on her carotid arteries, but her throat wasn't crushed or bruised. Usually someone who has been strangled has extensive bruising around their neck. The way it was done – it was so precise. Almost like whoever did it didn't mean for her to die, but wanted her to be in a coma.'

'To make her Sleeping Beauty.'

'If that's what they wanted, then it worked. At least for a while.'

'From what I know of Flora, freedom was important to her. This would be the ultimate cruelty – making her linger on and on. Especially if she was aware at all.'

I shudder. Tears are coming now. I try to push them back.

'Would cutting blood flow the way it was done mean it had to be a doctor or some other medically trained person to do it?' Saphy says.

'Not necessarily, though you'd have to know how long to stop the blood to her brain. If it was too long, she'd have died, not long enough and she'd recover and be able to name her attacker. Though there is sick stuff online about how to do this.'

'What? Why?'

I shake my head. 'They say it's a game – a choking game. To

cut blood off to the brain for a short time to get some kind of rush, whether sexual or not. People – children, too – have died from trying this.'

'I think I've heard of that before.'

'I'd had a patient – a fourteen-year-old girl – in an irreversible coma from a choking game. She later died, and it was...' My words trail off. I feel like my mind has one of those slot machine games inside of it where everything has to line up in a row – and they've just fallen into place.

'What is it?'

'I hadn't thought of it like this before – but maybe...'

'What?'

'The day that we had the dinner party, where Flora met Benji. I hadn't originally invited Benji, it was kind of last minute. That girl I just mentioned had been brought to A&E that afternoon. It was heart-breaking. I'd been struggling to deal with it afterwards. Benji took me out for a coffee end of shift and I ended up inviting him to come. Before dinner, he mentioned that I'd had a difficult time with a patient, and we'd all talked about it – the choking game. Being in a coma afterwards.'

'Who was there?'

'I'm trying to remember if everyone had arrived. I think so. So, me, Benji, Flora, Leo, Marley, Owen and Imogen.'

'Could it have been someone who was there, even if they didn't have medical training? If talking about this gave them the idea, and then they found stuff online about how to do it?'

'I suppose so.'

'You said the sedative Flora had been given was available in hospitals. Isn't Owen a pharmacist in a hospital?'

'He is. But he was a friend of Flora's – why would he hurt her?'

'Maybe he was just a friend because that's what Flora wanted, and he was secretly in love with her.'

Everyone was in love with Flora. I sigh. 'If there was anything going on with Flora and Owen, I didn't know about it. Regardless, I don't see Owen as the kind of person who could drug and strangle anybody, let alone Flora.' Or maybe I just don't want to believe it.

'OK. Next – who is Imogen?'

'Imogen was Flora's employer, but they were also friends.'

'Did Flora have an argument or fall out with any of those who were there, then or later?'

'Leo, as they broke up soon after – and he really flipped out at the time. But as I said, his alibi checked out. And she broke up with Benji about six months later, though if they had a big dramatic argument or falling out, I missed it. Nothing with any of the others as far as I know.'

'Apart from those who were there that night, do you know of anyone else who could be a suspect?'

I shake my head. 'Flora was the kind of woman that people had strong reactions to, love or hate. But no one I knew.' I hesitate. 'I should probably tell you I was working at the hospital at the time.'

Saphy shakes her head. 'You don't need an alibi. I know how much you loved Flora.'

Loved her. Hated her, too. Loved her all over again.

'Is there anything else you know about Flora that could be relevant?'

Imogen's words hang heavy in the air – smoke that won't disperse. Holding it in is like it's choking me.

'Maybe,' I admit. 'But I don't want to talk about it. I don't want to believe any of it.' I sigh. 'It's something Imogen told me recently. She'd written "you are stronger than you know" on a Christmas card to Flora. I asked her what she meant by that, and she got upset, angry. I went to see her to ask her why. She told me that Flora broke up with Benji because of me – that she ended it when she found out I had feelings for him. The thing is, I'm sure Flora didn't know how I felt about Benji. She wasn't great at empathy, and I didn't tell her.'

'Marley knew though, didn't she? Maybe she's the one who told Flora about your feelings, hoping Flora would end things with Benji. That she might get Flora back on the rebound.'

Another missing link slots into place. 'You might be right. Anyhow, later Imogen messaged, apologised, asked to see me to explain.' I pause. 'I wished I'd ignored her. She told me that Flora had been abused when she was young.'

There is shock in Saphy's widened eyes. 'Do you mean, sexually abused?'

'Yes.'

'Abused by who?'

'She didn't know, said Flora wouldn't say. I asked Imogen if she'd told the police – she said no, and that she wouldn't. And it sounded to me from what she said that it was more guesswork on her part, that Flora never came right out and said. I mean, I could tell the police what Imogen said, but if it's all hearsay and supposition, what's the point? Especially as it is something that would have happened a decade or more ago, if it did at all.'

'If it's true, who do you think it could be?'

'There has been an abuse scandal at her school that surfaced recently. Students complained about a teacher years ago and it wasn't actioned or reported to the police. It was the boarding school she went to when I was at university, and the dates line up. I just wish I could ask Flora. Know what really happened – if I could have done anything to stop it.'

'Oh, Fern. I'm so sorry. That must be hard to deal with.'

'And if I bring this up, what about Mum and Dad? They'd feel even worse than me and it might not even be true. Do you think I should tell the police?'

'I honestly don't know. It's so long ago. Could it be relevant now?'

'I don't know. But I do know that I have to go to work

tomorrow morning. I should try to get some sleep. If you feel safer here, you're welcome to stay as long as you like.'

'Thank you. I appreciate that. Jack's coming over tomorrow night, so I'll go home tomorrow and work out what to do next then.'

'OK. Thank you for being here.' I hug Saphy, find her a towel, show her where things are and head for bed.

I like having her here. I feel at ease talking to her about all the hard stuff. I don't think I'd realised how much I needed to be able to tell someone what I think, without judgement. And to say out loud what Imogen told me. Saphy agreed, didn't she? That if it is ancient history there is no point in raising it now? Though I realise now that I didn't tell her everything. I didn't tell her Imogen thought Flora was going to tell Benji who it was – just days before she was strangled.

I can't sleep. I stare at the ceiling, thinking things through. I can understand why Saphy is suspicious of Marley, especially after Marley has been so hostile to her. But isn't it precisely because of Marley being protective of Flora and Flora's family that she's been so harsh to Saphy?

Do the police know that Marley had a relationship with Flora? I'm guessing not. Even I hadn't worked it out, and I was living with Flora.

But thinking these things through is just trying to distract myself.

Was Flora abused? Could it have had anything to do with her death? I don't know but I can't stop thinking about it.

EIGHTY-TWO

SAPHY

I'm in Flora's room, in her bed. My head on her pillow. But there is no chance of sleep tonight.

What was it about Flora? Marley, Benji, this Leo that Fern told me about, and even Fern: they all seem to be obsessed with Flora in one way or another.

Me, too. She is always with me. In my thoughts, on the edges of what I do and say. And now, maybe whoever it was who strangled her and killed Debra will come for me. Before they can, I need to work out who they are.

Despite how Fern feels about Benji, he has to be on the list. The police charged him – they must have evidence. I want to meet him, look him in the eye. Ask him if he did it. And I tell myself that it's all to search for the truth, but that isn't the only reason. Flora loved him. I want to know why.

Then there is Marley. She lied about her relationship with Flora, and tried to drive a wedge between Fern and me. Is that because she's afraid I'm on to her?

I think through Fern's reasons for discounting Marley as a suspect. Fern thought it couldn't be Marley because we assumed Marley only found out from Flora that Benji was meeting her there when they were on the way to Dorset. But what if she already knew? Flora could have told her before, giving Marley time to plan, to source the sedative. Fern also discounted Marley because she said she was a good judge of character and didn't believe Marley could have hurt Flora. Yet Fern was wrong about me. Marley was right: I have been trying to worm my way into Flora's family. Maybe Fern is wrong about Marley, too.

There is also Leo – another possible suspect. Fern said she could believe he could have hurt Flora in a violent rage, but not in the calculated way that Flora was strangled. She could be wrong about that, but the police accepted his alibi.

And then there is Fern's bombshell – that Flora may have been abused when she was young. Did it have anything to do with how she died?

I feel like I've been getting to know Flora, through her friends, family, even the glimpses of her in my dreams. What do I know about her? Extrovert. Party girl. Juggling lovers and living in the moment. Being a victim doesn't immediately fit that picture, unless... it was all about denying it ever happened. Always being in control and not letting anyone have power over her, so it couldn't happen again.

EIGHTY-THREE

FERN

I get ready for work quietly the next morning. I leave a note for Saphy with a spare key next to it, repeating the invitation to stay if she'd like to. Then I head across the park and do what I'd decided to do in the middle of a sleepless night: get my phone out, and call Marley.

'Hi, Fern, how're things? Missed saying goodbye last night – didn't see you go.'

'It was a bit sudden. We got some bad news about a friend who died.'

'Oh no, sorry to hear that. Anyone I know?'

'I don't think so. It was one of Flora's recipients, that we had drinks with just days ago. She was injured in a knife attack and then died last night.'

'Oh God, how awful. I'm so sorry.'

'That's not why I was calling, though. There is something I want to ask you.'

'Go ahead.'

'A friend of Flora's recently accused me of causing Flora and Benji's break-up. She thought I'd told Flora I had feelings for Benji, and that was why Flora ended it. The thing is, I didn't. And I doubt Flora would have worked that out for herself, so what I'm wondering is, did you? Tell Flora, I mean?' There's a pause. 'Are you still there?'

'Yes. I am. Sorry. We did have a conversation about you in relation to Benji at one point, but I'm struggling to remember just what was said. Does it matter now?'

'It's just I never thought Flora would do something like that, for me – to spare my feelings. And if she did, did it have anything to do with what ultimately happened to her?'

'Fern, *don't*. Don't think that way. You couldn't have guessed what Benji would do.'

If he did.

'Fern? Are you OK?'

'I don't know. Everything feels mixed up at the moment.'

'It's Saphy, isn't it? You've spent too much time talking to her and she has you doubting things. Don't let her do that to you.'

We say our goodbyes. Marley didn't seem to twig that something happening to one of Flora's recipients might have a wider implication. One thing I'm sure of, though: she was less than forthcoming about what she told Flora in relation to Benji and me. She was the one who convinced Flora to break up with Benji, I'm sure of it.

Marley said Saphy has me doubting things. But is she really worried that I'm doubting *her*?

EIGHTY-FOUR

SAPHY

Fern had left for work by the time I got up. I'd guessed – hoped – that she was the sort of meticulous person who kept a written address book. I was right. I found it tucked in a kitchen drawer, Benji Lawrence's address neatly printed inside.

As my bus gets closer it's getting harder to remember why I ever thought this was a good idea. Benji by all accounts loved Flora. He may well have killed her, too; the police think so. No one knows where I am, where I'm going. He could be dangerous.

I hesitate when the bus approaches the stop for Benji's street; I don't have to do this. I could stay on the bus. Unde-cided, I don't press the bell, but there are people at the stop and the bus pulls in. At the last moment I slip out the door.

It's a row of small, terraced cottages in a pricey postcode. I'm walking slower as I get closer. A loud bang makes me jump and almost scream – a car backfiring, that's all it was.

And there it is – Benji's front door. His cottage has an unloved, unkempt look to it, curtains drawn and the tiny front garden is almost in as bad a state as mine. I'm scared but my curiosity is stronger than my fear. I have to look in his eyes. I have to know what he's done.

Maybe he's not even home.

Open the gate, step through. A few taps of the knocker.

The door opens a moment later.

'Yes?'

It's him – Benji. I recognise him from photos online but he's not looking great. Gaunt. Pale, like he's been avoiding the sun. I know I'm staring but now he is, also.

'Oh my God,' he says. 'Are you Flora's – I mean—'

Ah. The TV interview. 'Yes. I'm her heart recipient.'

'Why are you here?'

'I was hoping I could talk to you.'

'Why?' He looks part bewildered, part angry, and I'm thinking he's going to retreat back inside and slam the door in my face. Instead he shakes his head, stands aside and gestures for me to come in. I do so and he pushes the door shut, trapping me inside and I struggle to hide the fear that floods through me. I shouldn't have come.

We're just standing there, looking at each other – in silence so thick. His eyes hold mine, eyes of the man that Flora loved, and whether it is fear or something else, I'm finding it hard to breathe.

Then he turns away. 'I'll put the kettle on,' he says.

I follow him into the kitchen at the back of the house. Windows open, a mess of a garden beyond. Empty wine bottles stacked on the counter. He sorts cups, teabags, milk and gradually the tension seems less than before. A wry half smile when he puts a cup of tea in front of me.

'I'm just trying to think through my bail conditions, whether you count as friend or family of Flora's.'

'I'm guessing the law hasn't had to tackle this one before.'

'Maybe not. What's your name?'

'Saphy.'

'And I assume you know I'm Benji, accused of the murder that saved your life,' he says, his voice bitter. 'But sorry to disappoint. There's some other murderer out there you need to give a thank you card to, if that's why you're here.'

I shake my head, even though trying to put into words why I came is beyond me just now. Though maybe the best way is to be blunt, go for the shock factor. Watch his reaction.

'Did you hear what happened to the recipient of Flora's corneas?'

He shakes his head, puzzled but not alarmed.

'She was stabbed, in both eyes. And she's died.'

'*What?*' Horror and shock war on his face. 'Seriously?'

'Yes.'

'Why would someone do that?'

'I don't know. But if it's connected to Flora, I'm scared.'

Concern – perfected as bedside manner for patients, or genuine? – I don't know. He's been spikey – awkward – fair enough, in the circumstances. Yet there is still something about him, his eyes and the pain behind them, that draws me, even though I'm unsure what he did or didn't do to Flora. But unless he is a very good actor, he didn't have anything to do with Debra's death.

'Saphy, are you going to tell me why you're really here?'

Because you were a part of Flora's life, whether or not involved in her death. Because I want – *need* – to know everything about her that I can. Did you do it, Benji? Did you strangle Flora?

Before I can try to find words that won't drive him away, there is the sharp *tap tap* of the knocker at his front door.

He walks across to the window in the front room and pulls the curtain aside to look.

'Ah. The police are here. Probably want to ask me how sharp my knives are and if I have an alibi.'

EIGHTY-FIVE

FERN

Our police liaison officer leaves a message on my phone while I'm working: Benji is back in custody for breach of bail conditions. What's he done? I know he's not allowed to have any contact with Flora's friends or family, and now I'm worried someone saw us speaking in his garden a few days ago. But I instigated that; it wouldn't be fair. Is there any point in calling the police to tell them it was my fault? But if they don't know and he breached his bail some other way, telling them may get Benji in more difficulties. And – being honest, at least to myself – I don't want anyone to know what I did. I didn't even tell Saphy when we were talking everything through. Going to see Benji was a betrayal of Flora – at least, that is how most people would see it. Especially my parents.

I've spent most of the day debating whether I should or shouldn't call DCI Jennings, and, if I did, what I should say. I'm no closer to an answer.

EIGHTY-SIX

SAPHY

I'm exhausted: there's been way too much to deal with, for too long. The shock of Debra's death, talking it all through with Fern. Another sleepless night.

And then Benji. The police. They wanted to ask him some questions, they said. Could it be about Debra? But once they worked out who I was, Benji was arrested for breach of bail. Turns out that they did put me in the friends and family of Flora category. I told them it wasn't his fault; he didn't know I was coming. But they didn't seem to care.

And why was I there? They wanted to know.

Curiosity, I said. I know it didn't satisfy them.

Benji's eyes met mine as they took him out – not angry, and he should have been furious. More, resignation. Like what happened to him was of no consequence. Is that because without Flora, nothing else matters?

One of the police drove me home and I'm guessing my neighbours will be all atwitter at that.

I'm so tired that I consider telling Jack not to come. But I want to be with somebody who is just there for me, has nothing to do with Flora, Benji, any of them.

I try for a nap in the Chair of Sleep. It doesn't live up to its name, though I must doze at least a little; it's later than I thought when I hear the approach of Jack's motorbike. He knocks a moment later.

I open the door. 'Hi.'

'Hi. Can I come in?'

I stand aside; he comes in and shuts the door. Hermi isn't locked in the kitchen and gives him side eye that would fell most, but he withstands it with only a flinch. She slinks up the stairs, leaving us alone.

'Sorry I was so crap,' he says.

'Just to see we're on the same page, how were you crap?'

'I left when you were asleep without saying goodbye. Didn't message or answer your message.'

'OK, yes. That was kind of crap. Any particular reason?'

'Yes. But it's hard to explain.' A pause. 'I kind of freaked out.'

'Freaked out, why?'

'You. Us. It was too intense.'

'You felt something, so you ran away?'

'That's a pretty good summary. But I couldn't stay away.'

Does he move, or do I? His hands, light on my waist, thumbs on my hip bones – lips on mine and I'm falling, weak, he with me, and we're on the floor. He's remembering to be careful with me but I don't want him to be and I'm pulling at his clothes, digging my fingernails into his back, my body arching to join his.

It's over – so soon – but it is still perfect. He's sitting up, looking at me, lying there, a smile and I'm smiling back.

'There we go. Being intense, again.'

'Yeah.' I sit up, straighten my clothes, reach a hand to stop him from doing up his shirt, to see his tattoos. I trace the snarling bear on the left side of his chest and shoulder with a fingertip. On the right – over his heart. I draw in a sharp breath. It's a girl with waves of red hair half covering her face. A finger against her lips. Even though you can't see much of her face I have no doubt at all who it is.

'What's wrong?'

I'm afraid, but I have to know. 'Who is this girl?' I say, touching her face on his chest.

'It's just a tattoo.' We're both up now; he's doing up his jeans, his shirt, his face – turned away. Hiding.

'Not just a tattoo. Who was she to you, Jack? Did she break your heart?'

'Shut up.' His hands are on my shoulders now, but not like before – he's holding them so tight it hurts. There is rage in his eyes – his pupils, they're dilated, I didn't notice that before. He doesn't look *right*.

I'm scared now, whether of him or what he might say – if he'll confirm what I know in my gut – but can't stop myself saying the words. 'It was Flora. Wasn't it?'

He lets go. Starts to walk to the door. Opens it, then turns back to me, anger gone now – eyes full of bewildered pain.

'Just tell me one thing. How do you kiss like she did? *How?*'

I don't answer. How can I? I don't know.

He slams the door. His motorbike starts seconds later, roars into the night.

I have a hot shower, a long one. Still I'm shaking. I thought Jack was only here for me, that he had nothing to do with Flora, but I was wrong.

Have I been trying to be Flora and doing it so well that I've started to become her? *I kiss like she did* – that's what he said. Was that the only reason he wanted to kiss me again, after the first time?

Jack loved Flora. Not me, never me.

Am I broken-hearted? No. This was never about love with Jack – not to me, not to Flora. She played with his feelings, didn't she? I'm certain of that, even though I have no way of knowing. And you can't really tell it is Flora in his tattoo, but I know her face so well that I was sure – backed up by his reaction when I asked him.

The night we met, he'd been staring – came over – instigated it all. When he kissed me, I was so close to just leaving with him, without knowing anything about him. Maybe I would have if I hadn't got sick. That is *so* not me – nothing about this thing with Jack was ever me. It's Flora: it must be. Making me do what she wants, the way she would have.

But how did Jack find me in the first place? We met before the interview aired, so he couldn't have identified me from that. Is it some weird karma thing that he just chanced to meet me – the heart recipient of a girl he'd loved? Fuck. It sounds like some B-grade movie, not my life.

I'm losing it. I'm losing me. I thought I wanted to be Flora: beautiful, glamorous, fearless. Who wouldn't? But that wasn't her whole story, and I'm not sure I want to know the rest of it.

I don't want to be her anymore. I want it to stop.

I curl up in bed, alone. Too empty to cry. Too tired to sleep.

It's much later when I hear the faint ringing of my phone. I must have left it downstairs. Who calls in the middle of the night? I go down the stairs. Hermi is there, eyes glowing in the dark, until my hand finds a light switch. It has stopped ringing now. On the screen – it was Jack.

A message pings a moment later.

Please, Saphy – answer. I need to talk to you.

Seconds later it starts ringing again. Don't answer it, I tell myself. Don't.

Another message.

We have to be together. Nothing else makes sense.

And then another:

Answer me!

A moment later:

OK, maybe you're asleep. Call me in the next few minutes or I'll come over.

My phone slips out of my hand to the floor. *Not again.* I don't want to be Flora's plaything anymore. I'm getting out of here.

I run upstairs, throw on clothes, shoes. Pause, listen by the door. It's quiet. No bike in the distance. Open the door and run out into the night.

EIGHTY-SEVEN

FERN

There's a loud knock at the door. It's early. I look through the window to below and fear twists through my gut. It's the police. The last time police came calling, it was because Flora was attacked. It takes me straight back to that moment. I'm nauseous, shaking, as I rush down the stairs to the door, pulling on a dressing gown on the way.

One of them is Harry – the DCI who investigated Flora's murder. I spoke to him the other day about Debra.

'Sorry to disturb you so early, Fern,' he says. 'Can we come in?'

'Of course.' They step through, close the door. 'What's wrong?'

'A young man was stabbed last night. He's in critical condition.'

For a moment I'm puzzled why this has brought them here, and then it hits me all at once. I draw in a sharp breath. 'Was it Liam?'

'He's not conscious but his ID says Liam Flynn. Not official yet.'

All at once I'm dizzy, holding a hand against the wall:

Saphy. Since that interview, everyone knows about her. 'What about Saphy?'

'Officers went to Saphira Logan's house this morning. There was no answer. Concerned for her safety, they tried the door – it was unlocked. Checked the premises and there was no sign of her in or around her property. We spoke to a neighbour, who gave us Saphy's mobile number. It goes straight to message – switched off or out of battery. Is there anything you can tell us about where she might have gone if she has fled?'

'She's been seeing someone; I haven't met him. His name is Jack but I don't know his surname. Maybe she's gone to his?'

'Who might know more about this Jack?'

'Her best friend, Zoe. Zoe Hendricks, I think. I haven't got her number. But Marley – the reporter, Marley Jansen – might. Zoe took part in the interview my parents did with Saphy about organ donation. I could call Marley and ask?'

He nods and I fetch my phone from upstairs and call her. It rings four times, goes to message. 'Answer the phone, Marley. It's urgent.'

I ring again. This time she answers, with a sleepy mumble that might be hello.

'Wake up, it's Fern. Have you got Zoe's number? Saphy's friend. Police need it.'

'What? Yes. I think so, hang on.' She's back a moment later, reads out the numbers. I write them down on a notepad. 'What's going on?'

'I'll explain later. Bye.' I end the call, tear off the note and hand it to Harry.

'We'll find Saphy. In the meantime, if you hear from her or think of anyone else who might know where she is, let us know.'

'Now that two of Flora's recipients have been stabbed, it must have a connection to Flora. And Benji is in custody, isn't he?' He nods. 'So he couldn't have stabbed Liam. You need to go back – look at everyone who was originally a suspect in Flora's case.'

'We're considering all options at this time.'

After they leave, I call home. Thankfully, Dad answers.

'Good morning, Fern. This is early.'

'Yes, well, something has happened.' I fill him in about Liam, that Saphy is missing. 'Do you think Mum needs to know?'

'We'll see if he's named in the news. Thanks for calling. You'll let me know if you hear from Saphy?'

'Of course.'

Marley turns up at the front door soon after.

'Why did the police want Zoe's number? What the fuck is going on?'

'Who's asking? Is it Marley, who loved Flora and is my friend, or Marley, the reporter?' *Or Marley, the murder suspect.*

'Do you really have to ask?'

'I don't know.' I sigh, and remind myself of all the reasons it couldn't be Marley, and high on my list is instinct: it wasn't her. I'm sure of it. 'Sorry. I'm so worried. I told you how one of Flora's organ recipients had been stabbed and died, but I didn't give you the details. She'd had bilateral corneal transplants from Flora. The night she was attacked, someone stabbed her in each eye with a knife.'

This time she gets it. The shock in her widened eyes looks – and feels – genuine. 'I heard about that case – it was Flora's recipient? Oh my God.'

'I told the police Debra's link to Flora – and about Saphy, and the other recipient we met, who had one of Flora's kidneys. Liam. He's a student. Last night, he was stabbed. He's in hospital. And now Saphy is missing.'

EIGHTY-EIGHT

SAPHY

I'm walking. I don't know where I am, what I should do. I can't think straight.

Jack wasn't on Fern's list of possible suspects, but she wouldn't necessarily have known everyone that Flora did. Could it have been him who strangled Flora? I don't know. Maybe. The look in his eyes when he held my shoulders – when I asked if his tattoo was Flora. If just talking about her makes him that furious, who knows what he's capable of? And what about Debra – did he stab her? As soon as I have the thought, I dismiss it. If he wanted to kill Flora's organ recipients he's been alone with me several times. Now I'm remembering all the times he cradled me, a hand on my heart. Feeling it beat. Maybe he was building up to it.

Should I call Fern – ask her if Flora knew Jack?

I can't. I didn't bring my phone and I don't know her number. I don't want to go home to get it, either. What if Jack is there? I don't want to face him alone. That's when I realise: not only did I not think to take my phone, I didn't bring my medications, either. I need to take my morning immunosuppressants at ten—

Wait. Did I remember to take them last night? I was so tired, the evening is a blur. I try and try but can't remember.

Fern is a doctor. Could she get me a new lot of medications so I don't have to go home?

What about Zoe and Claire? She's a nurse; maybe she could help. I almost cry to think of being with them, talking all of this through.

But Jack has met Zoe. What if he tracks her to find me? What if me being there puts Zoe and Claire in danger?

I'm crying. I want my dad. I want him to fix things the way he always could when I was young. I'm longing to be that child again, certain I would always be safe, loved, looked after. Everything has gone wrong since he died.

Thinking of Dad reminds me of Flora's father, Charles. He emailed when we were setting up lunch; I think Fern was copied in. I could email her. Where can I check emails?

A library. I look around, try to register my surroundings. Nothing is familiar. I've been walking for so long – hours, as the sun came up and the day began – paying no attention to where I'm going. I have no idea where I am.

I wipe my face, try to look composed and go in a shop to ask if they know the location of the nearest library. They don't. I try another shop; they think they do, give me directions. I finally find it, try the door but it's locked. I can see a clock through the glass – it's ten to nine. The hours on the door say it will open at nine-thirty. Forty minutes.

There's a bench. I'll wait.

I sit down. The fatigue from another sleepless night is taking hold. I pull my knees up against me, wrap my arms around them. My eyelids are heavy, closing, and I fight to keep them open, to stay aware of my surroundings. Anybody could be looking for me – find me here. I need to stay alert, be ready to run.

Even with my eyes open, I'm drifting. Not awake or asleep

but somewhere in between. Then my eyes close, and I can see more clearly.

It's Flora. She's distressed.

Get up, Saphy. Run, hide; you're in danger. Run...

A distant siren penetrates and my eyes snap open. How long have I been asleep? Stiff, I stretch. The library is open now. I straighten my hair with my hands, go through the doors and to the front desk.

'Hi, is there a computer I can use?'

They get me to fill in a slip with details, point me towards a computer and give me the password.

My hands are shaking so much it takes a few attempts to get the password in correctly, then to sign in to my email. There is an email from Charles – sent just a few hours ago.

I open it.

Hi Saphy, are you OK? Fern told me about Debra. There's been another knife attack last night also, against Liam – Flora's kidney recipient. Fern has been trying to contact you and we're all worried. It might be a good idea to lay low for a while. I've got a safe place you could stay where no one could find you. Just let me know. Wherever you are, I'll come and get you.

Liam, too? *No.* Please, no. He was so young. Funny. I really liked him. Did he survive? Charles didn't say. Tears are rising in my eyes.

I'm not safe. Flora told me to run, hide – she was right.

And Charles – such kindness, offering help to someone he barely knows. And yes, it is complicated by why he knows me, but still. Could this be the solution I'm looking for? Unlike with

Zoe or even Fern, I don't think anyone would expect me to go to Charles. I should be safe with him.

I think for a moment, then hit reply.

> Hi Charles, thank you so much. You might be right – disappearing for a while could be the best thing. I'm in a library just now.

I give the name, the address, from the library letterhead with the computer passwords.

> I left home without taking my medications – I've missed at least one dose of immunosuppressants. Can you replace them?

I spell out what I take as best I can remember.

I send it before I can change my mind. What now? I hit refresh a few times in case he's online now, but nothing.

For distraction, I go through my inbox. Mostly the usual junk, though there is an email from Jenny – sent this morning:

> Hi Saphy, I need to talk to you. It's important. I've tried calling and it goes straight to message. Is everything OK? Please call me.

I haven't known her for long but she is my birth mother; I don't want her to worry. Should I answer? What can I possibly say?

I hit refresh again while I think about it, and this time there is a reply from Charles:

> Hi Saphy, I'm so glad to hear from you. I'll come and get you.
> I should be there in about an hour and a half.

I want to cry, but this time from relief: he's going to help me. What about Jenny? I think for a moment, then send this:

Hi, I'm fine, but I need to get away for a few days. I'll get in touch when I can.

I find Fern's email address in one of Charles' emails, copy her in, and Zoe – and then email Neeha, too, asking her to feed Hermi. Log out of my email and then the library computer. That's it.

All I can do now is wait.

EIGHTY-NINE

FERN

Marley has to leave for a meeting. After she's gone, I try Saphy's number, but as the police said, it goes straight to message. I don't know what to do with myself and feel so useless. I want to find Saphy, help her, but how? I should have noted Zoe's number down twice so I had it, too. I'm about to call Marley to ask for it again when I remember a childhood trick. I take the notepad where I'd written the number for the police, lightly sketch over it with a pencil and can just make out the impressions of the numbers I'd written on the sheet above.

Zoe answers straight away. 'Hello?'

'Hi, it's Fern. I'm hoping you've heard from Saphy?'

'I haven't. Neeha called me, said the police have been looking for her. Then the police called me, too – asking if I know where she is and what I know about Jack. They wouldn't tell me why they're looking for her – just said they're concerned for her welfare. Do you know what's going on?'

'Did Saphy mention about meeting two more of Flora's organ recipients? Both of them have been attacked by someone with a knife in separate attacks in the last few days. One of them has died.'

'*What?* Why would someone do that? Do they think Saphy is in danger?'

'She might be. Were you able to tell the police much about Jack?'

'Not really. I've met him twice, but I don't even know his surname. I've since got in touch with everyone I could think of who goes to the pub where she met him, but no one knew him. Everyone seemed to think he was someone else's friend.'

'That sounds odd. What did you think of him?'

'I wasn't sure. He made me a little uneasy, though I couldn't say why. I thought maybe I was being too protective of Saphy.'

'The knife attacks may have nothing whatsoever to do with Jack; she may be safe with him and there's nothing to worry about.'

'Or maybe he's involved somehow, and she's not safe, at all.' There is silence for a moment. 'I've got her spare key. I'm going over there to see if I can find anything that gives an idea where she might be.'

'I'll come with you.'

'I'll pick you up on the way – give me forty minutes or so.'

After we say goodbye, I get dressed, try to eat, but I can't. I'm pacing, worrying. Where could Saphy be? With the other knife attacks, the victims were found soon after they were stabbed. If anything like that happened to Saphy, we'd know, wouldn't we?

My phone vibrates: an email. It's from Saphy. Relief floods through me, but then I read it. She says she's fine, that she needs to go away for a while. Does she know about Liam? Has she put that together with Debra, and decided the best thing to do is to go away, hide? Is she by herself or with Jack? Jack that she met in a pub, but no one knows who he is.

I email her back – saying I'm worried and asking her to call, tell me where she is. Then I forward her email to Harry.

When Zoe arrives, I show her the email – she was copied in

on it, too.

'It's weird she emailed,' she says. 'She'd always call or message. She never emails me.'

'Maybe she lost her phone, or it's out of charge?'

'But then why wouldn't she say so? I'm not sure I'm reassured.'

'That's what I thought, also. I've sent the email to Harry – the DCI. I'll call him and see what they think.' Instead of going to message, this time he answers.

'Hello, I was just reading your email from Saphy,' he says.

'I'll put you on speaker. I'm with Zoe.'

'Hi, Zoe,' he says.

'Have you found out who Jack is?' Zoe says.

'No.'

'Me neither.' She explains she'd checked with the pub regulars.

'But now we have her email,' he says. 'And Saphy is over eighteen. I understand that you're worried, but if she wants to go away – understandable, in the circumstances – that's up to her.'

'But Saphy never emails me – she always calls or messages,' Zoe says. 'And sure, maybe something has happened to her phone, but why wouldn't she say that in her email? If she was on a computer she could have messaged even if she couldn't have called, and that's what she'd normally do.'

'Are you thinking it might have been faked, sent by someone else?'

'Maybe. I don't know. You're still looking for her, aren't you?'

'Of course.' He has to go, says goodbye. Asks us to let him know if we hear from her.

Zoe's face reflects mine: worried.

'It isn't like Saphy to vanish like this,' she says. 'Something is wrong. I just know it.'

NINETY

SAPHY

An hour and a half, Charles said. There are some comfy chairs
for reading but I don't dare wait in one of them in case I fall
asleep again. I wander, pretend to browse books without even
seeing what they are, regularly checking through the windows
in case Charles arrives early. When it's approaching time, I go
through the first set of double doors at the exit, stay behind the
others, and watch through the glass. I have no idea what kind of
car he'll appear in; I should have asked. A car pulls in front and
I'm about to go out, thinking it might be him, but then two girls
get out and it pulls back to the road.

Soon after, a black Range Rover pulls in. The passenger
side window opens and I can see through to the driver's seat. It's
Charles. He's here. I go through the outer doors and up to the
passenger door, check through again, to make doubly sure.
It's him.

'Hi, Saphy.'

'Hi.' I get in, shut the door, sag back in the seat. 'Thank you.
Thank you so much for coming.' Tears – relief – are rising in my
eyes. I'm not alone anymore.

He reaches a hand across and takes mine. 'It's OK, Saphy.

We'll work this out. I promise.' The way he says the words is so much like the way my dad would say them. A tear spills out, runs down my cheek. He releases my hand, closes the window. Pulls back onto the road.

I fight to regain control. 'Those knife attacks, on Debra and Liam. Who could have done this? Why?'

'I don't know. But I do know that we need to keep you safe while the police work it out. Right?'

'Right. Do you have any news of Liam?'

'Last I heard, he's in hospital. Seriously injured but they're hopeful he'll recover.'

'What now?'

'I've got a place where no one will think to look for you. You'll be safe. You can stay there as long as you like.'

'Thank you. Did you manage to get hold of my medications?'

'Yes. I'll get them out when we stop. You didn't tell anyone I was coming to get you?'

'No, no one. I just emailed a few people who might worry, told them that I was fine and was going away for a few days.'

'Good. Now, try to relax. You look completely exhausted.'

'I am. I've barely slept the last few days.' I'm trying not to yawn as I say that and failing.

'We've got a few hours to drive. Sleep if you can.'

A few hours? Should I wait that long to take my immuno-suppressants? He must think it's OK, and he's a doctor. The movement of the car. Classical music, on low. My eyes close, lulled, safe. Did he say where we are going? Doesn't matter. A few hours means not London. London, where knives seek out any part of Flora still living.

Her heart beats fast as if we are running. She whispers in my ear, low and urgent, but I can't make out the words.

NINETY-ONE

FERN

Zoe pulls up in front of Saphy's house.

'Police said it wasn't locked when they were here – would she go out without locking up?' I say.

'No. Well, not generally. I guess anyone can forget sometimes.'

We get out of the car, try the door. It's locked now.

'Maybe Saphy is home?' I say.

'Or Neeha, her neighbour, has a key – she might have locked it.'

We knock, wait a while – no one comes to the door. Then Zoe gets out her key; we go in.

'Saphy?' she calls out. No answer besides Hermi, meowing for attention.

'What next?'

'You know her better than I do – let's just have a general look around, see if anything seems out of place, unusual?'

'OK.' We look around the lounge room. Hermi is batting at something with her paw, just under the edge of the sofa.

'Have you got something there, cat?' Zoe says, has a look and then holds out Saphy's phone. 'Flat battery.'

We have a look in the dining room, kitchen. Go up the stairs. Her bedroom is a mess, slept in. Bed not made, some clothes on the floor. But no actual sign of a struggle or anything. Nothing unusual in the other bedroom, study, bathroom.

We go up the stairs to the loft. Zoe is ahead of me and she gasps.

'What is it?' She doesn't answer.

I get to the top of the stairs. There's a roll of something – wallpaper? – spread out around the room. Almost covering it are printed images of Flora. Some I recognise, more I don't. Recent ones, from years ago, too.

'Why would she have these?' Zoe says.

'I'm not a psychiatrist, but I've been worried for a while that Saphy focuses too closely on Flora. But this – it's worse than I thought. As if she's obsessed.'

'She'd had a photo of Flora on her phone lock screen. She got all embarrassed and defensive when I asked her why. But this is way beyond a photo on a lock screen.'

'Yes. So Saphy's mental health is in question.'

'Which makes me even more worried.'

'Me too.'

We go back downstairs to the kitchen.

'What now?' Zoe says.

'I don't know. I'll see if she's emailed back.' I check my phone. 'No, no reply.'

'Oh my God,' Zoe says.

'What?'

'Look.' She reaches for a case on the countertop, opens it. 'It's her medications – all set out by day. She wouldn't have gone away without this, not if she's in her right mind.' She looks closer at the days. 'And she didn't have the ones for this morning, or last night. How long can she be without her immunosuppressants?'

'Not long. Even missing a single dose so soon after surgery

gives an increased risk. At first they can treat it, reverse the process. But it might not work if it's been too long since she's taken them.'

I call Harry again; it goes to message. 'I'm at Saphy's house with Zoe. We've found her phone – flat battery. Also, she hasn't taken her medications with her. She could become very ill without them in just days; she could die. Can you ramp up the urgency?'

There are tears in Zoe's eyes. 'She would never go anywhere without them – she knows the risks. I'd been hoping maybe she was just off with Jack and everything was fine. This says everything is not fine.'

'Maybe she'll come back for them. Did you give a description of Jack to the police?'

She nods. 'Not sure it'd help much. All I could really say was that he was fit – well-muscled, but not heavily bulked out – good-looking enough that he turned heads – average height – brown hair. Long enough to tie back but it was loose. He had a pierced eyebrow and some tattoos on the lower part of his neck but I didn't see them well enough to describe them. The only other thing I know about him is that he told Saphy he's a personal trainer and manages a gym.'

Zoe's words might not be enough to recognise him if you didn't know him, but they are connecting in my mind. That could be Leo.

'What is it?' she says.

'Your description – it could be someone I know, an ex of Flora's. And he sort of manages a gym that his parents bought for him.'

'An ex of *Flora*? With Saphy? How?'

'I might be wrong. But his name is Leo, not Jack.'

'Have you got any photos of him?'

Phone out, I'm hunting back but all I can find is one from years ago – teenage Leo. I show it to her.

'It could be him. But I can't be sure.'

'I'll try Marley.' I call her, willing her to pick up.

She answers at the fourth ring. 'Hi, Fern. Any news about Saphy?'

'No. But Zoe has described Jack – someone Saphy has been seeing – and it might be Leo.'

'Fuck. Seriously?'

'Yes. Have you got a photo of Leo you can send me so I can show Zoe? Maybe from that dinner party? I know someone took some, but I can't remember who.'

'I'm not sure. Hang on, I'll check my phone.' There's a pause. 'No. No photos with him from that night. Maybe it was Imogen?'

'Yeah, OK, I'll try her.'

'Let me know.'

'I will. Bye.'

Imogen's phone rings once, twice—

'Hello, Fern? I was just about to call you—'

'Let me go first. You know that dinner party last year – the one where Flora met Benji. Did you take some photos?'

'I think so, but—'

'It's important. Do you have any of Leo? Can you send them across?'

'I will look in a moment, but I need to talk to you. It's about Saphy. I'm really worried about her.'

'Saphy? Do you mean Flora's heart recipient?'

'Yes.'

'How do you know her?'

'Not on the phone. We need to meet up.'

What on earth could it be that she'll only tell me in person? But right now, the photos are more important.

'Listen, Imogen. Saphy is missing and it's possible that she is with Leo. He might be dangerous. I've got Saphy's friend Zoe here, and she met Saphy's boyfriend, Jack. I need a photo of Leo so she can see if he is the same person.'

'Right. I'll look now.' There's a pause. 'Yes. Found a good one, I'll send it now. Let me know what's happening. And I really need to see you – as soon as possible.'

We say goodbye. A photo lands in my messages and I hand my phone to Zoe. She looks carefully.

'It's him. It's Jack. I'm sure of it. So, an ex-boyfriend of Flora has started seeing Flora's heart recipient, Saphy, under an assumed name. If that's not suspicious as fuck, what the hell is?'

'I'm calling the police.' It goes to message again and I swear. 'Harry, we've identified Jack as being Leo Baldwin – he's been seeing Saphy under an assumed name and is an ex of Flora's. Call me.'

My phone rings as soon as I end the call – Marley, wanting to know if we've found a photo of Leo for Zoe to check.

'Imogen sent a photo and Leo is Jack, Zoe is sure. I've called the police – left a message.'

'Fuck that,' Marley says. 'Let's go there.'

'To Leo's?'

'I dropped him off a few times, I know where it is. I'll come and get both of you.'

NINETY-TWO

SAPHY

I stir, open my eyes – groggy, confused for a moment, not sure where I am or what is going on. I'm in a car? It's slowing. Charles is driving. It comes back now. I stretch. We're on a narrow lane, fields all around. The smell of the sea?

'Ah, you're awake. We're almost there.'

'Are we near the sea?'

'It will appear past the next bend.' He's right. We're at the top of a hill, blue in the distance below. The lane dips down and it disappears again. After what must be a few more miles he pulls in by a gate, enters a code to unlock it and we go through. He gets out to lock it behind us. We go down a long driveway to a cottage.

'We really are in the middle of nowhere.'

'Absolutely.' He parks in front of the cottage. The sky is pulling in, heavy. Much colder than it has been. He gets out and comes around while I'm still undoing my seat belt. Offers an arm and we go to the front door. He unlocks it.

'We'll need to get provisions tomorrow. I did bring some milk and bread so we can at least have tea and toast.' We go through to a hall, bedrooms off the sides of it. Stairs up to an open-plan kitchen and lounge above.

There's a balcony and I open the door, step out. I can just see the stretch of blue beyond it before clouds obliterate the view. The wind is picking up and I'm shivering. I go back inside and shut the door.

'The kettle is on,' he says. 'Best take your immunosuppressants now.' He hands me a glass of water and the capsules, already out of the blister pack.

I swallow them down. 'You do have more?'

'Of course. I'll just keep them safe.'

What an odd thing to say, though it's true that I'm not very with it at the moment. Perhaps he's just being careful. I'm about to ask him where they are when a rush of understanding hits my befuddled mind. Family cottage, Dorset. Where Marley drove Flora, and Benji found her, close to death.

Charles has gone back to the kitchen, pours the tea. Stirs in milk and then holds out a mug but I don't take it.

'Is this the place? Where Flora...'

My words trail off but he doesn't seem to need more. He nods, sadness etched in the lines of his face. 'Yes. It's hard to be here, but it was the logical place to hide you away. No one would think to look for you here.' He hesitates. 'I didn't tell you ahead of time where we were going; I was hoping you wouldn't realise. I didn't want to add any more worry or distress when things are so hard for you just now.'

He holds the tea out again. I take it, hands greedy for its warmth even though I'm in shock at where we are. It must be so much worse for him, and he's doing this for me.

'I'm sorry. I know you're helping me and I'm grateful for that.'

'Despite the circumstances and the venue, I'm glad to have some time with you, Saphy. There is something I've been wanting to tell you for a while.' He gestures at the sofa and we sit there together.

He looks troubled, serious. Despite everything – I'm curious.

'I'm not sure where to start,' he says. 'I want to get this right.'

'Whatever it is – I'm listening.'

He nods. 'Well, here goes. Quite a few years ago, Margot and I were having a few problems – not that that is an excuse – and I had an affair. I'm not proud of that. But my girlfriend got pregnant. She had a baby girl, and I'm very proud of her, indeed.'

I don't understand why he's telling me this. And then something about the way he is looking at me – he doesn't mean—

'What are you saying?'

'Saphy, you were that baby. I'm your father.'

NINETY-THREE

FERN

Marley parks a few doors down from Leo's and we go on foot. Leo's bike is out front. I go to the door, knock – Zoe and Marley hang back so he won't see them at first. I knock – knock again. He's not answering. I get my phone out – message him.

It's Fern. I'm at your front door – it's important. I need to talk to you.

There are some sounds inside; the door opens. I'm shocked when I see him, dishevelled, face pinched with dark circles. His eyes, they're wrong – he's using again.

'Why are you here?' he says.

Zoe steps around from the side. 'Hi, Jack. Or should I say Leo?' He looks past her – sees Marley, standing further back, phone in her hand.

'Marley, too? It's the three musketeers. Have you got the police on speed dial there, mate?'

Marley waggles her phone. 'I'm always prepared,' she says. 'I should have been a Boy Scout.'

'Where is Saphy, Leo?' I say.

'I wish I bloody knew. Went round there early this morning – she was gone.'

'You don't mind if we come in, have a look around, do you?'

He shrugs, stands back from the door. 'Be my guest.'

Marley stays outside, phone in hand – ready to call the cavalry if anything goes wrong. Zoe comes in with me. It's a mess, rubbish everywhere.

We quickly check all the rooms – in wardrobes, even under beds. She's not here.

'Tell me one thing,' I say. 'How did you meet Saphy?'

'Just happened into a bar, and there she was.'

'Leo – come on.'

'Are you sure you really want to know? You told me about the interview. I followed you to Sky and then waited to see who came out. And there she was. I followed her until I had a chance to meet her, at that pub.'

He looks at me again, frowns as if something just connected. 'What's going on? Why are you looking for Saphy?'

'She's missing.'

'And straight away, you thought of me? That I had something to do with it?' He swears, punches the wall. Through the plaster. His knuckles are bleeding. 'I couldn't hurt her, Fern. I could never hurt her.' And tears are running down his face, but the way he said it – like he wanted to hurt her, but couldn't.

'The police will want to talk to you. You went to Saphy's last night, didn't you? You might be the last one who saw her.'

'Fuck the police – they're clueless. They couldn't work out who hurt Flora.'

Leo *hated* Benji. If there is anyone he'd rather see rotting in prison, it's him.

'You don't think it was Benji?'

'I fucking know it wasn't Benji. It's in the eyes, or it isn't. He didn't have it in him to hurt anyone. But the police wouldn't listen to me, would they?'

He pushes past us. Gets on his bike and disappears with a roar up the road.

The police finally arrive. We tell Harry how we worked out that Leo was Jack and everything else; he's unhappy with us coming here like this without waiting for them. He wants to both search the property more closely and find Leo and question him.

But they won't find any traces of Saphy here. Leo might have tracked Saphy down and then lied about his name for whatever reason, but I'm sure he wasn't lying now. He doesn't know where she is.

NINETY-FOUR

SAPHY

I stare at Charles in shock. Did he really say what I think he did?

'It's true, Saphy. I'm your father.'

I can't take this in, what it means, what it meant all those years ago. He groomed Jenny, that's what she said – she was a *child* – and he's my father? He doesn't know that I know Jenny and what happened to her. If he did, he wouldn't have said.

'Saphy? I know this is a shock. I'm sorry I haven't been there for you all these years. But I'm here now.'

I'm overwhelmed, confused, struggling to put things together.

'That means that Flora was my sister? Half-sister, I mean. And Fern, too?'

He nods. 'Yes. But they don't know; neither does Margot. We'll have to find a way to tell them.'

He wants to tell his family about me, and to be there for me now. He's looking into my eyes so earnestly and I'm both drawn and repelled. Drawn, as now I am what I always wanted to be: part of Flora's family. Repelled, because of what he did to Jenny.

'I know this is a lot to take in,' Charles says. 'Especially on top of everything else. You look exhausted. Why don't you have a nap before dinner, such as it is?'

'Yes. That's a good idea. Thank you.'

'There are three bedrooms – take your pick.'

I go back down the stairs. There are, as he said, three bedrooms. A bathroom. The largest bedroom – it has a bed with posts on the four corners. Was this where Flora was tied up? It must be.

Flora, my sister.

I back out, go to the bedroom that is the furthest away. Shut the door, curl up on the bed, hugging a pillow against me.

Try to close my eyes but all I can see is Flora. Images of her spin through my mind, along with a kaleidoscope of the things I know – the guesses, too.

There is something there, an almost understanding. But it stays just beyond my grasp.

NINETY-FIVE

FERN

Marley drops Zoe back to get her car, then takes me to meet with Imogen. I'd agreed to come in case whatever it is she wants to tell me might help us find Saphy.

I walk into her gallery. Imogen motions for me to come through the staff room door, closes it behind us.

'Now what is it you couldn't say over the phone?'

'Saphy is my daughter.'

'*What?*' I don't know what I was expecting, but that wasn't it.

'When I was younger, I went by Jenny, short for Imogen. Is that familiar to you, Fern?' I'm frowning, trying to pull it from my memory. 'I'll help you. My mother was Becky Turner.'

'Our last housekeeper?'

'That's right. I used to play with you sometimes when you were little.'

Now that she's said, I can recognise her, a little. Her hair is so different – everything – but I can see that it is her. 'I hadn't made the connection. But I think I remember you, now.'

'Fern, I'm sorry. This will come as a shock.' There is a sink-ing, sick feeling in my stomach before she says the words. 'Charles – your dad – is Saphy's father.'

I'm staring back at her, not just shocked but horrified. Is it true? How old was Imogen, or Jenny as she was then? School uniforms, I remember. It can't be, it *can't*.

Imogen's face shows compassion. 'It's true. Saphy is our daughter. I recently found out from the adoption agency that, according to their records, my representative requested her adoptive parents call her Saphira. Not a binding request but they honoured it. But I didn't have a representative and I never made that request. Also, I never received letters that were written to me by Saphy's adoptive parents – again, the representative I didn't have gave them the address to send the letters. It was a post office box that has since closed. I didn't know at the time, but just found out from my mum that it was your dad who arranged the private adoption. Mum didn't know he was my baby's father, she just thought he was being helpful.' There is so much repressed rage in her voice as she says that word. 'He must have set things up, received the letters. He must have known Saphy was his daughter. When I saw the interview on TV and realised Saphy was Flora's heart recipient, I didn't know what to do, what to say. Whether I should tell her or not. What it meant. I convinced myself it might be some random coincidence – that Flora was an organ donor and when they tried to match her to a recipient, they found Saphy – understandable that Flora was a good match, as they are half-sisters. But what if there was more behind all this?'

'I don't understand what you're getting at,' I say, but do I? I'm pushing it away, looking for the lie that makes the whole thing tumble down. 'If you have all this history with our family, how did Flora end up working for you? It couldn't be a coincidence.'

'That I can explain. I sought Flora out, got her to know her and then offered her the job. I wanted to hate her, to use her to find out things about Charles. To discredit him. But I couldn't hate her. Not when we may have both been victims of the same man.'

No. I can't hear this; I don't believe it. 'You're saying... Dad... abused Flora?'

'I said *may have*. She wouldn't confirm or deny that it was him. Take that how you like. But Saphy is missing. I'm scared for her if she's with him.'

NINETY-SIX

SAPHY

I finally give up trying to sleep under this roof, between walls that feel like they are closing in on me. Despite the cold, I open the window wide, but it doesn't help. I get up, go through the front door to outside – breathe in deep and try to calm my thoughts.

Shadows are lengthening. There's the feel of a storm coming. I'm shivering, the chill shaking off exhaustion and focusing my thoughts.

Charles. Jenny. She was fourteen years old. That makes him a paedophile, the worst excuse for a human being. And he wants to be in my life, as my father? Flora is gone now, but this is her family – what I thought I wanted. I'd have a claim to it all, but how could I stand to be around him, knowing what he did?

'Where are you going?' Charles says. He came up behind me so quietly, I almost screamed with fright to hear his voice.

'Nowhere. I mean, I was just having a look around.'

'Come inside,' he says. 'It's too cold for a ramble. Maybe tomorrow.' He hooks my arm on his, leads me back to the house. Shuts the door. Locks it and puts the key in his pocket.

He gestures for me to go up the stairs ahead of him, then to take a seat at the dining table. There's red wine, already poured into two glasses.

'I found some tins in a cupboard. I hope beans on toast are OK.'

'Of course. Though I'm not very hungry.'

'You've had a few shocks recently, and you've got to keep your strength up. You're still recovering.'

He's got that doctor bedside manner down perfectly, the right balance of sympathy and expertise that should make me feel better and cared for, but it doesn't. Fern has a doctor mask, too. Like she did that day I asked her about Benji. Something to hide behind but I'm not going to let him hide any longer.

'Charles, can you tell me about my mother?'

'She was a lovely girl. She didn't want to be a parent, that's all. I think I need to respect her privacy.'

A lovely *girl* and that is just the problem. 'I've met my birth mother – Jenny Turner. She never told me who my father was, but she told me she was only fourteen when it started with him. Fifteen when she got pregnant.'

'That's not true, and that isn't your mother's name. How did you meet her?'

'Through the adoption agency.'

'There's been some mistake, I promise you.' His face is so open, honest. His eyes are compelling and say *trust me*. But it was the adoption agency who put me in touch with Jenny; they confirmed she was my mother, even though they couldn't explain the missing letters. And there was Jenny's sister, who looked so like me. Had a congenital heart problem like I did. If Jenny is my mother – and I'm sure she is – then he's lying.

Being here feels so *wrong*, and it isn't just being in this house, where Flora was strangled. It's Charles, too. Locking the door and pocketing the key. Keeping my medication *safe*, safe from what? I'm a prisoner and the jailer has the drugs that keep me alive. But even as I think that I discount it, push it away. Why would he do that? It doesn't make sense.

If I'm not a prisoner, I should be able to borrow his phone. Send a quick message to my friends.

'Can I borrow your phone? I need to let Claire and Zoe know I'm OK.'

'I'm afraid not. I was rushing and forgot to bring a charger, it's flat.' He's making toast, stirring beans, and he's lying again. Isn't he? Because he's not sure if I believed him about Jenny.

'How about I go and charge it in your car?'

'Dinner's almost ready now. We can do that later.' He looks at me searchingly. 'Don't look so worried, Saphy. I know the last few days have been difficult for you, but I promise you: no one will find you here.'

A promise, or a threat?

I manage some beans on toast. Some conversation, too, as if by rote, but I can only half hear what he is saying. Part of me is still turning things over and over again in my mind, trying to make sense of everything.

Things we know, things we guess. Fern told me that a friend of Flora's said Flora had been abused. Fern thought if it was true that it must have been someone at Flora's boarding school. That whoever it was couldn't have had anything to do with her death, because how would they know she was about to talk about it now, so many years later?

But that was just a guess. One Fern might have wanted to make because the other possibility was too horrible for her to contemplate.

What if it wasn't someone at her school? What if, instead, it was someone far closer to home? Someone who would have a lot to lose if Flora spoke out.

I gasp in shock, stare at Charles.

'What's wrong, Saphy?' A mild voice, watchful eyes. I

shouldn't let him know what I've worked out, but I can't hide the horror from my face or stop the words that spill out.

'It was you – you strangled Flora. Your own daughter!'

'Me? Of course not. Why would I do that?'

'You're lying! It was you. It was thinking about what you did to Jenny that made me realise. You raped Flora when she was a child, didn't you? Then you strangled her all these years later to stop her from telling anybody.'

He's not shocked; he's not reacting in outraged disbelief. He's thinking, trying to work out how to explain it all away and I wish, so much, that he could. Make it all be a lie. Be my dad, my family. But he can't.

'I'd have done anything for Flora. *Anything*. But she didn't understand true love, or family loyalty. And I did it for you, too. You needed a heart that matched. But it was all for nothing, wasn't it?' He shakes his head, regret in his words, how he says them.

We're in the middle of nowhere.

Now his eyes are cold. 'I really wish you hadn't worked that out.'

A place where no one will think to look for you.

'What am I going to do with you?'

No one will find you here.

NINETY-SEVEN

FERN

I ask Imogen to give me a moment alone. She goes back through to the gallery. There are so many things spinning around in my mind and I want to scream, *no, no*. Saphy is Imogen's daughter? I swallow. And she says Dad... when she was a schoolgirl? That'd make Saphy my half-sister. And then what she said about Dad, and Flora.

It can't be true, any of it. Can it?

But what if it is?

Is there anything that corroborates what Imogen has said? I'm thinking back, to every moment with Dad and Saphy when she came for lunch. Any sign that he looked at her like his daughter. Instead, what I remember is that there was something odd, about her name – but it was Mum who raised it. I'll ask her. Which reminds me: does she know about Liam? If she does, she'll be in a panic about Saphy. For now, I won't mention him or that Saphy is missing unless she does.

I call her.

'Hi, darling.'

'There is something I need to ask you about Saphy.'

'What's that?'

'Her name – Saphira. I remember you asking her about her name at lunch that day. Was there a reason why that name was important to you?' There is silence. 'Mum?'

'It's painful. I lost a baby when you were small. She was stillborn. We called her Saphira. It was such a strange coincidence that she had the same name.'

My stomach is twisting. It can't be a coincidence, not with such an unusual name: it must have been Dad that requested that name – replacing the daughter he'd lost. It backs up part of what Imogen said and if it does that, what of the rest of it?

'By the way, darling, I just had the strangest call from Leo.'

'Leo? What about?'

'He demanded to speak to Charles, and when I told him he wasn't here, he was so rude.'

'Where is Dad?'

'Some medical conference asked him to speak last minute after another speaker pulled out.'

'I need to speak to him – do you know which conference?'

'No idea. Try his phone, darling.'

'Will do, thank you. When did Leo call?'

'Just a few minutes ago.'

We say our goodbyes and I sit there, staring at my phone. Numb.

I force myself to think what to do next.

Dad told Mum he was going to a medical conference. A quick search: I can't find any likely conferences he could be attending just now. Where is he?

Could Saphy be with Dad? She was scared, because of what happened to Debra and Liam. She might have turned to him for help. Where would they go?

A shiver runs through me.

Someplace no one would find them: our cottage in Dorset. The one Mum keeps pushing Dad to sell, since we'd never use it again after what happened to Flora there. The one place nothing needs booking; there is no one to see who is there or ask questions. It's isolated, no neighbours.

I leave the office, go to Imogen.

'I've thought of a place Saphy might be – I'll try to find her.'

'You'll let me know?'

'Of course.'

Quick goodbyes and I rush out the front, call Marley. Hope she hasn't given up waiting.

She answers.

'We've got to go to the cottage in Dorset. Now.'

'Why? What's going on?'

'I think Dad might have taken Saphy there. And Leo might have gone after them.'

Everything is running through my mind as I rush to the end of the road where Marley said she'll come for me.

Is Saphy my half-sister?

There were echoes of Flora in her. I'd convinced myself it was just her hair, what she was wearing – that I was seeing things that weren't there.

Could Dad... could he have abused Flora like that? I'd always been jealous of Flora. The pretty one who always got Dad's attention away from me. I tried, so hard, to please him – to get his approval. Nothing I did ever seemed good enough.

I'd thought Flora's attack couldn't have had anything to do with the childhood sexual abuse Imogen claimed happened – that if it happened at all, it must have been at her boarding school, and how could anyone from back then have known if Flora was about to talk? But if it was Dad... maybe she said something, so he either knew, or suspected. Maybe that is the reason why everything was so strained at Christmas. Just days before she was strangled.

Everything around me is dissolving; nothing is sure. I swapped shifts with Benji – family synched calendar, Dad would have known I was filling in for someone. He called, didn't he? What did I tell him? I can't remember. I can't. Did he work out from what I said that Flora had gone to Dorset, and when Benji might arrive? I don't know. Maybe.

Saphy needed a transplant to survive. Dad probably knew about her heart condition from the letters written by her adoptive parents. After that, he must have been tracking her medical history – either he knew one of her doctors, or he found a way to access her NHS records. He knew Saphy would die without a transplant. And Flora – her half-sister – was a perfect match.

The police thought whoever strangled Flora had meant to kill her. That has always bothered me – what was done to her was too precise.

Maybe, they're wrong. Maybe it was timed and done deliberately to put her beyond reach, but not dead. Perfect for organ donation.

NINETY-EIGHT

SAPHY

I run down the stairs, trip and come down hard on my ankle, fall and sprawl on the floor below. The pain is so intense I almost pass out but I push it away. I remember now that the front door is locked. But the window – I left it open in the back bedroom. It's dark. The wind is howling; we're miles from anywhere. But I have to try. I try to stand and cry out in pain.

Charles follows more slowly down the stairs.

'We can do this the easy way, or the hard way. Your choice. I've got pills you can swallow and gently drift away.'

'Why make it easy for me? You didn't make it easy for Flora.' I lunge down the hall but he grabs my hair, jerks me back.

'The hard way, then,' he says. His hands are closing around my throat, pressing and constricting and I'm struggling with all the strength I have but it isn't enough. Everything is starting to fade.

He lets go. I fall back, gasping, coughing, not understanding, but then see someone else is here now. It's Jack. Did he get in through the window? He's pulled Charles away from me – they're struggling, fighting. Charles is bigger, taller, but Jack is younger, stronger. Full of fury. He slams Charles into a hall window and it shatters, glass everywhere. Charles is stunned, his body going slack.

'You bastard,' Jack says. 'I was listening. I heard what you said upstairs. I'd only suspected – you'd already be dead if I'd known what you did to Flora.'

Jack punches Charles in the face – hard. The crunch of bones. Blood.

I have to get away. I crawl, through shards of glass, to the back bedroom. I manage to pull myself up and through the open window at the back – and fall to the ground in the night.

NINETY-NINE

FERN

Marley is breaking speed limits by a huge margin.

'Tell me again why you think Saphy and your dad have gone to the cottage in Dorset, and that Leo is on his way there. Because nothing you've said so far has made any sense.'

'I don't know if it's true.'

'If what is true?'

'About Dad. And Flora.' I fill in what Imogen told me, and she's swearing, driving even faster.

'If it's true I'll fucking kill him myself. But how does Saphy fit into all of this?'

'She's his daughter, too. My half-sister.'

'*What?*'

I explain – about Imogen. How young she was when she had Saphy. 'All of this is from her – she could be delusional and none of it is true. I don't know. But Saphy's name backs up her story.' I explain about the stillborn baby with the same name.

'And Leo?'

'He called Mum, demanded to know where Dad was.'

'And you think that he might have connected the same dots and is heading there, too?'

'Exactly.'

'So, either your dad is a paedophile and raped Imogen and Flora,' Marley says, and I flinch. 'Or he isn't, he just took Saphy away to keep her safe, but Leo is going to kill him because he thinks he's to blame for Flora's death.'

'That's it.'

'And you called me instead of the police, because?' She holds up her hand. '*Don't* answer, I get it.'

'Slow down, we're nearly there.'

Leo's bike is here, against the fence by the gate. He must have climbed over it and walked down. I rush to enter the code to unlock the gate and we speed down the long driveway.

A car is parked to the side of the cottage. 'That's Dad's car,' I say when we're close enough to see the reg. The front door is damaged, hanging at an odd angle. Light spilling out. We rush through the door and check every room – no one is here. But there's broken glass, blood, from a smashed window in the hall. What's happened? Where are they?

'Headlights,' Marley says. She gets back in her car and does a slow spin to point her high beams along fields, then the cliffs past the cottage. *There*: figures moving, struggling, by the cliff. Outlined in light.

Fear and pain twist in my gut so much I can hardly breathe. I start to run toward them. Hear Marley's footsteps coming behind me – car lights left on and showing the way. She's swearing, says there is no signal to call the police.

It's Leo and Dad. Leo has him in a chokehold, blood dripping down Dad's face. Leo is blinking in the light from Marley's car, squinting.

'It's me, Leo – Fern. Let him go.'

'He deserves to die! He killed Flora! And he tried to kill Saphy. And that's not all.' And now Leo is saying things I don't want to hear, to believe – what he did to Flora. When she was a child.

'Dad? Is it true?'

'None of it,' he says. 'Don't listen to him – he's lying.'

My father. The one I always wanted to impress, but somehow never quite managed to, did I? It was all Flora in his eyes. But I was the lucky one.

Dad's eyes are fixed on mine, sure of me, my loyalty. After all, he could always make me believe anything – make me do anything. How could I have been so stupid? He's still protesting, choking on his blood.

'Stop lying! I don't believe you. How could you? Your own daughter!' Grief, shock, rage flood through me. But rage is winning.

'And now he's going to die,' Leo says, and he's pulling Dad to the edge of the cliff.

'Don't do this, Leo. Think of yourself. What good is it if you're in prison the rest of your life? You don't deserve that.'

'Yes, I do. I deserve worse! I was going to kill Saphy – to give the police a reason to look at Flora's case again and nail this prick's ass to the wall. I couldn't do it. But I followed her – when you met that woman with Flora's eyes. That student, too. I did it, Fern – I stabbed both of them. I didn't mean for her to die, I swear it. But she did. And now we're going to go to hell together.'

They're at the edge of the cliff. I should try to stop Leo, say something, go to them, anything – but I'm frozen in horror, can't move, can't think—

Another step – they're gone. There is a strangled scream – which of them, I don't know. An impact on the rocks below. And then silence.

Marley must have found a phone signal. She's calling the police.

Daddy? You really did all those horrible things? So many memories, good and bad, are whirling around inside of me, and the worst pain of all: I didn't save Flora. I failed her, again and again.

My feet want to take me to the edge of the cliff, whether to see if they're dead or join them.

But then I remember: I have another sister.

Where is Saphy?

ONE HUNDRED

SAPHY

I'm cold, so cold. The stars in the sky above me move and shift like a kaleidoscope, in and out of clouds. Focus, instead, on the ground. I have to get away. There's a steep path behind the cottage. I can't walk; I crawl. Grass and scrub become grit and rocks. My hands and knees are cut, bleeding, but Flora is urging me on and I can't stop. But it isn't the Flora I've felt I was getting to know. Instead, it is Flora, the child. The terrified child. But she was always hidden inside, wasn't she?

Never again. Make it stop.

I'm more Flora than Saphy now, sobs shaking through my body. The path goes down, down. Rocks give way to sand and the breeze off the sea carries salt and more sand that stings against my face.

'Saphy? Saphy!' Voices carried on the wind from above.

Clouds shift; moonlight dances on the water. 'I think I see her!' A distant cry. Footsteps pound down the path behind me but I'm at the water's edge now. So cold. It will wash it all away, make me clean again.

'Saphy! It's safe now – come back.' It's Fern's voice and I want to believe her, but I can't.

'No! You left me. I don't trust you anymore.' The waves splash over me, support me, too, feet off the sand below. Lying on my back and looking at the stars. Then hands grab me, pull, and I'm struggling, going under. Coughing and choking.

'I'll never leave you again, I promise. I love you, Flora.' It's Fern who is holding me now.

I'm wracked with sobs. 'I love you, too. But he'll never leave me alone.'

'He'll have to now. He's gone. He's dead.'

'Dad? He's dead?'

'I promise.'

The fight is slowly leaving me, the cold taking hold. Fern is dragging me through the water, to the beach, saying she's sorry, over and over again.

'I forgive you,' I whisper, and slump in her arms.

Flora's arms are around me, too – the woman and the child, whole and together again. *Hang on*, she whispers. *Hang on.*

ONE HUNDRED ONE

FERN

Saphy is air-lifted to hospital and I go with her. I'd promised her that Dad was dead, without knowing for certain – but I was right. Leo, too.

Mum comes to join me, holds my hand while we wait. Zoe and Imogen are here, too. I know Marley told all three of them the basics of what has happened. There is so much pain and confusion in Mum's eyes, but the past can wait. I retreat into what Benji used to call doctor brain: listing details, treatments, numbers, reducing the life-or-death moment to all the minutiae. In Saphy's case, cuts and blood loss from the glass she crawled through. A broken ankle. Concussion. Hypothermia. Bruising around her neck and a multitude of more minor bruises and scrapes that still pose serious infection risk to a heart transplant recipient. Rejection episode, too, after missing several doses of her immunosuppressants. I'm going through how each can be treated in an attempt to hold my emotions at bay, but it's not working. I need Saphy to live. I need to have saved one sister, to save myself.

It's approaching dawn when one of her doctors comes to see us. I've been that doctor so many times. I search his exhausted face for answers as we listen. Body temperature stabilised, vitals going well. Broken ankle set. Optimistic rejection caught in time. Some of the deeper cuts needed stitches. Intravenous antibiotics to fight any infections. I sift through all he said, looking for the 'but' and not finding it. And that's when I can finally cry.

ONE HUNDRED TWO

SAPHY

Hushed voices. Footsteps, beeps and other rhythmic machine noises. I'm in a hospital? My thoughts feel sluggish, confused, and then everything rushes back at once. Charles – his hands, around my neck – pain, fear. Flora, the terrified child. A scream is rising inside but when I open my eyes, Fern is sitting next to me.

'Hush. You're safe now, Saphy.' She's holding my hand.

My eyes dart side to side. 'Charles?'

'He's gone – he's dead.'

'How? Jack – he was there. Jack saved me?'

'He did. But the rest is a story for another time.'

Gradually my breathing is calming, details coming back. Flora – taking over. Running away so it could never happen again. The cold sea.

I'm crying. 'I'm so sorry...'

'Why are you sorry?'

'He was your father.'

'Do you know...' Her words trail off.

'That he was my father, too? Yeah. He told me. If he hadn't, I wouldn't have ever worked out what he'd done to Flora.'

'Are you sorry he's dead?' Fern says.

'No.'

'Neither am I. I'm sorry for what you and Flora went through. I'm not sorry he's paid for what he did, what he tried to do.' There is so much pain behind her words. I know she means what she says, but it's not as simple as that. It never can be. Not when she's lived all her life with him, part of her family.

'Benji will be free now. Won't he?'

'Yes. Marley has spoken to the police on the scene already. They want to interview both of us. Once they know what really happened to Flora, they'll have to drop the charges against Benji.'

'She was there, with me.'

'Flora?' I nod, and Fern's eyes: she believes, or she wants to. 'And now? Where is she now?'

'She said she forgave you, then she slipped away soon after. I don't think she's coming back.'

Fern's tears fall now, with mine.

* * *

It's a few days before I can leave the hospital. Even before then, I start writing, filling page after page. The urge to write has been growing since my transplant, and now I know the story I want – *need* – to tell. Ours. Three sisters who became two, but Flora will always be part of us.

Faced with dying that night, one thing became so clear: I don't want to die. I want to *live* and breathe and experience everything I can, as long as I can. Despite the uncertainty with my health and grieving my parents; despite the horror of knowing what Charles did, and that Flora died, at least partly because of me.

Stories like Flora's need to be told. No one – not her father, a boyfriend or any other man – ever owned her. Girls and women need to *know*: that they can be heard. They can survive.

And this is for Flora – to finally set her free.

EPILOGUE

FERN

'Are you sure about this?' I'm looking up at the fastest zip wire in the world, people ahead of us hurtling along – Saphy's idea of the best way to mark the day.

'You're not going to chicken out, are you?' Marley says.

'No way.'

'That's the spirit,' Saphy says, then holds up a hand for a group high five: us three and Zoe, Claire, Neeha, Imogen and Mum, all along for this girls' weekend in Wales.

It's the one-year anniversary of Saphy's heart transplant. The year mark is a big deal with transplant recipients: make twelve months and things are looking good for the future. She wasn't sure if it was right to celebrate this – it's also a year since we lost Flora. But we talked it through and agreed: to celebrate Saphy's life and Flora's memory, together.

Benji was released, the charges against him dropped. But he's gone. He said he couldn't stay, not after everything that happened. He's left the UK, joined a medical charity. Working in war zones to save other people, because he couldn't save Flora.

I'm so glad Marley and Saphy are friends again. Marley was key to us being there in time to save Saphy from the sea, and anyway, Marley can't complain about Saphy trying to be part of Flora's family anymore – because she actually is.

Far harder was mending my relationship with Mum. She told me things I never knew, like why she quit garden designing – so that she could always be there for Flora. To stop her being alone with Dad. The same reason she sent Flora to boarding school. Mum knew, and didn't do anything? She insisted that she didn't, that she suspected, but when she confronted Dad and he denied everything, she believed him. I know better than most how manipulative he could be – how he could make you believe almost anything. But she couldn't have been convinced, not completely, or why the boarding school? But the guilt was killing her enough. I didn't need to add to her pain. I told her I forgave her, even though I wasn't sure if I did. She's been drinking less since then, as if having everything out in the open has eased her. But I know we both failed Flora.

Saphy's obsession with Flora, her insomnia and all the stress and fear, brought on a psychotic break that night – where she really thought she was Flora. She recovered once she knew Dad was dead, though I know Saphy believes Flora was really with her that night. I'm a doctor: I believe in science and things I can test and measure. But the way Saphy spoke to me that night? It was with Flora's voice – not as an adult, but from so many years ago – and there, in that moment, I believed. Now, of course, I can explain it: I needed Flora's forgiveness. I projected that onto Saphy. Made myself believe that Flora, whether her ghost or some other form of consciousness, was there, and could grant it.

But I'll never forgive myself. Leo was right. Flora had been coming back from her coma, bit by bit, becoming more and more aware. She was paralysed and that was unlikely to change, but you could ask her questions and she'd blink once for yes, twice for no. Whether her memory was intact enough to name her attacker, we'll never know. She didn't get a chance.

Dad convinced me Flora wouldn't want to live the way she was. Freedom was so important to her – how could she bear to linger on and on, silent and paralysed? He said it was an act of love and mercy to set her free. I slipped the drugs he gave me into her IV to depress brain stem function. It was a medical puzzle to give her just enough that she'd fail the brain stem tests, but not too much, to keep her organs healthy for transplant. Dad was insistent on Flora being an organ donor. I didn't question that at the time – it's the right thing to do – but he had a reason beyond general altruism: Saphy.

Did Flora say something to him that made him realise she was going to tell Benji what he'd done to her? Did he strangle Flora to keep her quiet, or to provide a heart for his other daughter? Or maybe even both. That must have been another medical puzzle: how long to cut off blood to Flora's brain to put her in a coma, but not actually kill her.

Dad had the letters that should have gone to Imogen – we found the originals in his things. I can't reconcile the father who abused and strangled Flora with the one who went to such lengths to name, monitor and eventually save the life of another daughter. And then he tried to kill her, because she worked out what he'd done to Flora. It's like, to him, we weren't human beings in our own right – we were his creations, to do with as he willed. To eliminate if he felt threatened.

Was Flora aware of what was happening to her at the end, when we were saying goodbye? I don't know. I hope not. But I do know that I risked my career, my freedom and effectively killed my sister – all because Dad asked me to. Yet the worst thing of all is that I'm not sure I can say that was the only reason. I could see a long, slow future stretching out, one where I'd always be caring for Flora – my life defined by her, to the end.

'Earth to Fern,' Saphy says, and I focus on her, on now. On being strapped in and hooked up, ready to fly into the unknown. And on my second chance, to be the best big sister I can be.

A LETTER FROM TERI

Dear lovely reader,

Thank you so much for choosing to spend time with Saphy, Fern and Flora in *The Patient*. If you'd like to keep up to date with all my news and latest releases, it's easy to do: just sign up at the following link. Your email address will never be shared and you can unsubscribe at any time.

www.bookouture.com/teri-terry

I hope you enjoyed reading *The Patient*. Reviews make so much difference to authors! If you can spare the time to write a review, I'd love to hear what you think. It really helps new readers discover one of my books for the first time.

I love hearing from my readers – you can get in touch with me on social media or through my website.

Thanks,

Teri Terry

KEEP IN TOUCH WITH TERI

teriterry.com

facebook.com/TeriTerryAuthor
x.com/TeriTerryWrites
instagram.com/TeriTerryWrites
threads.net/TeriTerryWrites

ACKNOWLEDGEMENTS

For so many years, my mom has been saying, why don't you write a book for adults? So here it is.

I fell down so many research rabbit holes with this one. Thank you so much to heart heroes Andrew Ward and Jan Markley, for generously sharing their experiences. Thank you also to Dr Melanie Thornton for patience with my endless questions, and Dr Yvonne Underhill for fielding initial enquiries. Of course, any diversions from reality in furtherance of plot or any errors are all my own.

Thank you to everyone at Bookouture, especially eagle-eyed editor Jayne Osborne: my first adult novel, her first Bookouture acquisition! This is the start of a partnership that I hope continues on and on.

Organ donation saves lives – like Saphy's, Andrew's and Jan's. I always ticked the box to opt in as a donor back when that was how things were done. It's a huge step forward to make the assumption the other way around, but families of donors still play an important role in these decisions. This is a plot spoiler if, like me, you skip ahead to acknowledgements, but any inference that a degree of consciousness of donors like Flora comes along with their heart or other organs has no basis in fact – likewise for any suggestion that a donor might be locked in but conscious, like Flora was until the end. I want to stress that this was only because Flora was given drugs to mimic brain stem death. In the real world, patients are carefully assessed and screened to eliminate any possibility of reversible causes of brain stem death.

Massive thanks to Tania Tay and all the Furies! My new tribe of crime buddies did more than support and encourage, as it was entirely conversations with Tania and a few others that led me to submit to Bookouture in the first place. See you at CrimeFest!

Thank you to my other tribe, the Slushies. And especially Addy Farmer, who coined and let me borrow the awesome word 'miaowls'.

And finally, first, last and always – thank you to Graham and Scooby for helping me keep one foot in the real world.

PUBLISHING TEAM

Turning a manuscript into a book requires the efforts of many people. The publishing team at Bookouture would like to acknowledge everyone who contributed to this publication.

Audio
Alba Proko
Sinead O'Connor
Melissa Tran

Commercial
Lauren Morrissette
Jil Thielen
Imogen Allport

Data and analysis
Mark Alder
Mohamed Bussuri

Editorial
Jayne Osborne
Imogen Allport

Copyeditor
Donna Hillyer

Made in the USA
Las Vegas, NV
22 February 2024

86134739R00208